Haunted Island
A Love Story

Martin Berman-Gorvine

For Jackie. Who else would I write a love story for?

1

It was a small shock seeing a woman standing alone atop the dunes in the deserted stretch of Assateague Island where I was walking with one eye on my pedometer, waiting until I had to take another sample of the clear seawater. I had been lost in my own thoughts as usual. The cool salt breeze off the Atlantic Ocean was delicious, and I was dreading the sweltering hours I had ahead of me in the mosquito-infested marshes, taking water samples from the bay on the other side of the dunes on the way back. To my left, the waves crashed into the sand, leaving irregular damp semicircles for the sandpipers to peck at, till they rose chittering at my approach. To my right, the irregular line of the dunes, each with its own unique shape, formed a natural fence hiding the belts of pine forest and marsh that formed the western fringe of the island.

The woman stood at the peak of the tallest dune in sight, silhouetted against the bright blue of the late May sky. The brisk offshore breeze stirred her chestnut hair and the long brown skirt she was wearing, but she seemed even more lost in thought than I had been a moment before, as she stood with her arms folded gazing out at the hard blue line of the ocean horizon. My instinct was to leave her alone with her thoughts, but I was also drawn to her solitary strangeness.

I tried to work out what was so odd about her as I approached. Certainly her dress, I thought as I drew nearer. It looked much too warm for a day like today, and anyway it wasn't the sort of thing you expected to see anybody wear to the beach. It was the color of milk chocolate, the blouse extending to her wrists where it ended in frilly cuffs, while the skirt fell to her ankles. Maybe she belonged to a really religious sect—there were pockets of Mennonites, who were like the Amish, in this part of Delmarva. Her clothes were wet and muddy and clung to her body, and her hair was damp and matted as if she'd just been for a swim and the wind hadn't yet had time to dry it out. As I drew near enough to make out the features of her face, which had been obscured by the sun's glare, I was startled to see that she was much younger than I had thought, as if she'd just graduated high school. Her skin was pale, paler than the sand, as if she'd been inside all winter and spring. Her nose, chin, and cheekbones traced delicate lines, and as she turned to look at me I saw her eyes were a startlingly bright green.

For a moment I almost turned and fled. But for once curiosity and yearning won out over bashfulness and I climbed to the top of the dune, carefully avoiding trampling the roots of the delicate grasses that held it together. I stopped when I was almost close enough to reach out and touch her.

"Um. Hello," I said. "Sorry to bother you."

"Oh. No. That's quite all right," she said with a faint smile. Her voice was low and a little breathy, as if she'd run to reach the top of the dune. But she hadn't moved since I first spotted her from far up the beach, probably at least fifteen minutes ago.

"I just saw you standing here. It's a hot day. I mean, it seems awfully hot for you to be standing here in that dress. I mean, not that what you wear is any of my business! I just thought, well, I wondered, well, I've got lots of water in my backpack and it doesn't look like you have any and would you like something to drink?"

She chuckled gently. "No, that's quite all right," she said. "I'm not thirsty, really. But you go ahead and have a drink if you are." Her green eyes glittered as if she had turned her face to the sun, though it was actually almost directly overhead.

"Okay, thanks, I think I will," I said, sitting in the sand as my knees suddenly gave way. She sat down beside me, her damp skirts clinging to her legs as I fumbled around in my backpack for a water bottle.

"I'm Darren, by the way," I said between gulps.

"Hello, Darren. I'm Anne Marie. My friends and family call me Annie," she said.

"Are you from around here?" I asked.

She gestured vaguely. "I'm from Green Run," she said. "It's just a short walk from here."

I presumed that was a slip of the tongue. Assateague is a wild island. Green Run must be some little village on the Delmarva mainland I'd never heard of, I thought.

"*You're* not from around here," she stated with certainty.

"Well, I am from Maryland," I said. "I grew up in Columbia. It's near Baltimore," I added when she looked blank. "I'm in college now at the University of Maryland."

"A college man," she said, a little wistfully. It seemed an odd phrase, slightly old-fashioned or literary—I had a minor in English.

"Yeah, I guess I am a 'college man.' I'm studying marine biology."

"What's that?"

"You know, plants and animals of the briny deep. I want to help preserve all this," I said with a sweeping hand gesture, "these beautiful barrier islands, the marsh birds and the fish and clams and oysters. You know, the waters around here are still famous for their blue crabs and oysters, but they're not a shadow of what they once were."

"Not a shadow of what they once were," Annie murmured to herself with a sad little smile. She gripped her knees with both hands and shivered. For a moment her outline blurred, and I blinked. My eyes must be watering in the harsh sunlight. I had an impulse to reach over and hug her, just to give her comfort, but I didn't dare. After a long moment Annie made an effort to tear her gaze away from whatever inward space it was turned on and said, "You sound like a natural philosopher."

"A natural philosopher?" I said with a puzzled little laugh. "I don't think I've ever heard anyone actually use that phrase aloud. It's what they called Thoreau, isn't it?"

"So you've read 'Walden, Or Life in the Woods?' I didn't think anyone else had."

"Well, sure I have," I said. "Old Henry David helped inspire me. Though it's a lot easier to be a 'natural philosopher' now than it was in his time. Take this, for example," I said, reaching into my backpack.

She looked intently at the metal tube I pulled out. "What is it?" she asked.

"It's the reason I'm here today," I said, putting it down in the sand with the tapered end pointing in my direction, so she wouldn't think it was some kind of weapon. "It measures the electrical conductivity, pressure, temperature, and pH of seawater, but Professor Wilensky is mainly interested in the pH part—how acidic the water is. The oceans absorb about one-quarter of all the excess carbon dioxide produced by greenhouse gas emissions, and that means seawater around the world is becoming more acidic, and who knows what that'll do to sea life—nothing good, that's for sure. He's one of the researchers on a worldwide project to gather data on that, and I'm one of his minions, tramping along the shore measuring the acidity of the water every couple hundred yards."

"It looks heavy," she said doubtfully. "And how does it measure how much acid is in the water?"

"It only weighs about 16 pounds. And it's got a digital display," I said, turning it on for her to see. She did a double take, then leaned in, fascinated. It was a perfectly ordinary, greenish LCD screen that would have been at home on any digital watch or calculator. She murmured something to herself, then sat back, clasping her hands around her knees again.

"I'm sorry. I'm boring the hell out of you," I said. "But at least this research gets me out here to Assateague, which I love, and I can observe the birds and other wildlife here at the same time. Wait, what's the matter?"

She was blushing. "I just wish you wouldn't swear."

"Swear?" What had I said? "Hell"? Even in rural Delmarva, that's not much of a swear word. But I reminded myself she was just a kid. Maybe she was home schooled.

"I'm sorry," I said, blushing myself.

"Oh, that's all right," she said with a sigh. "Pa sometimes forgets himself and uses blue language." Then she brightened a bit. "You keep mentioning birds and fish and clams. But you haven't said a word about the ponies."

"Of course I love seeing them too. The famous 'Chincoteague ponies,'" I said. "But come on, that's all tourist stuff. *Misty of Chincoteague*, and all that." She looked blank, and this time I did roll my eyes. "The children's book? By Marguerite Henry? The one that put Chincoteague on the map? I've never met anyone from around here who hasn't heard of it."

She smiled. "Well, now you have," she said, standing up. "Would you like to see them anyway? I know a place they live that no one ever comes to."

How could I resist? I followed her over the crest of the dune, down into the hot sheltered hollow of bare sand behind it, and beyond that into the cool piney woods. I must have noticed that no sand spilled off Annie's long brown skirt when she stood up, nor did she have to brush herself off. But as I followed her I was preoccupied with the way she moved, and enchanted as always by the sights, sounds, and smells of the island all around me. The loblolly pines towered tall and straight above our heads, their fallen needles cushioning the sandy ground beneath our feet. A dragonfly bumbled past, and in the near distance there was a rustling and the snap of breaking twigs as a big animal passed, probably a deer. We came to a thicket that Annie pushed her way through seemingly without effort, but I stumbled and nearly fell. She didn't notice, though I certainly made much more noise than the deer had. "Come on," she said, turning around and calling from a sandy, sunny glade up ahead. I withheld my "swearing" and followed her onward as the ground turned boggy. The trees gave way to savory-smelling bayberry bushes, then to the lush green grasses of the marsh, my boondockers squelching in the muck. I'd come far enough from the site of my last pH measurement, over on the ocean side, that I knew I should probably whip the meter out again for my first bay-side measurement, but there was no time—Annie was moving so fast it was hard to keep up. Then she stopped so abruptly I bumped into her. I started to apologize, but she hadn't lost her balance as I expected, and I realized I hadn't felt the contact.

She was pointing at something. "Look," she said simply.

In a circle of trampled grass several yards across a band of nine or ten ponies stood grazing, their bellies swollen from a diet of salty grasses. In their midst, a foal so new I could see the sheen of his afterbirth stood suckling from his mother. The coats of mother and son were quilts of large brown and white patches, but whereas the mare had a tiny white spot above her eyes on an otherwise all-brown head, her foal had a generous white stripe running from just below his eyes almost to his nose.

"I knew Terry was about to give birth," Annie whispered as we crouched in the tall grass watching. "I've been watching this band closely for years now."

"Years?" I said. "How do you find time to go to school?"

"In the old days, there were very few piebalds like Terry and little Jamie," she said, ignoring my question. "They were all one color or another. Chestnut or off-white, mostly. They got these patterns through cross-breeding with new ponies people have brought to the island."

"You sound like you know a lot about it."

"I love horses," she said. "I know them all by name. Or anyway, by the names I make up for them. This stallion here is Scotty."

He was a gentle ruler. Annie pointed him out to me where he stood a little apart from the others, sniffing the onshore breeze. He'd been like that his whole life, ever since he was a foal himself, she said. I couldn't remember how long horses lived, but it seemed odd that Annie could have watched him from birth, unless she really did live on the island. But how could that be? The whole thirty-seven-mile-long expanse of Assateague Island was national and state parkland, you couldn't live there. Many questions like that came into my mind as the afternoon wore on, but every time I was about to ask her something she told me some amazing little story about the ponies, like how they looked after each other during storms, and I'd forget all about it. Besides, I loved listening to her voice. The longer she talked, the less she sounded like a kid. It was as if she was shaping the wind itself into words, as if a flute could speak. Her voice blended with the murmur of the ocean waves, and I found myself, not quite falling asleep, but drifting into a half-trance where I could still make out the individual words and sentences if I made the effort, but they seemed to convey something more than their plain meaning. I felt something deeper than ordinary drowsiness, but with a restless note within it, and I thought of a line from Keats' Ode to a Nightingale: "I have been half in love with easeful death…"

Suddenly I started wide awake as if someone had goosed me. Scotty noticed me and reared up on his hind legs, upsetting his whole band. The mares milled around for a moment, then set off after him deeper into the marsh, with the foal Jamie bringing up the rear. For a moment they were silhouetted against the gaudy scarlet of the setting sun. What the hell time was it? I jumped to my feet, slapping at the mosquitoes that I suddenly noticed were all over my bare arms and legs. *That's what I get for dozing off and not putting on bug spray for hours,* I thought ruefully. And where had Annie gone? I called her name but there was no answer.

2

Would I ever see Annie again? The question kept me awake that night in my crummy motel room. When I finally dozed off, I had strange dreams that I couldn't remember the next morning, Sunday, though they left me with a feeling of aching loss. But I didn't have time to sit around brooding if I was going to catch up on the measurements I'd failed to make for Professor Wilensky yesterday. I grabbed a quick breakfast of cold cereal and set out in Mom's ancient green Geo Metro, which she'd let me have after she was able to buy a newish Toyota Camry with the divorce settlement from Dad.

As usual I parked at the roundabout that marked the southern end of the road into the National Seashore, grabbed my pack and set off on foot across the sand in the clear, cool morning light, wondering where exactly I'd emerged out onto the beach after that long strange afternoon in the marsh. Had the whole thing been some kind of weird fantasy or daydream?

And why would I fantasize about a high school girl? I walked to the edge of the surf and took a pH measurement. That wasn't hard to answer—my psych class last fall gave me all the info I needed. Ultra-nerd? Check.

Uncomfortable around people, especially girls? Check. I retreated a bit onto dryer sand. So who would be safe enough for me to talk to? Someone young, innocent, and covered up. I sighed. Check.

"Hello again," a low, breathy voice said. I jumped about a mile and landed flat on my ass in the sand. "Sorry," Annie said, scrunching up her face so she wouldn't laugh. She was wearing the same brown long-sleeved blouse and ankle-length skirt as yesterday. Her clothes and her hair still looked wet. And even though there was a light overcast, her eyes still sparkled like the sun reflecting off a green sea. It was strange, but kinda hot.

"You made me crush some of the dune grass," I complained. "Don't you know the dunes blow away without it?" She wasn't offering her hand to help me to my feet. Well, I guess that wasn't a surprise. At least she was real and not a figment of my overheated imagination, but seeing her did raise an awkward question—what business did I have hanging out with a girl who might be underage?

"I meant to ask you, yesterday was Friday," I said as casually as I could, "and, uh, well, shouldn't you have been in school?"

Her amused expression turned faintly sad. "I'm not in school," she said, clasping her hands together and looking at the ground.

"Umm, homeschooled then?"

"What's that? No, I'm not in school anywhere," she said. "Not for a long time. I—I used to be married."

I almost lost my balance again. She looked barely old enough to go to prom, much less to have been married and then divorced.

She raised her head and gave me a quick look. "Come on," she said. "I see you brought your instruments with you. I'll show you a shortcut to the marsh." Turning her back on me, she set off quickly over the crest of the dune without looking back to see whether I was following her. I was panting by the time I caught up. I still couldn't think what to say, but of course I had to blabber away anyway. "Married? How did your parents let you get married so young?"

"Everyone does. At least, everyone in my village," she said, still not looking back at me. "Maybe it's different in the big cities. Anyway, I didn't mind. I've known Will my whole life."

"But did you love him?" I asked, then clapped my hand over my mouth.

She lifted her skirts daintily as we stepped over a narrow brackish stream, or "gut," but I saw out of the corner of my eye that she didn't make a splash as she waded. "I liked him well enough," she said. "I am sorry I won't ever be able to see him again."

What did she mean by that? Had I really stumbled on some odd little isolated world back here? The Eastern Shore of Maryland was different from the rest of the state, sure, but not *that* different. Ocean City in June was just like College Park, really, except with a boardwalk.

But what Annie had said so matter-of-factly seemed so sad. I wished I could kiss her, but it would be better, I thought, to treat her as a younger sister.

Maybe she felt the same way. "If you are willing, I would like to keep you company while you make your scientific measurements," she said as we strolled on through the trees.

"Well, I. Uh. Of course," I stammered. Scientific measurements, she had said. It made me feel absurdly important, as if I were a real scientist, rather than just a drudge for Professor Wilensky! Of course I wanted her along. I squelched over to the bayshore several yards away with Annie beside me. She watched intently as I took my first measurements, and the meter beeped to let me know it was done. I explained again about the various characteristics of the water I had just measured.

"Aren't you going to write the numbers down in a notebook?" she asked.

"There's no need. This thing can record up to ten thousand sets of readings, and of course they can all be uploaded to any computer with a regular USB cable." I glanced at her and once again saw puzzlement on her face. "Like I said yesterday, the point is to measure all the changes in the environment that people are making. So we can try to save what we can."

"Save what you can," she murmured. She looked up at me with those amazing green eyes. "But everything passes. In the end, you can't save anything, or anyone. Nothing abides."

I blinked, at a loss for anything to say.

"My father used to own a hotel here," she said. "It was the biggest building in the village. On the whole island, in fact."

"A hotel? A village? But I thought this was all National Seashore."

"It was torn down a long time ago, after he died," she said. "The pieces were all shipped to the mainland."

"I'm, I'm so sorry," I stammered. "That your father died, I mean."

Again that heartbreaking tiny smile. "That was a *very* long time ago. But in its day Wright's Ocean House was the most popular hotel in this part of Maryland. People used to come from all around. From Baltimore, from Philadelphia, even from way out west in Ohio and Illinois. They didn't mind the boat ride across the bay. It was all part of the adventure for them."

"Couldn't they just drive over the bridge?" I asked, gesturing northward. There are two bridges onto Assateague Island, actually, but the one on the Maryland side, which is named after the explorer Giovanni da Verrazano, was much closer to where we were.

"This was before the bridge was built," she said. "Before there was a park."

But the park had been there a long time. Surely it had been set up before either of us was born. But I kept my thoughts to myself.

She continued to talk about her father's hotel. "Pa loved to greet the guests. If they looked tired he'd offer them a glass of sherry, or even a little brandy, on the house. He'd take their coats and have me personally escort them to their rooms. They loved him for his courtesy, though at first we couldn't have afforded to pay a boy to carry their luggage anyway. But he would have been like that even if he could've afforded more staff, though it would have been nice if there'd been anyone around other than me and Will and Jim to spell him. But no matter how tired he was, he'd get the guests all settled, make sure they had everything they needed. He'd even trim the wicks on their lamps for them!"

"He'd do what?" I asked. She didn't hear. I wondered if she was even talking to me. What she said sounded as if she was suddenly speaking aloud a conversation she'd been having with herself for a long, long time.

"Will and I helped him build the place with our own hands. It was good to see him throw himself into something, after all he suffered in the war, after Ma's death. He had to get away from the big city, and Assateague Island seemed like the answer to his prayers. Mine, too."

"Your mother died too?" I asked. I reached out as if to touch her arm but checked myself.

"She died of consumption," she said. "It was hard for me, but I was sent away before the end so I wouldn't see the worst of it, the blood she'd coughed up on her sheets and pillowcase. Pa couldn't be at her side as he longed to be, for he was still away at the war. Only Violet was there to tend to her as she lay dying." A tear sparkled on her cheek.

My gesture had brought her back to herself. "Come on," she said, standing up and forcing a smile, "I am keeping you from doing your duty as a natural philosopher."

But I didn't want to move from where I sat in a nest of pine needles at the edge of the salt marsh. It was the word "consumption" that had finally gotten through my thick skull. Consumption was what they called tuberculosis in the nineteenth century. It had killed our mutual hero Thoreau at the age of forty-five. Nobody would call tuberculosis consumption now.

I'd known there was something strange about Annie from the moment I'd first seen her. Uncanny, in the true sense of the word: *of supernatural origin.* Uncanny Annie. I couldn't move. I looked up at Annie and I saw her green eyes flash with dismay. "You're a ghost," I said.

"Yes," she replied softly. "Yes, it's true. I am sorry."

"Sorry for what?" I asked hoarsely.

"It's just that I hadn't spoken to anyone for so long," she said, again as if talking to herself. "But I hadn't the right. I knew that the first time I tried. You know?" Her eyes brimmed over with tears, which fell sparkling from her face but never reached the ground. I stared at her. Now that I knew what she was she seemed to glow with an unnatural light in the dim of the forest's edge.

"I went to church," she said, "of my own free will. Isn't that a laugh? Pa wasn't much of a churchgoer, especially after Ma died—he was a freethinker who considered himself a Transcendentalist. But he wanted me to go to Pastor Scarburgh's Sunday services in Andy Birch's cabin so we would fit in with everyone else, and although I skipped church more often than not, after we were married Will insisted I start going again. I wanted to be a good wife, I *so much wanted to.* So I did as he asked, even though I hated those hellfire sermons Pastor Scarburgh preached. He always seemed to be looking at *me* when he spoke about 'the fire everlasting, the terrible fire that shall melt the flesh of the unrepentant sinner.' Even—even *before,* I wanted to shout at him. Who did he think he was? Just a backwoods preacher. But I didn't dare."

I spoke her name.

"I went to church one Sunday," she said, staring past me. "A year to the day since my funeral. Pastor Scarburgh, the fool, was preaching on grace." She dropped her voice an octave, and for a moment I could picture the ignorant old country preacher standing before me, in a shabby black suit and a broad-brimmed hat to match. 'The innocent girl so tragically taken from us a year ago surely dwells at Jesus' right hand, with the angels in heaven,' he said. I couldn't stand the lies anymore! The solemn lies he kept ladling out to my poor father, whose hotel prospered more and more, like a curse! To Will, who had lost all his joy in life and sat staring at the pastor with brimming eyes! So I leapt at him, at Scarburgh, in full view of the congregation. I roared at him to stop his lying, and tell everybody the truth that there is no heaven and no hell and no Day of Judgment. That there is no G-G-G..." She stopped and seemed to struggle for breath, though an unthinkably long time had passed since she last drew one. I stared at her, stricken.

"No one saw or heard me, of course," she continued more quietly. "No one except Andy's little daughter Addie, two years old and still not speaking, who began to howl and point at me. Her mother Betty tried to quiet her, and took her outside for a sound thrashing when she could not." She paused, staring off into the distance. "So I was wrong, after all. There is judgment and there is a hell for sinners such as me. Only it is no burning place of fire and brimstone. It is merely this world, which I am condemned to wander forever, never speaking to a living soul."

I didn't dare speak. For a long moment there was no sound but birdsong and the lapping of the little waves in the marsh behind me. When I tried to talk something stuck in my throat. Not the usual "lump," but something more like a hard little pebble. Finally I managed to speak around it. "But that's not true," I rasped. "Addie saw and heard you. I can see and hear you. There must have been others."

"My father saw me once," she whispered. "But I avoid

people. I would have run from you too, but you came upon me so suddenly. It was so easy to start talking to you... as if I were a living person, and not..." Abruptly she turned and dashed off into the woods. I jumped over the gut to follow her and almost fell into the shallow, brackish water.

"Annie, slow down, please!" I called after her.

But she didn't listen. She moved swiftly and steadily as if she knew exactly where to place her feet, while I had to skirt dense patches of brush and nearly twisted my ankle countless times as I stumbled over hidden tree roots. After a quarter of an hour we suddenly emerged into a clearing. Annie stopped. When I looked around a prosaic scene of picnic tables and two bright green porta-potties greeted me, and off to the side by the water's edge, a ramshackle abandoned building that might once have been a hunting lodge. There was a sign at the edge of the clearing. I staggered over to it.

"Green Run Backcountry Campsite, Assateague Island National Seashore. Permit required."

I turned and shot Annie a puzzled look. "This is what you wanted to show me?" I asked.

She shook her head. "But it's close to here. I wanted to give you a chance to catch your breath and drink some water. I forget about those things sometimes," she said.

Forget about breathing and drinking water? Yes, I suppose you do.

She walked northeast from the clearing, into the woods that separated it from the oceanfront dunes. I followed her to a sparkling cove, on the other side of which a herd of the wild ponies stood grazing the saltmarsh cordgrass against a backdrop of graceful, dark green loblolly pine trees. The trees came right down to the edge of the water, without an intervening stretch of marsh. It was beautiful, but that didn't keep the mosquitoes from biting fiercely, and I slapped at my arms, restraining myself from cursing through sheer effort of will as I followed Annie around the little cove. It wouldn't have been so bad if my sweat hadn't washed away all the bug spray. I wanted to jump into the water, which was so still it reflected the trees with hardly a ripple.

"Annie, where—"

She slipped away from the water's edge into a thick stand of brush and trees. Thin, bony twigs reached out as if deliberately to scratch me, and even my jeans were no protection against the briar thorns that were everywhere. If only the variety of nature was a little less various!

The ground was sloping upwards, following the curve of an ancient dune. At least the mosquitoes weren't eating *her* alive. I was panting heavily by the time I reached the top. Annie had stopped walking but had her back to me. She hiked up her skirts and crouched low to the ground. I peered over her shoulder and saw a gray stone. No more than an inch or two of it poked above the sandy soil. What was a large stone doing on a sandy barrier island like Assateague? I squinted in the mottled sunlight that filtered through the pine branches. Were those the tops of letters? I crawled forward and began brushing sand away. I needed something better to dig with. The best I could come up with was the cover of the pH meter's battery compartment. Using that as a makeshift trowel, I began to dig. Birdsong and even the distant rush of the waves died away as I worked, till the scrape of metal against stone sounded loudly through the silent forest. Finally I stopped to mop away the sweat that was streaming down my face and stinging my eyes. Now I could read what was carved into the stone.

ANNE MARIE PEARSON
BELOVED WIFE AND DAUGHTER
TAKEN FROM US BY THE CRUEL SEA
DECEMBER 12TH, 1874
AGE 18 YEARS, 2 MONTHS, 28 DAYS

It has to be a hoax. Somebody's playing a practical joke on me, the skeptical part of my mind whispered. But my vision was blurring with unshed tears. And Annie was saying something.

"I'm sorry, Darren. I'm so sorry! I should have kept my vow. I have no right to bother the living." I looked up just in time to see the side of her pale face dwindling as she moved away through the trees.

"Annie! Annie, come back!" But the forest was silent. A moment later birdsong pierced the too-bright sunshine.

3

When I tried to stand up I found I had sprained my ankle and couldn't put any weight on it. Luckily I had enough juice in my cell phone to call the park rangers, but they told me it was going to take a while till they could send a boat for me. In the meantime I took pictures of Annie's tombstone and the clearing with my cell phone camera, the better to find it again. Then I piled sand back on the tombstone till it was even more deeply buried than it had been when I'd tripped over it. I didn't want someone else stumbling over it, or worse, stealing it for a souvenir—it looked small and light enough for a strong man to carry away. I had to protect Annie. Though what I could protect her from, when she'd been dead for nearly a century and a half, was a good question.

I wasn't frightened, sitting in the glade waiting to be rescued. It was much too sunny and peaceful for that, and far from wanting to hurt me Annie had seemed ashamed by her very existence. I had a lot of time to think about what I'd seen, about how real she was. I'd never believed in ghosts or the supernatural. Dad was a medical researcher at Johns Hopkins University, which was the reason, he said, he was death on any kind of "superstition." He used to make fun of Mom for going to synagogue on the High Holidays. Let's just say I wasn't exactly shocked when my parents told me the summer before my sophomore year that they were separating. They both seemed far less upset about their marriage breaking up than they were about the effect the news might have on my grades, but I didn't disappoint them. It was a relief, really, to throw myself into examining the blue-green blood of horseshoe crabs and writing papers for Wilensky. Even at its worst, nature was far less scary and confusing than people. You could understand the natural world completely with science, that's what my dad and Professor Wilensky and I all believed.

So I had no mental framework into which I could fit Annie. Ghosts were ridiculous. Cartoonish white swirls, little kids wearing old bedsheets on Halloween, modestly entertaining special effects in movies. Dead was dead, and that's all she wrote, although at age twenty death was more than slightly unreal to me. And yet, Annie was real. I had no reason to doubt what I had seen, heard, and felt. And now I had the picture of her tombstone on my cell phone, which I would never have found if she hadn't led me to it. But there was an additional reality I was sensing, one my strictly empirical father would never have accepted as evidence. Annie was a real person, realer in some ways than anyone else I knew. True, she knew nothing about computers or cell phones or TV or any of the other stuff we all take for granted. But weren't those things full of the unreal? Take the people you saw on TV that you imagined you knew well, sitting in their cozily furnished, homey sets that were a glamorous but familiar extension of your own (far messier) home. Or the people you formed online friendships with through Facebook and email, the ones you never got to meet in person, so that you had to take their identity and even their existence on faith. Who was the real ghost, then, and who the real person?

And if I could see Annie and talk to her, and more

important if she could see and talk to me, if we were interacting, that is, like any two people… I didn't know quite where that thought was leading me, but I knew I wanted her to come back. I wanted to figure out some way to help her, to comfort her, if only by letting her know that she wasn't all alone any longer as she had been for close to a century and a half. I couldn't even imagine that amount of time. It was seven times longer than I had been alive. Hell, it was longer than any living person had been alive. No wonder she loved the Chincoteague ponies so much. Did they sense her, in some weird animal way? Did they ease her loneliness somehow? It seemed they couldn't ease her guilt. But guilt over what? What could she possibly have done in her life that the memory of it plagued her long after everyone she had known had died—long after the *grandchildren* of everyone she had ever known must have died? Perhaps if I could get her to talk to me again, I could figure out what it was, and that would ease her suffering. It would put her at rest. And then she would no longer be a ghost, right? But then would she just fade away?

"Annie," I said aloud. There was no answer except the wind and the birds. "Annie, whatever it is, whatever you once did, it's all right. It's over, don't you see? It ended so long ago. And whatever it was couldn't have been that bad anyway." I wondered whether she could hear me. Whatever the case, I remained alone in the clearing as the sun passed the zenith and started its long trek downward toward the bay, which I could just catch blue glimpses of through the gaps in the trees.

#

When the shadow of the tall loblolly pine across the clearing from me had climbed most of the way up the trunk of the tree I was resting against, a distant thrumming on the bay woke me from a doze. The noise grew louder as its source grew closer, then sputtered to a stop. A voice called me. I called back, and less than a minute later the crackling of dry twigs heralded the arrival of my rescuer. I struggled to my feet to greet a guy in his late twenties, wearing the light gray uniform shirt and olive-green trousers of a National Park Service ranger. As he emerged into the clearing he took off the traditional round hat with the black band and wiped his streaming face on his sleeve. "Mr. Trachtenberg, I presume," he deadpanned.

"Guilty," I confessed, shaking his sweaty hand. "Call me Darren." The shine on his name tag was a bit dull, but his name was easy enough to remember: Truitt, a widespread Eastern Shore clan. He had a friendly, slightly pudgy sunburned face.

"I'm Paul. Let's see that ankle of yours," he said, kneeling down. "Left or right?"

"Left," I said, sitting down and taking off my shoe and sock. My ankle had puffed up like a balloon. He grunted.

"You'll be off this foot for a couple of weeks if you don't take it easy," he said, producing an ace bandage from his pocket and wrapping up the ankle with quick, efficient motions.

"I just feel, well, sort of stupid for making you come out all this way."

He chuckled as he helped me back to my feet and put his hand under my right arm to help me down the hill. "Rescuing tourists is part of the job description."

I blushed. "I'm not a tourist, though." I tried to reach into my pack for the pH meter with my free hand and almost toppled both of us over. "I'm a marine biology student at College Park."

"Ah. That must explain what you were doing on top of a twenty-five-foot hill fifty yards from the water's edge. Watch your step, now," he said, helping me into his motorboat. As soon as he had me settled with a lifejacket belted firmly on, he started the engines, pointing us north toward the bridge and the ranger station.

"Yeah, I guess I wasn't doing what I was supposed to," I shouted over the roar of the engine. "To be honest, I was poking around looking for the ruins of a village called Green Run. Ever heard of it?"

He nodded. "Tell you about it when we get to the ranger station," he said. Getting there took a very pleasant quarter hour of chugging across the bay, with the orange of the lowering sun to port and the wooded fringe of the island to starboard, slowly giving way to marsh and sand dunes. The breeze was a relief. Just before we reached our destination we passed another band of the Chincoteague ponies. A minute or so later we tied up at a dock and Paul helped me off the boat.

The ranger station was crowded with campers checking in for the evening, but he led me to a back room where a fan was laboring hard to cool things off. "Do you need to call someone to come get you?" he asked.

I explained that my Geo Metro was parked in the roundabout, and he agreed to run me out there after he finished some paperwork. The drive was less than five minutes long, barely enough time to pump him for information on Green Run.

"There's not much to tell, I'm afraid," he said. "My grandfather told me about it when I first applied to work here. His Aunt Adelaide was born there, though her family moved to Berlin over on the mainland when she was four. She came along on a boat trip once and showed Grandpop what was left of the house where she'd been born—he told me it looked like it had been little better than a shack even in its glory days. He told me where to look for it, but I couldn't find anything. On an exposed island like this it's pretty hard to find any 'ruins,' and any reusable timber would have gone for salvage long ago."

"Could I talk to him?" I asked eagerly.

"Who, Grandpop? I'm afraid he died three years ago."

The fact he was dead didn't necessarily mean I couldn't talk to him. I stifled a hysterical giggle.

"Green Run was never much of a village," Paul said. "No more than a couple dozen families ever lived there. Everyone either worked at the Green Run Life-Saving Service Station, like Aunt Addie's father Andy, or at a hotel called Wright's Ocean House. Or they were watermen—oyster harvesters."

My ears perked up. Annie had mentioned her father owned a hotel. But there wasn't much left of that building, Paul told me. "It was all waste not, want not out here in those days. After the hotel was abandoned, it was taken apart and the lumber shipped over to the mainland. You can still find the brick foundations if you hike out to Wright's Landing, which is north across a bayside inlet from the campground."

That would be the Arcadian stand of trees I'd glimpsed across the water from Annie's tombstone.

"But who took it apart? And where did the lumber end up?" If the building had been reconstructed somewhere nearby, it might be haunted by the ghost of Annie's father. (But not by her husband's ghost, I hoped.)

Paul shrugged. "Beats me. This was a hundred years ago, just after World War I. Personally, I've been down around the cove where the village used to stand many times over the years, and everything else is long gone, apart from a boarded-up hunting lodge near the campsite that includes part of the old Life-Saving Service station—which they moved from someplace else, after it had been turned over to the Coast Guard and then closed down. But don't get any ideas about poking around inside there. The Park Service closed it up for good reason, so nobody breaks an ankle, or worse."

Damn. What else should I ask him? But we had already pulled up behind my car. Paul opened the door for me. "Need help getting on your feet?"

"That's all right, I think I can manage," I said, leaning on the side of car for support and wincing when I put too much weight on my sprained ankle. "Oh, there is one more thing," I said, trying to sound casual. "Are there any summer jobs open on the Park Service staff?"

"Not at the National Seashore. And even if there were openings, you have to apply months in advance and, if you want to become a ranger, undergo a lot of training. But my cousin Bob Cropper works at the Maryland State Park—you know, the beach that's straight ahead just after you come over the bridge, before you make the right turn to drive down to the National Seashore—and I think he said something about one of their gatehouse operators having quit just last week. Left them in the lurch just at the start of the season, he said. Let me talk to him and get back to you. What's your cell number?"

4

At dawn I woke with my heart pounding and Annie's name on my lips. No more sleep for me. I had a shower, got dressed in shorts and a T-shirt and hobbled over to the motel office for some coffee. The place was so cheap we didn't even get breakfast, but at least there was always a pot brewing. The girl behind the desk, whose name tag identified her as Lakeisha, was yawning when I came in. When she saw me she covered her mouth with the back of her hand and smiled apologetically.

"S'alright," I mumbled, "I know how you feel."

"Been on shift since eleven o'clock," she said. "Nancy's supposed to relieve me at seven, but she's always late. I got to get some sleep before I go to my other job."

I nodded. "Live around here?" I asked lamely.

She nodded. "Just up the road in Berlin. My boyfriend Kevin's gonna be here any minute. My day job at the State Park starts at four. You tourists come down here to hang out at the beach in Ocean City, but if you live here you've gotta find work wherever you can."

"Aren't there more jobs in Ocean City?"

"Yeah. Kev and I will move to Ocean City—he's a cop there—once our stupid lease is up in two months."

A light bulb went on in my head. When Kevin arrived the three of us worked out a deal. If I got the job at the State Park gatehouse—and Lakeisha promised she'd put in a good word for me—I could sublet their place in Berlin for a hundred dollars a month off the regular rent.

"It's pretty comfortable for a trailer," Lakeisha said.

The next step was to land that job. I drove across the Verrazano Bridge to the Assateague State Park offices and asked if anyone there knew where Paul's cousin was.

He wasn't in the office, but they radioed him and relayed his request that I wait, he'd be back in twenty minutes from a quick patrol up and down the beach. In less than ten minutes he strode in the door, his hand out. Bob Cropper was taller than his cousin, and dark where Paul was fair, with a thin face dominated by a sharp nose. He was as intense as his cousin was laid back. Were they really related? "Good to meet you, Darryl," he said briskly.

"Darren Trachtenberg," I corrected him, trying to extract my right hand from his crushing grip.

"So, you're the one who wants to take the 8 a.m.-to-4 p.m. shift. There's not much you have to learn. Lakeisha can talk you through it in like fifteen minutes when she gets here this afternoon and you can start first thing tomorrow morning."

I shook my head. "Sorry, I can't start that soon. I've got finals coming up this week, but I'll be happy to start right after that."

"Well, I can't guarantee the job will still be open for you if you keep me waiting all that time!" Bob snapped, and stormed off to do another patrol.

#

I went back to my car and caught up on my textbook reading while waiting for Lakeisha, who laughed when I told her what Bob had said. "Don't pay him any mind, it's not as if they're beating the doors down," she said, tucking in her uniform shirt. She looked crisp and clean. "Now I'm guessing 'Commandant' Bob didn't bother telling you what you get paid. It's minimum wage plus a dollar twenty-five an hour," she said briskly. I did a quick mental calculation and groaned. Between rent on the trailer and food I might be operating at a loss. I didn't think my parents would be all that excited about my taking a summer job that *cost* them money, instead of helping me pay toward college.

"It could be worse," she said. "At least you won't be running patrols, dealing with all the fools who sneak beer in and tease the ponies."

Green Run was pretty far from the State Park entrance. "Actually, I think I'd prefer that."

Lakeisha looked at me as if her respect for my sanity had vanished. "Lucky for you, you can't do that job anyhow. You need to pass a physical, and then you have to go on a training course. It ain't worth it, trust me."

"So how come you work two jobs?" I asked.

"Saving up to start my master's in criminology at UMES in the fall." The University of Maryland's Eastern Shore Campus was an hour's drive to the west, in Princess Anne.

But if I got to ask personal questions, so did she. "A little bird told me you're a college kid," she said.

At least Annie called me a college man. I nodded.

"So if you're up in College Park, why the hell do you want to come all the way down here for a summer job? You won't get much time to work on your tan, I can tell you that. Bob wants us working six-day shifts."

"That's okay. The island's a special place for me." That much at least was true. Lakeisha raised an eyebrow, but smiled. Then she took me out to the gatehouse at the park entrance and showed me how to collect payment or note down visitors with weekly or annual passes. Bob was wrong, it didn't take fifteen minutes. It took all of ten. I offered to stay longer and help out, but Lakeisha shook her head.

"Go relax on the beach till Kev gets here. I talked to him and he promised he'll get off work early so he can show you the trailer."

"That's nice of him," I said.

"You're the one doing us a favor. Now scat."

#

In the end, though, Kevin couldn't keep his word because there'd been a bad accident out on U.S. 50, the main road that funneled all the Washington and Baltimore tourists to Ocean City and funneled them right back out again in multiple lanes of honking, snarling gridlock, as if they'd moved the Beltway two hundred miles east. Some drunk classmates of mine had gotten mixed up about which way was which and half the police department had to work overtime to clean up the mess, Kevin explained to me apologetically by cell phone. But he gave me directions to the trailer, which was located an easy ten minutes' drive up the road to Berlin, so I swung past it.

At least it wasn't part of a trailer park. It was about twenty feet long, an aluminum can painted white that gleamed in the late afternoon sun, and it sat in lonely splendor on a quarter-acre fenced-in lot with a neatly trimmed lawn shaded by a rickety-looking old oak tree that leaned familiarly towards the front door.

#

Professor Wilensky seemed bemused when I stopped by his office the next day to tell him about my summer plans.

"It's not as if I can give you extra credit just for working in Assateague State Park and spending time on the island, you know," he said. "Look, I don't mean to discourage you from getting as much field experience as possible. But there are so many fantastic summer programs you could be doing instead. Have you looked into doing an internship up at Woods Hole?"

"I don't think my parents would want me to go all the way up to Massachusetts," I lied. Actually, they were both too busy to notice much of anything I did, unless it cost them money. So I added, a little more truthfully, "I need the money from an actual paying job."

He sighed. "Yes, I know how that is. Look here, I'll check the departmental budget and see if I can get you a stipend to conduct some bay grass counts in Chincoteague Bay. I can't promise anything, but I'll try."

Counting seaweed had to be more interesting than just sticking the pH meter in the water, especially if I could get paid for it. The professor came through, and the extra $1,000 meant I could vary my diet of Ramen noodles with boxed mac-and-cheese.

5

Moving into the trailer for the summer turned into much more of an adventure than my previous trip to Assateague. The sun was setting as I drove east on U.S. 50 from College Park. It was sunset, and through the window to my right I could see the orange sun staining the water with light as I crossed the bridge over the wide Choptank River. *Nor now the long light on the sea*, I thought, remembering an Archibald Macleish poem I had read in high school, *and here face downward in the sun, to feel how swift how secretly, the shadow of the night comes on.* I told myself my shivers were due to the air conditioning, and turned it down. But it also had something to do with the reading material I'd brought along: a collected edition of Edgar Allen Poe. Research, I guess, though Annie's predicament made me feel sad, not scared.

Kevin was waiting for me at the trailer. "Come down here for all those 'June bug' girls?" Kevin asked, nudging me as he helped me manhandle my old window air-conditioner into the window frame.

"You mean those high school graduates who come to Ocean City to party? Nah, not really."

Kevin chuckled. "I can tell from the way you answered

me that you've got a girlfriend."

"Sort of, yes. No, not really."

"Well, which is it, man? Never mind, I won't interrogate you. You're smart enough you'd probably lawyer up anyway. She's the reason you came down here for the summer, am I right?"

"Something like that." I had to find a way to change the subject before I ended up blurting out that I was into a ghost. "Are you from around here?" *What an original line. Good going, Darren.*

He nodded. "My family goes way back. Matter of fact, some of my ancestors were slaves around here. We know which white families were the slaveholders, too."

"That must get sort of weird when you bump into them at the supermarket."

"I won't say I don't get a secret thrill out of pulling over those guys and writing 'em a ticket when I get the chance," he said. "But mostly we don't think too much about it."

"That's good, I guess." He picked up my heaviest suitcase over my protests. Following him with the smaller bags, I asked casually, "Did anyone in your family ever live on Assateague Island, at a place called Green Run?"

"Green Run? No. My folks mostly lived around Pocomoke City, down by the Virginia line." He insisted on helping me with the rest of my stuff. There wasn't much, just a duffel bag, a backpack full of books, and my beat-up old bike. The place came with battered but usable furniture, and Kevin said I was welcome to his old linens and some mismatched plates and utensils, too. "Least I can do for you, for taking this place off our hands. You're welcome to the landlord. He'll leave you alone, long as you pay the rent, but he won't fix anything either. Oh, and you have to mow the lawn. Mower's in a shed out back. Let's see, what else? Keisha left you some peaches and a roll for breakfast, so you don't have to go shopping till tomorrow. There's a Food Lion less than a mile away, on the other side of U.S. 113. Call if you need anything." We shook hands and he gave me his police business card, which gave his rank as sergeant. And then I was alone in my new home.

I slept badly that night, with more nightmares that I woke from feeling sad and drained. Fortunately Cropper had agreed to let me start Tuesday, so I had a day to get myself organized. I quickly figured out that U.S. 113 was a sort of Berlin Wall—with the eastern side, the one my trailer was on, being all African-American and the western side being all white. It seemed that history hadn't quite been left behind. I got a few curious looks from my new neighbors as I walked back from the Food Lion with my groceries—two bags full of milk, bread, orange juice, breakfast cereal, peanut butter and jelly, and bananas; I'd need to save for the rent. I nodded shyly to one or two of my new neighbors and explained that I had sublet the trailer for the summer. They were polite but distant, which suited me fine. I got everything squared away and then rode my bike to the public library on Main Street to see what they might have about the history of Assateague Island.

There wasn't much, and what there was, was very general. Both the National Seashore and the State Park had been set up more than fifty years ago, so Annie's village of Green Run must have been abandoned a long, long time ago. I found a passing reference to the Green Run Life-Saving Service Station, which was taken over by the Coast Guard and then abandoned in 1939, later to be converted into the hunting lodge I'd seen at the campsite. But the hotel, and the village itself, might as well never have existed for all the information I found on them. By midafternoon I gave up and went back home for a peanut butter and jelly sandwich. I brought several library books back with me—everything they had on Assateague, including children's books, and more famous ghost stories such as Henry James's *The Turn of the Screw*—but none of them told me anything important. I was going to have to go out there and learn what I needed to know myself.

6

The first half of June passed without any sign that Annie was anything but a figment of my imagination. My schedule was rigid and dull. I'd get up at 6 a.m., eat breakfast, pack sandwiches, fruit, water, sunscreen, and bug spray in my backpack and drive down Assateague Road, heading eastward out of town, past overgrown fields and a dilapidated, abandoned farmhouse on the left, until I came to State Highway 611, Stephen Decatur Highway— the hero of the War of 1812 was a local boy—where I made a right and wheeled through a tunnel of regularly spaced tall trees that shaded most of the roadway. So early in the day there was little traffic and it was usually pleasantly cool. Passing a little shopping center dominated by "Island Market," a combination restaurant, camping supply store, and gift shop, I'd take a left at a crossroads, emerging out from beneath the trees onto open marshy ground. The parking lot and buildings of the National Seashore headquarters and the attached, shiny new Visitor Center appeared on my right. It would be weeks before I set foot in there; on Wednesdays, my day off, I was always so tired I slept through most of the day with no company but the droning air conditioner.

Next came the Verrazano Bridge, a bold and grand name for what was after all just a little two-lane bridge over the narrow neck of Sinepuxent Bay. Often there were Chincoteague ponies grazing on both sides of the road as I came down the gentle slope onto the island. One or two would raise their heads to look at me as I drove past. This, with the bright red sun just starting its climb out of the ocean dead ahead, was the best moment of the day.

What followed next was usually the worst moment of the day, with Cropper hollering at me to hurry up with my clocking in and get my skinny ass out to the gatehouse, but not before making a sweep of the parking lot for garbage left behind by the previous day's visitors. It wasn't too difficult, with my bright yellow long-handled broom and dustpan, to remove whatever debris Lakeisha hadn't caught the previous evening, or that might have been left behind by overnight campers, but it was a tedious job, and I soon grew to loathe the squeaking cawing of seagulls fighting over the scraps of food I hadn't gotten to yet.

By eight o'clock I was in my booth, ready for the first cars to pull up. I preferred that first early hour or two when I was still fresh and the early beach blanketers and recreational surf fishers were cheerful about having beaten the rush to the cool of the morning beach. By late morning the lines were longer, sometimes stretching back toward the bridge as far as the eye could see amid a wavering heat haze under the powerful sun, and tempers were growing short. The hour before lunch was the worst. From noon till 12:30 Bob would relieve me and I would eat my now-sticky sandwich in the cool of the back of the gift shop in the park headquarters. In early afternoon there was a slight lull, though the traffic usually picked up again toward the end of my shift at four o'clock. Even on rainy days, of which there were only one or two in that first half of June, a fair number of people would still come to the beach, perhaps hoping to wait out the shower; or in the fishermen's case, perhaps they expected the rain to stir up their prey.

Rain or shine, as soon as Lakeisha came to relieve me I would get in my car and head out, turning left before the bridge to follow Bayberry Drive south down the island toward the National Seashore. For the first few days I had to flash my annual pass when I drove past their gatehouse a few miles down, but after that my counterpart would just nod to me. Woods crowded in on both sides of the road, but the effect was less tunnel-like than on Stephen Decatur Highway, and of course they were not planted regularly. It wasn't uncommon to see a white-tail deer or a smaller sika deer, the latter actually a Japanese miniature elk descended from a herd that a troop of Boy Scouts had brought to the island for some reason in the 1920's, grazing by the side of the road. If there was a band of ponies ahead I knew it first from the cars pulled over on the shoulder, or stopped in the middle of the road if there was no shoulder, so that the tourists within could take pictures. You would think they had never seen a horse before; well, perhaps they hadn't, and certainly not "wild" ones like the Chincoteague ponies.

I'd drive clear through to the end of the road in a roundabout south of the National Seashore campgrounds. There I'd park and set off on foot over the sand to Green Run, eight miles further south. At the beginning I was out of shape and couldn't jog the entire way, instead jogging for a hundred yards or so and then slowing down to a plod for the next hundred yards of surf line, taking more than two hours to cover the distance. By mid-June I'd cut that time almost in half. Rainy days were actually easier because the damp sand made good footing for the entire width of the beach, so I didn't have to hug the surf line and dance out of the way every time a particularly energetic breaker climbed higher than usual. Kilometer posts planted along the way helped me keep track of my progress, with thirteen of them for the eight miles, and as post 29 came into view I'd jog up the beach, over the dunes and through the loblolly forest, bypassing the campsite and coming out on the bayshore. I got to know the hill where Annie's tombstone was hidden better than I knew my own room in the trailer, which was only a place to lay my head. I spent hours there, at first in silence, just sitting and listening to the sea breeze tossing the treetops. Each time I arrived I'd clear away enough sand so I could read her name at least, reminding me again and again that she was a BELOVED WIFE AND DAUGHTER / TAKEN FROM US BY THE CRUEL SEA and the date of her death. And every time I left, as the sun approached the landward western horizon, I'd carefully replace the sand to protect her resting place.

As the days went by without any sign from her, I began to talk as if she could hear me, on the assumption that she really could, that she was only hiding in the forest somewhere nearby. The woods should have been foreboding, sitting as I was by a lonely tombstone waiting for a ghost. But they were filled with sunlight, and the trees were much shorter than in any mainland forest, so that wandering among them it was as though I was surrounded by a quiet, friendly crowd that listened patiently to me chattering away to Annie as if she were actually there. If someone had happened along it might have looked odd, although they might have just assumed I was talking to someone over a cellphone earpiece. When I ran out of breath or stopped to take a drink of water, I had to fall back on my own thoughts or the soughing of the wind in the treetops.

I spoke about my life, about my parents' divorce and the years of quarreling that had come before it, which would die down for months only to break out with renewed fury like the Centralia coal seam fire. The carbon monoxide had killed that Pennsylvania town, and in the same way I was being slowly poisoned by the fumes my parents gave out. Yet I had nowhere to go. I couldn't drive and I had no friends to hang out with. So I'd shut myself up in my room and read, play video games, or waste time on the Internet—I found trying to describe those last two activities to a listener who had grown up in the nineteenth century an interesting challenge. I sensed that Annie was listening, though she never showed myself, and over time I reached deeper into the torment of my childhood, describing how I had been teased and bullied from the moment I entered kindergarten until the day I graduated high school. I never knew or understood what there was in me that made it so much fun for my classmates to call me a nerd, a geek, and a teacher's pet, to make sure I was always picked last for teams or to trip me up when I was walking along minding my own business. But my favorite teacher, Ms. Laramie, told me things would be different when I got to college. And they were. I was accepted, but still intensely lonely, a feeling I tried to push away by working hard in class, so hard that even Professor Wilensky had told me to lighten up.

The second week of June melted into the third and nothing happened. On the summer solstice I jogged out to Green Run as usual—I could now run the whole eight miles with barely a short water break or two—but this time, I had brought a pup tent and sleeping bag that I'd bought at the Wal-Mart on U.S. 50 outside Ocean City. I set my things up at the campsite, which I had to myself, and then, rather than walk to the gravesite as usual, I skirted the hill where it stood and made my way out to the westernmost tip of Wright's Landing. There, hidden among the trees, I did indeed find the brick foundations of the hotel that Ranger Paul had described to me, half-hidden under bayberry bushes and long grass. It looked as if the building had been surprisingly large. Would Annie be there? I didn't see her but the hairs on the back of my neck were standing up.

"Annie," I said. There was no answer but the distant rush of the waves on the ocean side of the island, and the cry of a marsh bird somewhat nearer. "Annie, why are you still hiding from me? You can't think by now that you were 'bothering the living' by talking to me. I *want* to talk to you." I paused. After so many weeks of speaking into the silence I was no longer self-conscious about it. I chose my words carefully. "I'm sorry I've been talking so much about myself," I said at length. "But until you stop hiding from me, there's no way I can ask about you. Aren't you—" my voice dropped to a whisper—"aren't you even lonelier than me?"

There was still no answer and no tangible sign that she was anywhere nearby. My heartbeat skipped, then slowed as if a cold November rain had somehow penetrated deep within me. I struggled for breath—the air too had gone cold, and clammy, with a cloud covering the face of the westering sun. Did this soul-killing sadness come from within me? It seemed much older and much stronger than I was. My vision began to blur and darken. "Annie," I gasped. But the icy weight vanished from chest suddenly. My vision cleared and there was only the placidly setting sun, the rippling bay water and the distant cries of seagulls. I walked slowly back to the campsite and set up my tent.

The night was clear and cool. I lay on my back looking at the stars through the transparent mesh at the top of my tent. What had happened at the ruins of the hotel? Whatever it was, had I gotten a glimpse of what Annie wanted to spare me from? And was I really strong enough to bear the weight of her sorrow?

I said softly, "I WON'T abandon you!"

Gazing at the stars should have been soothing, but my mind was racing in circles to no purpose, and I couldn't forget that the stars I saw were themselves ghosts, their light having traveled for decades, centuries, or millennia to reach me. For all anyone knew half of them might have burned out or gone supernova, and the sky, if we could see it as it really was, should be much darker. At some point I slipped from this dismal philosophizing into sleep. I saw the stars bursting one by one with a blinding light, leaving a deeper darkness behind them. "That can't be right," I said. My voice sounded strangely tinny in my ears, as if I was hearing it through a bad phone connection. "Stars don't die all at once. That takes millions of years. Billions!" At the same instant I knew what was wrong with my voice. It was no longer contained within the tent, which had vanished. I was out under the open sky, and the air was thinner than it had been. I had to breathe in great gulps of it to get enough oxygen, and when I did it tasted dry and dusty, without a hint of salt tang. The ground beneath my feet—I was now standing—was still sand, but much finer than it had been before, as if the sea had ground and reground it countless times over numberless geologic eras before drying up. This dry talc stretched away in all directions, as far as I could see, unbroken by trees or grasses or hills. Even a rock would have been a welcome sight, but there were only wind-sculpted ripples.

"Annie?" I gasped, and began to cough. "Annie, where are you?" A brilliant starburst cast cold shadows over the sand. The wind rose, with nothing to block it, blowing harder and harder until the tiny particles of sand stung me like billions of tiny bees. *Damned*, the voice of the wind slurred in my ears, *Annie is damned to wander the Earth forever, and you are damned with her.*

My eyelids slammed open like a window flung up in an airless room. The stars were fading in a deep blue predawn sky. I pawed at the tent flap, frantic to escape so I could see, hear and taste the rush of the waves up the ocean beach, which lay a couple hundred yards away along a winding path through forest and dune. My stumbling run startled a large animal—perhaps it was a whitetail deer—which went bounding away through the brush. In the distance I heard a pony whinny, and the sound was as great a comfort as the tumbling waves I heard half a second later. Still I ran on, determined to get the first glimpse I could of the banked fire of the dawn over the ocean glowing brighter and brighter till it gave birth to a rosy sun. There was a figure standing at the crest of the dunes, a wavering silhouette against the luminous sky. "Annie!" I shouted, straining to go faster and faster while my feet sank into soft sand. "Annie!" But when I reached the top, I found myself all alone in the glorious sunrise.

7

On Saturday I drove to the Reform synagogue in Ocean
Pines and borrowed a prayer book so I could look up the
text of a memorial prayer I remembered vaguely from my
grandfather's funeral when I was a high school freshman.
Then I drove to Salisbury to do some research on Green
Run at the university there, but found nothing of interest.
In the late afternoon I was hungry enough to want a break
from pb and js, so I drove to town and had a whole
medium pizza before returning to practice the *El Malei
Rachamim* prayer until I no longer awkwardly stumbled
over the Hebrew words—I had to do this right.

When I was done I lay on my back in bed and stared at
the ceiling, thinking about the meaning of the words I had
just recited. *Oh God full of mercy who dwells in Heaven, grant
perfect rest to the soul of Annie, who has left this world, under the
wings of Your divine presence, among the holy and pure souls on high
who shine like the glimmering heavens, for I will give charity in
memory of her soul. The Garden of Eden will be her resting place. So
You who are the source of all mercy, shelter her beneath Your wings
forever, and bind up her soul in the bond of life. God, You are hers,
and let her rest in peace. Amen.*

But wasn't that a little dishonest of me? If her soul

enjoyed perfect rest, whatever that meant, then she wouldn't be around to talk to me, would she? On the other hand, wasn't I trying to help her find some kind of peace, at least so that she wouldn't be so unbearably lonely (what would it be like not to be able to talk to anybody for more than a century)? Maybe too I could ease her terrible guilt, help her see nobody deserved what had happened to her. But how was I to go about it?

Eventually I dozed off, and though I kept waking up from nightmares that left me a wreck by morning, it wasn't as though working in the gatehouse at Assateague State Park required great mental concentration. Still I was relieved when Lakeisha showed up ten minutes early.

"Going off into the National Seashore again?" she asked as she sat in the broken-down swivel chair that was our only creature comfort in that booth. The lull before the late-afternoon surge of visitors gave us a minute or two to talk.

I shrugged. "Every day," I said.

"You sure must like it down there," Lakeisha said, giving me a quizzical look. "What's so great about it that you don't just hang out on the beach right here?"

"I find the walk relaxing," I said, adding with almost complete truthfulness, "It's the reason I came down here to work for the summer."

Lakeisha took this in skeptically. "Didn't you tell me you're studying marine biology over by College Park?" I nodded and she said, "Then what're you doing working here, collecting money from a bunch of sweaty tourists? You sure can't be getting much research done."

"Actually," I began, but just then a car rolled up and I was able to make my escape. Still, I mulled over what I could tell her in the future as I parked in the roundabout and set off on the now-familiar jog, with the waves on my left and the dunes on my right. Maybe the best tack would be to say something vague about historical research on the vanished settlements of Assateague Island and then turn the conversation around to her. Even a social misfit like me knows that most people love to talk about themselves.

If only that were true of Annie. I felt absurdly like some kind of amateur magician as I puffed along with my borrowed yarmulke and prayer book in my backpack. If she didn't want to see me, what difference would it make to her if I recited a Hebrew prayer over her grave? Maybe I should have figured out what kind of church she had attended so I could recite a prayer that would actually mean something to her. But no, she had rejected her own religion, if not the idea of God.

Today the weather fit my gloomy mood. It was cool, with a light mist in the air that made the familiar landmarks I looked for, like those funny-shaped dunes, hard to identify. I would have been lost without the kilometer posts, but finally I found the right gap between the dunes and made my way down the sandy path toward the campsite, turning right before I reached it and plunging into the woods to reach the hill where Annie's tombstone stood. I climbed slowly, not wanting to turn my ankle again in the fog. Her grave looked the same as always. I knelt and brushed the slightly damp sand away from it. Feeling more than a little ridiculous, I pulled the yarmulke and prayer book from the backpack and began to recite the *El Malei Rachamim.* My voice sounded strange in my own ears, deeper, more resonant. I finished. *This is it. This has to end. I can't keep doing this.*

"I'm sorry, Annie," I whispered, touching the top of the stone with my fingertips. "So sorry I never got to know you." I turned and got up to go, and she was sitting there with her wet hair, her feet tucked under her mud-spattered calico skirt and her hands on her knees, looking up at me with those sparkling green eyes.

"That was beautiful," she said. "I wish I could rest, like the prayer says."

I found my voice. "You understand Hebrew?"

She looked surprised, but only for a moment. "I find I

can understand whatever people say—what they are *really* saying, that is, not necessarily the words they use. Sometimes they match, but more often than not they don't."

"People don't say what they mean."

"No, they don't." She smiled sadly. "That's another reason I avoid them. It's confusing to stand there watching a family enjoying themselves on the beach, talking about how they're going to spend the rest of their vacation, while the father is thinking about how much he'd like to be with the girl in the bikini sprawled out on the towel next to him, the mother is thinking about her lover back home, and the little boys are scheming about how to get each other in trouble."

I winced. She could be describing my own parents. "Surely everyone isn't a hypocrite."

She gently laid her hand on mine. Such a normal human gesture. Did I feel cool fingertips on the back of my hand? No, there was nothing there but the fog. Well, almost nothing. There was a slight but definite tingling sensation, and the fine hairs on the back of my hand stood up, then bent slightly. Annie jerked her hand away, a gesture so sudden her fingertips actually went *through* my hand. We both flinched.

"N-no," she said. "Not everyone is a hypocrite. But most everyone has some reason to conceal at least part of what they are thinking all the time, from themselves as much as from those around them. You, for instance. You kept talking of your pH meter the day we met, how the blessed thing worked and why you were using it, just so you didn't have to say aloud that you were falling in love with me."

There was a long silence. I was intrigued by her story and felt sorry for her, that was what I had been telling myself. But falling in love? How could you fall in love with someone you barely knew? Someone you couldn't even touch? I hated to think of my actions as cliched, but wasn't love at first sight one of the biggest cliches? So how could I be guilty of it? I tried to answer her, tried to say anything at all, and failed. Several times. It was Annie who finally broke the silence.

"Of course I knew it at once. And in my selfishness, I didn't run away. It had been so long, you see, since I'd spoken to another human being..." She trailed off, and closed those amazing green eyes for a moment before continuing. "That's why I've done my best to avoid you these weeks past. So that you would give up hope of seeing me again, and you would go back to your college and your real life."

"And you would be all alone again," I said, trying to take her hand. Again the tingling. This time she did not jerk away. *I want to help her. Why can't I make her understand that?*

"I do understand it," she said, and I gave a start, not realizing I had spoken aloud. "But there is no way of helping such a one as me, Darren."

Her strange old-fashioned language was going to take getting used to, too. But it was part of her. "Maybe not," I said. "But I can be with you, talk to you. Help ease your loneliness." I tried a smile. "I can even try to talk about things other than the pH meter, or marine biology. There's my job, for instance. My completely fascinating job collecting payments from the visitors to the state park."

"What job? I thought you were in college."

"I am. I, uh, I just took a summer job down here to help pay for tuition. You know, work-study..."

"I don't know what you're talking about, Darren, but of course I know you deliberately took a job down here so you could look for me." She smiled at my stuttered confusion. "You can't even tell me a little white lie. I'm not human anymore."

"Yes you are!" I cried, jumping to my feet. My cheeks flushed as she sat still, gazing up at me. "You are more human than anyone else I know! More alive, too... I know that sounds ridiculous, but I'm not lying, I'm not!"

"Those are a child's denials, Darren," she said, and pain lanced through my heart as she climbed to her feet and faced me. Standing, she was almost as tall as me. It was so easy and yet impossible to imagine taking her in my arms. "Still, I know you mean what you say. But I'm dead, Darren. I was dead before your great-great-grandfather drew his first breath. And even when I was alive, I was nobody you would have wanted to meet. I was a backward country girl, already a married woman when I was eighteen. My duty and my destiny was to bear Will sons and daughters and raise them to adulthood—if I did not die in childbirth, or they of the diseases that killed so many children. It would have given Pa so much pleasure if I'd lived to give him grandchildren to play with, new lives to make up for those lost in the war."

"The Civil War, you mean."

"The Civil War, yes! Do you understand now how long ago all this was? Will was also a veteran. I lived through the war myself as a child. If not for—for what happened to me, if I had lived to grow old, I would still have died so many, many years ago, Darren."

"But what you said isn't true," I said. "The important part of it, I mean. That I would never have wanted anything to do with you when you were alive, because you were a 'backward country girl.' What kind of 'backward country girl' reads Thoreau and talks knowledgeably about 'natural philosophy'?"

"One with too much time on her hands," she said.

"'As if you could kill time without injuring eternity,'" I quoted.

She smiled. "Thoreau. I could kill all the time I wished and still not injure eternity in the slightest. It is all that is before me."

I shivered at that, though the day was warm. "Tell me then what it was like when you were alive," I said. "Everything you can remember."

She hesitated.

"You said something about duty, and destiny," I said. "Most people laugh at those words these days. Duty especially. Everyone's highest duty is to please himself." *But not me,* I was too shy to say; of course she knew I was thinking it, anyway. I struggled to express my next thought aloud: "I have a duty to you, though, because I—I choose to."

Her gaze locked on mine. I struggled not to blink or turn away. "And you believe that if I tell you the story of my life, we will discover why I became what I am, and I will be released," she said.

I nodded wordlessly.

"I think you will only learn how very ordinary a girl I was," she said.

"Nothing could make me think that."

She added softly, as if to herself, "And how sinful." And so she began to speak, softly at first, though her voice gained strength as the sun burned slowly down in the western sky.

8

My first memory is of a fire in the night, glittering off shards of broken glass, and angry shouts from somewhere outside. I was four years old, woken from a deep sleep, too terrified to scream. It did not matter, though, for in an instant my mother was there and had scooped me up in her arms.

It was a good thing, because the torchlight and the shattered window were but the beginning. No sooner was my head cradled against Mama's breast then a terrible pounding started up, a thundering as if God was stomping upon the world with His heaviest boots. I pressed closer to poor Mama, probably hurting her with my heavy head, in the vain hope of blotting out the awful noise. Far from stopping, it grew ever louder. I had a sense of motion, when all I wished of Mama was that she would stay still and make the din go away. I was too little to understand that that was not within her power, but not too little to fear being carried toward whatever monster was trying to break down our house.

Cool night air on the back of my neck told me she had flung the door open wide. "What is it you want!" she shouted at the monster.

It answered in the ordinary, rather nasal tones of our Baltimore neighbors. "We want that damned Yankee, Captain Josiah Wright!" a man's voice demanded.

My mother tossed back her long red hair. "He is not here. He has gone to serve his country."

"Gone to serve the tyrant Lincoln, you mean!" the voice sneered. "Or so you say, you bog-trotter! Stand aside and let us check he is not hiding behind your skirts!"

"Can you not see I have a sleeping child in my arms!" Mama said, just as I found my voice and began to wail. The world began to violently shake and a voice roared, "Quiet that brat!" as my mother added her screams to mine.

An enormous explosion close at hand silenced everyone. For a moment there was no sound but the hiss and crackle of the torches the men crowding round the doorway were carrying. Then I heard a new voice that sounded much like the others, only calm where theirs were agitated.

"So, these are the brave rebels of whom we have heard so much tell since the firing on Sumter," this voice said. "So brave are you that it takes only a baker's dozen armed with pistols, torches, and brickbats to stand up to a woman and a babe in arms."

I'm not a baby, I wanted to protest. *I sleep all by myself, in a real grown-up bed!* But terror kept me quiet. I dared to lift my head and look around. The faces of the men who wanted to harm my father were gaudy in the torchlight. I recognized one of them by his large, drooping ginger mustache and remembered he had shouted at me when a ball I was playing with bounced into his yard. The others were strangers to me, but Mama must have recognized some of them because she began to give them a tongue-lashing. "Timothy Weatherby, does Emily know you're here?" she demanded. "And you, Fred Haskins, what would your father say?" The men began to look at their feet, and one by one to slink off into the darkness. "I shall expect your payment for the glazier!" Mama shouted after them.

Our rescuer was left in shadow. He was tall and skinny, and carried a shotgun with a few wisps of smoke still escaping from the muzzle. That was all I could see of him at first. But I wriggled in Mama's arms enough to make her put me down. As soon as I was on my feet I walked over and looked up into his face, which was further darkened by the slouch hat he wore. "My mother and I thank you for your assistance, sir," I said, lisping a bit over the word "assistance" and curtseying in my nightgown.

The man shifted the shotgun to his left hand and bent down to shake my hand solemnly. "It was my pleasure," he said, his voice cracking on the last word.

"You are but a boy yourself!" Mama exclaimed, stepping closer so she could get a good look at his face. I thought that she was wrong. Surely this was a man who had come to our rescue. He was the taller than Mama, after all.

"Ma'am," he said, tugging at the brim of his hat. It was too soft and shapeless for him to tip easily.

"I beg your forgiveness for failing to offer you the poor hospitality of my home, but, as you see, my husband is not here," Mama said, her voice barely faltering at all.

"Captain Wright is doing his duty, serving his country in the 'Potomac Flotilla.' I hope to join him soon," the man, or boy, said.

"But surely you are too young," Mama said. "Have you even seen eighteen summers? What do your parents say?"

"My older brother, Kent, has already volunteered for service. I can do no less." He paused and added, "If there is any way you can get word to your husband that I would be proud to serve under him…"

"He's been gone more than a month," Mama said. "I do not know when we can expect to hear from him next. But I shall certainly try to get word to him. There are not enough brave men to serve, I am afraid."

The man snorted. "It took little bravery to stand up to that bunch of drunkards," he said. "It seems they are determined to justify our city's disgraceful nickname of Mobtown. But I thank you for your kindness. You may tell your husband to ask for William Pearson—they call me Will—in the big white frame house over yonder hill."

"Mrs. Josiah Wright—Peg," Mama said, with a graceful curtsey.

Then Will knelt down and put his hands on my shoulders. I looked into his smiling brown eyes. "You have your duty too, little girl. Now you must be brave and take good care of your mother." I nodded wordlessly. He stood up, winked at me, tugged once more at the brim of his hat, and walked off into the darkness.

["How can you remember all that?" I asked Annie, as we sat in the gathering dusk. Her hands were clasped around her knees, like anybody's, and but for the eerie fact that her hair never dried I could have forgotten for a moment that she was a ghost.

She pondered my question. "It seems to me I can recall all the moments of my life with the utmost clarity," she said. "Re-call them, literally. They are called up, from who knows where, to take place again before my eyes and ears. Even smells come back to me as they originally were. When I was telling you just now about the mob that came for my father, I could smell the daffodils that grew in front of our house—for it was springtime—though I doubt very much I noticed them at the time." She smiled slightly. "It is strange, isn't it, after all the time that has passed. A century, is it? Or more? Sometimes it seems to me that I have passed eternities wandering alone on these dunes. Other times it seems to me that I—I passed only yesterday. If not for the ponies, I think I would have gone mad. But shall I continue?"]

For the remainder of that night I slept in Mama's bed, for there was broken glass strewn all around the nursery, and come morning I helped her and our housemaid, a Negro freedwoman named Violet, to clean up the mess. Or at least I tried to, but after I cut my fingers and Mama bandaged them she told me to run along and play, so I took my dolls out to the front yard.

Even those of our neighbors who weren't Southern sympathizers considered us outsiders. Pa hailed from Truro out on Cape Cod, and Mama was Irish, with the accent to prove it, although her father had brought her from the old country when she was a child. Daddo— grandfather, in the old Irish language—was a railroad worker, which made him little better than a Negro as far as Baltimore's "quality" were concerned, though he was always gentle with me. Pa's family must have wanted nothing more to do with him after he married an Irish girl, for he never spoke of them. He worked on a whaler when he was a young man, and met Mama when his ship put into Baltimore for repairs after a nor'easter. "Your father was such a dashing young sailor, and so wise for his years," Mama would say when I begged her to tell me of my father, for until I was nine years old, he was away at the war except for rare visits.

"Did he already have his beard, Mama?"

"Yes, and he'll never shave it off no matter how many times I beg him to," she sighed.

I liked the beard, which was nice and soft when he kissed me. But I may have been partial, for when he did visit us I could not have been more excited had it been Mr. Lincoln himself come to pay his compliments. He always brought fresh seafood for us, since "we are often anchored in some cove with nothing to do but wait for some smuggler to show himself, and what better disguise than as simple fisherfolk?" It sounded terribly exciting, but he assured me it was not. Once I overheard him tell Mama that the war for him was like drifting on a becalmed ocean on a windless overcast day, except on the rare occasions when he and his crew actually did catch sight of a smuggler or a rebel boat out to make trouble and gave chase.

"I don't like to think of the danger you're in," Mama said, very low.

"There's no danger!" Pa bluffed. "Not as long as I've

got trusty men like Will Pearson by my side!" That wasn't true, of course, as we learned to our horror when the rebels sunk Pa's ship—a captured smuggler's sloop he had named the *Anne Marie* after me—in the winter of 1862. This was just weeks after the battle of Antietam, which had taken place less than eighty miles to our west. You couldn't avoid its terrible reach even if you were as little as I was, thanks to the posting on every church wall of the endless lists of dead, not to mention the aimless crowds of women dressed in black wandering the streets of Baltimore like shades. I had just turned six years old. But after a brief visit home for Christmas, with faithful and handsome young Will in tow, Pa was soon back to battling Rebs and smugglers on the Chesapeake Bay and the normally quiet rivers that fed into it.

9

The last of the sunset had long since faded from the sky above the mainland, far behind me beyond the treetops, when Annie fell silent. I stood up and brushed long brown pine needles from my jeans. The bright yellow moonlight and the soft glow Annie gave off made everything look surreal. An owl hooted in the woods and I shivered. Annie looked up at me with concern. "It is late," she said simply. "I got lost, telling you these stories. For a while I was alive, and a child again."

"Then it was worth it," I said absently. Without quite thinking about where I was going or what I was doing I started down the hillside toward the ruins of the hotel, and the water beyond it. As I emerged from the trees, the soft night sky opened up to me, a sky washed of most of its stars by a full moon that was swelling and darkening as it sank toward the black uneven line of the mainland. There was no sound but the lapping of the little wavelets that filled the bay and the cry of a heron somewhere in the marsh. Annie came and stood silently beside me, watching the moon. If she had been there for real, in the flesh, I have no doubt we would have kissed then.

Instead she said abruptly, "This is where I died." I kept

my eyes fixed on the moon because I was afraid to see the expression on her face. "How?" I whispered, and she replied softly, "You know how." Yes. Her clothes and her hair always looked wet. She stared at the moon.

"It was an accident," she said, flatly. "Will and I were returning to the island from the mainland in a catboat. It was winter, with Christmastime coming. A storm blew up out of nowhere. I heard Will shout out a warning, but it was too late. The jibboom swung around and hit me on the head, and I fell overboard. And so I drowned." She told me how she had woken up on the dock beside the hotel only to see her father coming in off the water bearing her dead body, a burden he refused to pass on to her husband. How she saw her father keeping a deathwatch over her body as it lay on an ornate sofa in the lobby ("I always hated that sofa, the upholstery was so scratchy. But how I wished I could feel it now!"). How he leaned on Will, sobbing openly, at her funeral.

"You know the muffled whisper a shovel makes in sand," she said, smiling slightly as if at a fond memory. "And that was all. The stone came later. When I happened on it one day, it was a surprise. The woman it spoke of was a stranger. Beloved wife and daughter? Taken by the cruel sea? It sounded like somebody else's tragedy that you might read about in the newspaper. You know the kind of thing. 'A Melancholy Accident.'"

"What about your funeral?"

She sighed. "I try not to think about it. But I can't forget Pa's face—it looked like he was the one who had died—and a blue jay that landed on a pine branch high above and chattered noisily over Pastor Scarburgh's eulogy." She smiled sadly again. "For a moment I actually did believe in God's justice, hearing that hypocrite's voice drowned out by a simple bird. Well, it is a strange experience hearing yourself described as seven kinds of angel and blessed saint, when you know full well you're not, and that you are sitting at Jesus' right hand in Heaven

57

when you're only staring at the pastor's too-handsome face."

"Why did you hate him so much?" I asked. "This Pastor Scarburgh."

"He was a rotten hypocrite, I just told you so," she snapped, a bit too quickly.

"Is that the whole story?"

"Isn't that enough?" Her face softened after a moment. "But I am forgetting it's nighttime. And you have to go home to rest so you can work tomorrow. I know you're not looking forward to that long run up the beach and then the drive home in your horseless carriage, don't bother to deny it."

"Come home with me," I said suddenly.

She stared at me. "I didn't mean," I stammered, "I didn't mean it in *that* way... I don't ever forget that that's not even possible..."

Annie brushed my cheek with her hand. Again there was that faint tingling. Could the sensation be electrical? Could there really be some kind of scientific explanation for what I was experiencing? But what kind of explanation could account for the overwhelming sense that Annie was fully human, in her torment as much as in her warmth and shyness?

When I told her what I was thinking she chuckled. "I'm not a bolt of ball lightning," she said. "I wish I was! Then I'd have only a few seconds of this half-existence... And I know what lies behind your invitation. You wish only to ease my loneliness, and your own. No, don't blush again! There is nothing shameful in that. But I cannot leave the island. I cannot even move very far from where the village of Green Run used to be. A mile or two at most."

I frowned. "But you just told me you lived in Baltimore when you were little. Can't you return there?"

She shook her head. "Never. I've never been able to stray far from where I died, in all the years since then."

"Then I will have to keep coming out here, until you've

finished telling me your story and we can figure out what to do about it—about your situation," I said.

She rolled her eyes, and in that moment she might have been a twenty-first century girl. "Darren, I'm not a problem to be solved. Perhaps there is no solution, and I must wander here forever."

"That can't be true! Or anyway we can't resign ourselves to it. Not till I've heard everything about your life, and we can be sure there was nothing left unresolved. And if there *is* something, then I will make sure to resolve it for you. Or, I mean, with you." I didn't want her to think I was arrogant. But didn't women of her time expect men to take care of them? I had no idea what approach to take. She must have sensed my confusion—I could see it in her eyes, and in the way she raised her hand to my cheek. Again that tingling. I closed my eyes and pretended it was flesh and blood I was feeling.

"Darren, nobody has tried to help me since Pa walked this earth," she said quietly. "If we had lived at the same time... if we had met in life... but we didn't. Will you waste your whole life coming out here to be with a whispered memory of a woman—one who suffers for her sins—instead of looking for a living woman as good and sweet and kind as you?"

"But I choose to do it," I said. "I have chosen. Or put another way, maybe I can't choose. Being in love with you, I can't walk away and leave you all alone again. Besides..." I hesitated a moment, not sure if I should dare speak my thoughts aloud. "Well, I think like a scientist. I can't bear not to investigate a mystery."

She was silent for a long time. And I saw her looking at me the same way I imagined I must be looking at her— with pity and yearning and compassion all mixed up together. Was that mishmash of feelings the same thing as love? I didn't have enough experience to know, and although she had been born so long ago and had once been married, I suspected she didn't, either.

"Well then," she said, "I will tell you my story to the end. But on one condition. You have to go back home and get some sleep before work tomorrow."

She was right. But trudging up the beach in the darkness seemed to take much longer than in the afternoon. By the time I reached my car, I could have fallen asleep standing up, like one of the island ponies. I managed to drive home, only to have a night full of dreams like the one where I was all alone in a desert world.

Naturally I was a wreck at work the next day. All day long I kept giving people the wrong change as I brooded about Annie. She remembered the Civil War. Could I ever hope to understand what her life had been like? And how was I going to figure out how and why she had died so young, and why her spirit was still unquiet all these years later?

When four o'clock finally arrived, Kevin drove up to drop off Lakeisha, who took one look at me and announced that I looked like hell. "What you been doin' to yourself?"

"Nothing," I said, swallowing a yawn.

She put her hands on her hips and snorted. "Honey, you can barely stand up straight."

Kevin called from his car, "When was the last time you had a decent meal?"

"I've been eating fine!" My voice cracked.

"Uh-huh," Kevin said. "Go clock out, then follow me to Island Market for a crab cake sandwich. My treat."

My protests did no good, and less than twenty minutes later I found myself being manhandled through the old-timey wooden plank door of Island Market.

"Ain't my business, kid, but Keisha is starting to get worried about you," Kevin said as he shepherded me inside. He probably wasn't more than six or seven years older than me. But he was so much more self-confident and mature. "Two crab sandwiches, please, Jodie," he said to the woman behind the counter, a heavyset white lady who wore thick glasses and was nice to me whenever I stopped in.

"Comin' right up. Hey Darren."

When she ducked back into the kitchen, Kevin said, "Keisha tells me you head off into the National Seashore, all by yourself, every afternoon, after a full day manning that damned gatehouse."

I turned away from him and sat down at one of the small collection of flyspecked tables. "I'm doing research." Could Kevin see through me as easily as Annie? So I laid it on a little thick, telling him about the bay grass count and the bigger ocean acidification study and my minuscule part in the latter. "It's a worldwide project. At first it looked like a good thing that the oceans soak up about a quarter of the carbon dioxide people produce by burning fossil fuels, but if the seas turn all acid, what'll happen to all the fish and wildlife?"

He shook his head. "Nothing good, that's for sure. Pretty scary stuff. My father's side of the family has lived down here on the shore since the seventeenth century, and once we got free of slavery, a lot of us worked as watermen, or in canneries. Time was, you could practically put your bare hands in the Chesapeake and harvest oysters. Now, though…" He let his voice trail off, and a glint came into his eye. "But Keisha tells me you hike away down the beach with only a little backpack for drinking water, hauling your scientific equipment. So tell me the truth. It's something to do with that girl you moved down here for the summer for, isn't it?"

I'd forgotten I'd more or less copped to that. The simplest thing to do was just admit he was right, and try to change the subject. "Yeah, I meet her down there," I said, nodding.

"Every day? What's she do, live down there?"

"Sort of. Not really." Had Annie come to hate Assateague? She hadn't been born there, but now she was a prisoner, tied to a village that had vanished.

"Mystery island girl, summer romance. Sounds like a bitchin' rock ballad," Kevin said, smiling. He took a final swig of his Coke and stood up. "Well, let's get you home. Oh, and don't worry about coming in to work tomorrow—Keisha is telling Cropper that you need a sick day."

I nodded. I needed to get some sleep and think over everything Annie had told me.

As he was dropping me off at the trailer, Kevin said, "Oh, I almost forgot. Remember how you were asking me whether any of my family ever lived at Green Run, and I said no?"

My heart raced. "Yes."

"Well, I was talking to my granny—actually my great-grandmother Hattie. I went to see her at the nursing home up in Delaware. She can't see anymore, but her mind's still good. Well, I mentioned your question, and she said her Uncle Jim—her great-uncle, her grandfather's brother—worked at a hotel in Green Run, when he was young. The place was called Wright's Ocean House. Can you imagine, a hotel out on Assateague Island back then, when the only way to get there was by boat?"

I wished I could tell Annie about this new development right away, but I really was exhausted, and I ended up sleeping through the night until midmorning. I got up and stretched. My legs ached but I was otherwise refreshed and very hungry. My fridge was empty but I hadn't been spending anything, so I decided to treat myself to another crab cake sandwich at Island Market on my way out to the island. Jodie smiled at me. "You're looking better than you did yesterday."

I shrugged. "I was pretty under the weather."

"I see you drive past here every morning in your State Park uniform, hon, just as I'm opening up," she said, sliding my sandwich across the counter to me. "But you don't come back till I'm closing up, or sometimes not at all. What do you do out on the island?"

Did everyone have to know my business? I gave her the line about doing oceanographic and bay grass research and she nodded sympathetically. "My husband Bill likes to fish in the bay when he gets off work, and he says it's getting harder all the time to catch sea bass. Maybe they're sensitive to changes in pH?"

I said I didn't know but it was more likely to be a local problem, runoff from the chicken farms that crowd the Eastern Shore being the likeliest culprit. She scowled at that and I wondered if Bill worked for Perdue or some other industrial chicken concern. You can't blame people for having to earn a living.

I sped past the State Park entrance hoping Bob wouldn't see me, and headed off down Bayberry Drive. Sparkling puddles on the road shivered in the breeze, and fat drops fell off the trees. There had been a thunderstorm earlier in the day, when I was still sleeping. But it was bright and sunny as I parked my car and set off down the beach at a brisk jog. The damp sand underfoot made the going easy. Annie was waiting for me, smiling, atop the same dune where I'd first seen her.

"Darren, I hope," she began.

"I'd like to kiss you," I interrupted.

"Well, I—I don't think that's possible." Her smile had turned a bit crooked. But it was still there.

"I'm going to try," I said, and flung my arms around her—around the space where it looked like she was standing—and closed my eyes. A sharp tingling like an electric shock began at my lips, shot down my arms to the tips of my fingers and exploded down my chest, which was pressed against hers—or would have been, if Annie had had a body. Sparks cascaded down my legs. I unclasped my arms and staggered backward, till I sat down hard in the warm sand. The day had darkened, and my ears buzzed. Gradually my senses cleared and I became aware of Annie leaning over me, her face framed by the bright blue sky but glowing with an inner light of its own. She was saying my name over and over, her perfect forehead wrinkled with worry.

"I'm all right," I said, sitting up straight. Annie just looked at me. I smiled at her. "That was quite a kiss."

"I felt something too," she whispered, her eyes wide. "I did! I felt something, Darren!" She made an abortive gesture as if to take my hands in hers, but jerked back.

"Is that so amazing?" I asked with a half-smile.

"You don't understand. Well, you can't understand. Ever since—ever since that day on the boat, I experience the world through sight and sound alone. I feel nothing, I smell nothing, I can taste nothing, except in memory." She twisted her hands in her lap, her gaze still locked on mine. "How could you understand?" she said again. "Sensation is linked to the body. But I am nothing. I am merely an image, a memory of what once was."

"But that's not so!" I protested. "You may not be able to feel, but you have feelings—emotions—responses to me, and to your memories. No picture on a TV screen could say the same." *A TV screen? She won't have any idea what I'm talking about!* But she ignored that.

"I do feel, now. I felt something when you tried to kiss me," she said, plaintively. "A faint tingling."

"Let's go for a walk in the forest, and you can pick up your story where we left off the day before yesterday."

"Of course! You are getting too hot in this bright sun," she said, jumping to her feet and darting away through a gap in the dunes—not the broad, well-marked path to the campsite, but a narrower valley that led to a winding footpath between tall loblolly pines. She led the way to an old sand dune that had become covered with dead brown pine needles over time until it resembled a haystack. This offered a comfortable place to sit and I sank down with a grateful sigh in the dappled shade and guzzled the water bottles I had brought with me while Annie resumed her tale.

10

Mama had come down with a cough that got worse as the winter wore on. Bad spells of it left her wheezing and gasping for breath and massaging her chest as if it hurt. Selfish little girl though I was, even I began to grow concerned, and Violet took to asking her whether she was all right after these spells, and offered to prepare herbal poultices for her. But Mama only smiled and said, "There is nothing to worry about. We McGonagles have weak chests, that is all. I'll be right as rain come spring, you'll see!" But she wasn't.

In the meantime that winter of gloom was lifted by the amazing news out of Washington City that Mr. Lincoln had freed the slaves with a stroke of his pen! Violet was beside herself with excitement. "I'll be seeing them again soon, as freedmen, Tom and little Jimmy!" she exclaimed, leaving the washing board for a moment to ruffle my hair with wet, soapy hands. I didn't mind—her joy was infectious.

[At this point I interrupted her and said, "I meant to tell you— there is a policeman in Ocean City—an, er, a Negro whose trailer I'm renting—and he says the brother of one of his ancestors worked at your father's hotel. A man named Jim. Could it have been the

same person?"

"Yes, it must have been the same Jimmy I am telling you about," she said, an expression I couldn't read flitting across her delicate features. *"But to continue—"]*

"Don't get too excited, Violet," Mama said, coming into the room with her arms full of laundry from the clothesline outside. Not only were the skirts and blouses stiff from drying in the wind, they crackled with tiny ice crystals from the cold snap that had set in after Christmas. I hoped they wouldn't be too damp when they thawed. How I hated the moist clothing that we suffered from all winter! You would have thought I could have spared my pity for my poor father and Will, huddling against the chill wind over the water in a new boat he had doubtless named after me, not daring to light a fire lest the smoke alert the rebels to their position. Or for Mama—well, I *was* concerned about her, but only because it was she who fed me and clothed me and kept me warm.

["Don't you think you're being a little hard on yourself?" I asked. How I wished I could hold her! "All children are selfish, Annie. It's just the way they are."

She stared at me. "It is not! A dutiful girl is not always thinking of her own petty wants. She is thinking of how best to help her parents. And then when she grows up and is married, her duty is to her husband. I failed at all of these, hence my punishment." Her eyes held the calmness of a long-settled despair. I gave up on arguing with her for the moment.]

Violet looked at Mama with resentment, but she was only counseling her sensibly not to get her hopes too high. We had no way of knowing whether Colonel Greer's farm, near Montross, Virginia, was still in rebel hands or not. Pa had been vague on that point. Even if the area had been restored to rightful authority, the colonel might have fled south with his slaves.

"Oh, I know all that, Miz Margaret," Violet said softly. She refused to call Mama Peg no matter how many times she had been invited to do so. "But this is the end of slavery. Pharaoh and his horde are goin' down in the Red Sea."

"I thought Pa was going to sink them in the Chesapeake Bay," I said. Violet and Mama both laughed, and Violet ruffled my hair again. The warmth of that moment has stayed with me all this time, to the grave and beyond.

The spring thaw was welcome, but it did little to improve Mama's "weak chest." The pay packets Pa sent us could not keep pace with the food I ate in ever greater amounts and the dresses and shoes I wore out, and Mama was forced to take in sewing, a task she undertook with a handkerchief ready at hand for her prolonged and frequent coughing spells. Violet and I helped her with the jobs she got, but my clumsy, childish efforts were clearly of little worth next to the skilled, rapid piecework Violet could turn out with her strong, nimble fingers. Sometimes I sat with my own work in my lap and just watched. Eventually Mama took pity on me, or more likely on Violet as the object of my open stares, and told me to run along and play or go over my lessons. I'd scowl and stick out my lower lip at that. "It's boring, practicing all those curlicues Mrs. Wintergreen wants!" I had begun attending the neighborhood school—Pa had said no daughter of his would grow up illiterate.

Instead of the swat I deserved, Mama would smile her patient, tired smile. "Annie dearest, if you don't learn to write like a lady how will anyone know what interesting thoughts you have to share?"

"Run along, child," Violet would add in her kindly way. "When I was on Colonel Greer's farm I would have been lashed within an inch of my life for practicing curlicues! I never did learn to read and write until I got my freedom."

"And how was that, Violet?" I loved asking rude questions that were none of my business, and that should by rights have earned me a spanking. "That you got the money to buy your freedom, I mean."

"Run along now," Violet would say, bending her head back to her work.

#

The warm weather seemed rather to worsen Mama's cough than to give her relief. Sometimes she would complain of heat, even on cool days, and a flush came to her cheeks. At school the boys ran wild, throwing things at Mrs. Wintergreen when her back was turned and then blaming me, so that I got a caning! When I ran to Mama to complain she murmured something soothing but her eyes were sunken and her movements apathetic. I was not even seven years old and my fear took the form of tantrums of wild screaming and crying and kicking at the walls. More than once I left a dent in the plaster. I was so bad that even Pa, endlessly patient and loving Pa, had to give me a spanking when he finally came home on three days' leave in early June.

He was worried about Mama, I could see that. From my eavesdropping post I heard Pa ask whether she had been to see Dr. Sherman about "that terrible cough of yours."

"Don't exaggerate, Josiah, 'tis nothing but a summer cold," she said.

"And when last I was here you said you would be better when the warm weather arrived. I don't like it, Peg."

"We've no money for a doctor, Josiah, and besides I know perfectly well what he would say." Mama put on an uncannily good imitation of the doctor's nasal Chesapeake country twang. "You need to move up to the mountains for your health, Mrs. Wright. The cool, dry air will do your lungs a power of good!"

Pa chuckled dutifully, but he was not to be deflected. "And what's so bad about that idea, Peg? This city is awful in the summertime. If you aren't sick already, you're liable to get sick from the soggy, foul air. There are rumors of yellow fever spreading all along the seaboard, and with all these extra people in town because of the war—"

"Which is worse in the mountains than anywhere else, Josiah, you know that."

"But you aren't safe here either, Peg. There are rumors that Lee's army is on the march, heading north. Everyone knows the rebels would like nothing better than to cut Washington City off from the rest of the country, and what better way to do that than to invade Baltimore? Lord knows there are more than enough traitors here who would welcome them."

"I need no reminder of that," Mama said.

"Well then. You must leave, with Annie. You are right that the mountains west of here are too dangerous, so it's best you go to the Far West. You have never seen mountains so tall and beautiful, with snow atop them the year round!"

"Nonsense. I shall not go so far from you!"

"Come on, Peg. You must, for your health! You can take the train to Kansas City, and then a stage—"

"Never! I refuse to leave you behind. I shall stay here and recover my health!" The effect of this declaration was spoiled by a prolonged coughing fit. I went charging down into the sitting room, where I jumped up and down like a perfect little maniac and shouted, "Train! Train! I want to go on a train! I want to see mountains! Oh, please, Mama!"

Pa laughed and swept me into his arms. He smelled of pipe tobacco, sweat, and a harsher smell under it. Gunpowder? "See, Peg, the child wants to see the West! How can you refuse her?"

Mama ignored me, her eyes fixed on Pa. "I tell you, I won't go so far from you, Josiah."

Pa shook his head, his salt-and-pepper beard brushing deliciously against my cheek. "You're a stubborn woman, Peg."

She forced a smile. "You need a strong woman by your

side. And I swear I will be here for you when you come back from the war."

11

"Who would have guessed that it was my poor mother, not Pa, who would not survive the war?" Annie said. Every line on her face drooped, and to my alarm, I glimpsed a tree trunk *through* her body. What if she evaporated completely, from inconsolable grief? How could I stop that? Forcing a smile, I said, "Let's take a break, okay? Why don't we see what Scotty's band is up to?" I stood up and offered her my hand, an automatic gesture. She and I both smiled, and she put out her hand as if to take mine, but left a gap of an inch or so between us. When she was on her feet, she made as if to brush her skirts off—so I was not the only one affected by force of old habits. Though the habits were *very* old, in her case!

"We're in luck," she said, pointing, "They're grazing in the marsh just behind that stand of trees."

So we set off through the forest, Annie on my left. After a moment I put out my hand, intentionally this time, as if to take hers, and she moved her hand toward mine—closer this time, the gap was half an inch at most. I squeezed my eyes shut for a moment, yearning to feel my fingers entwined with hers. I was sure she was wishing for the same thing.

A few more steps, and Annie halted. "Let's stop here. This bunch is a little skittish—especially Terry since she foaled Jamie. If you climb that old sand dune over there, you should be able to get a good view of the band through the trees."

The ponies milled around, grazing on the bright green salt marsh hay. There was no need to ask which ones were Terry and Jamie. The colt, still only a few weeks old, was much smaller than the other animals, and he was galloping in lazy circles around his mother. After a minute or two he tired of this and ducked under Terry's flanks to nurse from her. She turned her body at an angle to help him, swishing her tail around to keep the flies away.

"Uh oh," Annie said softly.

"What is it?" I whispered.

"That yearling over there—the one bobbing her dark brown head—I call her Jenny—she's trying to get in on the act."

Sure enough, the filly she had described was attempting to nuzzle up to Terry, but the mare turned her head and bared her teeth at her, and she backed off.

"Poor thing," Annie said softly. "Her mother, Ellen, died last winter. She was pregnant, and carrying a new foal while trying to nurse Jenny was too much for her. Mares won't allow anyone but their own foals to nurse from them. You can't blame them, of course, but perhaps Jenny just misses her mother."

I looked at Annie. "You might be talking about your own grief."

"Yes. I miss my mother every day," she said, watching the mare and her colt. "Every day for the past fifty thousand days since I wore mortal flesh, I have missed them."

"Your mother died before you," I said slowly, "but what about your father? Did he live long after your death?"

"Yes." A barely audible whisper.

"Did you—could you—did you ever speak to him

then? I mean, as you are now?"

"I tried. He could neither hear nor see me. Except once… It was a cold winter night, the anniversary of my death. I knew that because he had walked to my grave, brushed the snow off the stone and the dead leaves and sand from in front of it, and stood motionless and silent with his head bowed in the freezing wind for close to an hour. He could not bear to visit it at any other time, even when Will was away and there was no one else to tend it. He could have asked one of the people who worked at his hotel to do it—I know he thought of asking Betty, and I would have been touched if he had, since she was almost like an older sister to me. But in the end, he couldn't bear to ask her to do it. I didn't mind, though. I wouldn't have minded if he had never visited my grave. I knew his heart, and he would never be whole again now that I was gone.

"This time, it was almost sunset when he made his way up the hill, and darkness had already fallen by the time he made his way back. He lit a fire in the deserted lobby and fell asleep in front of it. I sat in a chair opposite him and watched him. After a time the fire burned low. If I had been flesh, I would have brought a blanket to cover him— his left knee had bothered him ever since he banged it when the rebels sank the first *Anne Marie*. Perhaps the cold and the pain were what woke him now. His eyes opened, the pale blue irises flashing strangely in the light of the dying fire, and he saw me. He thought he was dreaming, and I knew I must not tell him he wasn't—remember, he was a hard-headed, skeptical Yankee. What would happen to his mind if he had to accept that ghosts were real? As part of a dream, though, he could accept my presence, could say my name.

"I cried then and told him how sorry I was. 'Sorry for what?' he asked, and I couldn't explain. He shook his head, then bethought himself to ask where Mama was, why she wasn't there. 'Because she is in Heaven, Pa,' I said. 'Or wherever it is the righteous go. I must go on walking the earth for my sins.' He began to cry, and I fled the hotel, walked as far away as I could in the troubled dark, out to where I could watch the ocean spend its senseless fury on the sand. When I ventured back an hour later he had fallen asleep again. I was glad of it. Let his soul forget I had ever lived, I who had brought him nothing but sorrow."

I could think of nothing to say for a long while. We watched Scotty's band graze peacefully as the sun slowly drew near the western horizon. Jamie tilted his head back and drank in the breeze that had sprung up. I said, "I thought you couldn't lie."

"Excuse me?" There was surprise and a hint of outrage in her voice.

"I thought you could speak nothing but truth. Yes, you never quite said so, but what's the point of telling me the story of your life if you're going to *lie* to me?"

"How can you say that, Darren? Every word I've said to you has been true!"

I shook my head. "No, Annie. You told me you brought your father nothing but sorrow. That can't be true, when he loved you as much as he did."

"It *is* true, *because* he loved me as much as he did. He made a terrible mistake, to love such a worthless girl, even if I was his daughter. The same mistake you are making, Darren, except now there isn't even a wicked girl to love. There is nothing but a tormented wraith."

"Annie—"

"I am nothing!" she shouted. "Nothing, don't you see? There is nothing here!" And she spun around and fled into the darkness of the forest. There was a commotion in the marsh to my right, and I turned, startled, as the stallion Scotty reared up on his hind legs and whinnied loudly, his eyes rolling. Then he took off running across the mud flats, with the rest of the band close behind him, and little Jamie laboring frantically to keep up.

I stood there stunned in the gathering dark. At last I turned back toward the forest, to cross the line of dunes and start the long trek back up the beach to where my car was parked. But something was wrong, a tiny sensation that was out of place with the muggy summer night air. It took me a long, slow moment to place it, but then I lifted my left arm toward my face as if in a dream. There was a cold spot on my wrist, and I thought of how Annie had spun wildly around, tears spattering in a sudden storm from her overflowing eyes. I touched my wrist to my lips and tasted salt.

12

Annie was waiting for me the next day in her accustomed spot on the crest of the dunes, a half-smile on her face. We stumbled all over each other's awkward apologies and insistences that no, it is *I* who must apologize. It was almost funny, except that it hurt too much.

"I don't like to remember that time," Annie said when I asked if she wanted to resume her story. "It was a hard winter. Our hopes that the war would end quickly and Pa would soon return to us faded. Mama stopped reading the papers and spent a lot of time huddled near the fire, drinking the herb teas Violet fixed her. It was Violet who had to get me ready for school most mornings, and eventually she simply moved in with us. 'Saves me money on the rent and the streetcar fare both,' she smiled when I asked if she didn't miss her own home. Of course, she hadn't really had her own home anyway—she shared a room with four other domestic servants—so maybe it wasn't such a sacrifice for her. I felt safer and better with her around, and I think I began to behave better too—she was so cheerful she could make Mama smile even on her bad days, but she was also stern enough to keep me in line and make sure I did my schoolwork before getting up to my deviltry in the streets."

"Deviltry?" I smiled. "What 'deviltry' could you have been up to, Annie?"

She scowled at me. "You imagine little girls are all smiles and dimples and playing with their dolls, or at least *I* must have been like that because I grew up in such a 'quaint' time."

I opened my mouth, and quickly snapped it shut.

"It is lucky Mama never bought me any dolls, because I would surely have pulled them apart," she said grimly. "No matter how much Mama, Pa, and Violet spoiled me, I was always angry because Pa was away at the war. Mrs. Wintergreen's school was a rough place, I told you that, and I soon learned to use my fists and my feet in a most unladylike manner to keep those boys from tormenting me."

"You were defending yourself."

"But I didn't know when to stop. That winter I'd pull on the gloves Mama had knitted for me and go out to the woods on the hill behind our house. On the other side of the hill was a broad carriage road that led to the turnpike out to Frederick. I'd find small rocks, pack the snow carefully around them until they were smooth, hard balls of ice, and stockpile these ice balls until a fine carriage rattled past." She shut her eyes. "I convinced myself that all those carriages were the property of plantation owners, that all their wealth came from slaves. That is how I justified myself. If I broke a glass window, I imagined I'd won a battle for General Grant. If I heard someone inside the carriage cry out in pain, I imagined it was General Lee himself! I was never even caught, though a coachman came very near, once." She bowed her head.

I didn't know what to say. "Did you ever aim at a horse?" I asked.

"Me, hurt an innocent animal? Never! Which was lucky, because if I'd panicked a horse and it bolted, I could have killed someone."

"But you didn't," I said gently. "Kill anyone, that is."

"Not for want of trying, Darren."

"No one would think it was strange if a boy without a father had acted like that," I pointed out.

"Perhaps, but it was unnatural in a girl. And I wouldn't help with the chores at home. For all my fine beliefs about freeing the slaves, I was more than content to let Violet do all the work around the house."

"But you were a child."

"An evil one."

I bit my lip. How could I get her to stop condemning herself? How could she stop? She'd had nothing to do but mull endlessly over her "sins," no one to talk to but her own tormenting conscience, for two whole human lifetimes.

"If I were to vanish, it would be a most wonderful gift," she whispered, a tear rolling down her cheek. I reached out as it fell. Once again I managed to catch it, and wordlessly I lifted my hand. The shining drop rested in my palm. She stared at it, then into my eyes. "What does this mean?"

I shook my head.

"You," she said. "You are taking on my pain, my guilt. You mustn't do that, Darren!"

"I'm not," I said. I paused and wracked my brains for some way of cheering her up. "It looks like it's going to be a beautiful sunset," I said after a moment, reaching out my hand to her, "would you like to walk along the beach?"

"Darren, I—"

"Come on. Your eternal shame will still be waiting for you when we get back," I said, then clapped my hand over my mouth.

But Annie laughed out loud. "Okay, Darren, I will walk along the beach with you."

It was a gorgeous evening. Once we were out on the open sand, a fresh breeze off the water blew away the humidity that had settled in smothering waves over us in the forest, and blessedly kept the mosquitos away as well. The orange sun was just brushing the tops of the dunes as we set out, casting strange stretched-out shadows that reached for us where we strolled along the water's edge.

"I wish you could feel the breeze and smell the sea," I said.

"I can see your face, Darren, and sense your delight, and that is almost as good."

"I wish you were here, in the flesh, to enjoy this moment."

"But how is that to happen, dear Darren? There is no way for me to live again. My poor bones lie moldering on the other side of those dunes. Perhaps God could give them flesh again, as it says in the Bible; but if He exists, He has chosen not to, and so I am forced to conclude that He has judged me a sinner and condemned me to wander this earth in this half-life forever."

I shivered, remembering the scientific meaning of *half-life*: the length of time it takes a radioactive element to lose half of its radioactivity. In the same amount of time again, the element will lose another quarter of its original strength, and then an eighth… until it "decays" to the point that its radioactivity becomes undetectable. *Until it fades away.* Which was worse, oblivion or being a ghost forever? I had to save Annie from those fates. In that moment, a desperate inspiration came to me. "I want you to come home with me!"

Annie boggled at me. "Come home with you? Darren, I've told you, I can't leave this island. I can't go far at all from the spot where I once lived—and died."

"How do you know?" I said.

She closed her eyes and shook her head. "Don't you think I've tried?" she whispered. "An invisible force pushes me back every time I try to cross the bridge."

Wait. That was strange—individual strands of hair swirled around her face, as if they were drying in the wind.

But what did it mean that her hair, still wet from her drowning a century and a half ago, was now appearing to dry?

When I pointed this out, she looked at me, her eyes suddenly aglow. "It means I'm changing, Darren. It means that somehow you're changing me!" She began to laugh, a sound I had rarely heard before.

"You see!" I said. "Anything is possible. You are pure spirit, not tied to a body. You can do anything you want, go anywhere you want. Nothing can stop you!"

Annie took off running, laughing her way up the beach as I followed breathlessly behind. If not for all the practice I'd had jogging down to meet her over the weeks, I'd never have been able to keep up. It wasn't until much later that I realized what I had missed in my explanation of what kept her tied to the site of Green Run.

I hadn't mentioned her husband. And neither had she.

In the moment there was only the exuberance of chasing her up the open beach. Was she dead, and a ghost? It seemed impossible—no one had ever been more alive! The casual beachgoers I saw in increasing numbers as we drew ever nearer to the end of the road, where my car was parked, were looking strangely at me as I dashed giggling past. They probably couldn't see Annie and thought I was just running up the beach shouting and laughing like a madman. But so what? I didn't care what any of them thought. I had found love—I loved Annie, and she loved me back—and so what if she was a ghost? People found love when they were in wheelchairs. People fell in love when they were blind, or deaf, or both. Why was it impossible to have love even if you couldn't have physical contact? People did it all the time over the Internet. And I did have Annie near me, I could see her and hear her, and something happened when we tried to touch. We weren't so badly off. We were very lucky!

I collapsed in the sand by my car, gasping. Annie danced around me. "Come on, Darren, come on! This is no time to rest. I want to go with you! I want to get off this island, to be free!'"

"Just give me a second," I groaned, fishing my last water bottle out of my backpack and holding it up to my dry lips with shaking hands. Annie was lucky not to have to catch her breath or drink water!

But she was too excited to notice, or care. "Come on, come on!" she cried, stretching out her hand toward me.

There was something strange in the appearance of her outstretched arm. I got to my feet, holding onto the car door handle for support, and fished for my keys, but my hands were trembling. I managed to get the door open at last, and gestured to Annie to get in. "Your carriage awaits, milady!"

She giggled, though there was puzzlement in her eyes as she gingerly climbed inside. "So, this is what a horseless carriage looks like from inside!" I was a little confused myself. Who ever heard of a haunted Geo Metro? At least Annie couldn't smell the dirty interior, or feel the stale heat of the air that had been trapped inside all day. As soon as I got in I rolled down the windows, though I had to stop myself from reminding her to buckle up.

"Come on, then!" she said, leaning over the dashboard until her forehead touched the windshield. "If there are no horses to whip to a trot, this should be quick, right?"

I started the car and drove into the gathering dusk. Annie was shouting with laughter, and her hair blew around in the breeze. But whatever it was lighting her up from within was getting stronger, too. It shone through the windshield and lit up the road before us brighter than the headlights.

"Come on, Darren, faster, faster!"

Maybe I could outrun whatever was happening to Annie. I stepped on the gas, and we whizzed past the darkening forest on either side of the road. But the faster I drove, the brighter shone the glow we cast on either side, the shadows of the tree trunks spinning eerily from before to behind us as I zoomed past. Already we were at the entrance to the National Seashore. Paul Truitt was just closing up the gatehouse, and he turned and waved. Why didn't he notice the blinding light coming from my car? Why didn't Annie? She whooped as I raced along the winding curves in the road.

"We're almost there, Darren!" Her voice came thin and high. "We're almost off the island! Don't slow down now!"

I turned left toward the bridge. Then I made the mistake of turning to my right to look at Annie. Only the faint outline of a woman was visible, but the searing light where her chest should have been was brighter than the sun. I let out a gasp.

"Darren, what is it! What's the matter!" She sounded like a bad phone connection. I turned my eyes back to the road, but red afterimages filled my field of vision.

"I can't see!" I shouted. Then came the loudest noise I'd ever heard in my life, followed by blackness.

13

I have only shards of memories of the next couple of hours. The shock of cold seawater pouring in through the broken car windows. Staring up at Kevin's dripping face while he said my name and asked if I was all right. Lakeisha checking me over with a professional eye before helping Kevin carry me to their car. Lying on the back seat asking them over and over again if Annie was all right, till Lakeisha finally asked, "Who's Annie?"

I don't remember whether or what I answered. Then I was in a hospital, white light everywhere. The overhead fluorescent lighting was surrounded by rainbow halos. Maybe my headache explained the halo. My head had never hurt so much in my life. The pain only got worse when they rushed me out of the emergency room and took me for an MRI—I never realized the things were so loud. I wanted to clutch my head to keep out the unbearable racket but they warned me to keep still as they pushed me slowly through the huge white metal tube.

"No swelling or bleeding in the brain, far as we can see," the tech said, as much to Kevin and Lakeisha as to me.

#

Things made more sense the next morning. They kept me overnight for observation, though they finally did let me go to sleep. I woke to Kevin and Lakeisha peering down at me. I tried to sit up but lots of new pains called attention to themselves. I fell back with a groan and Lakeisha placed her hand on my chest, a stern frown clouding her face. "Don't you dare move, you idiot! It's a wonder you're not dead."

"What are you, a doctor?" I said, wincing at the sound of my own voice.

"No, but it's a good thing I have paramedic training," she snapped.

"I'll second calling you an idiot," Kevin said. "I was driving back to the island with Keisha since she'd left her cell phone at work. We saw you drive your car off the Verrazano Bridge, lucky for you, or you would've drowned."

Which was precisely how Annie had died. I wiggled my fingers and toes experimentally. No casts. So I had been lucky, all right. But what had happened, in that moment before the accident? Had Annie finally gotten her wish—had she vanished? I had kept asking about Annie last night, but Kevin and Lakeisha didn't know who I was talking about. They must not have seen her.

"What happened to my car?" I asked.

"Totaled, I'm sure," Kevin said.

"How am I going to get to work tomorrow?" I moaned. "I'll have to ride my bike."

"Uh-uh Darren, you're not riding your bike or going to work anytime soon," Kevin said, shaking his head for emphasis. "The hospital ain't ready to discharge you just yet, and when they do, you'd better stay in bed a couple days at least."

I tried again to sit up. "But what about my job?"

"Cropper's just gonna have to man the gatehouse

himself till you're better," Lakeisha said. "And he won't give you any trouble. I spoke to Paul Truitt and he promised to make his cousin behave himself."

Just then a nurse walked in and called a doctor, who shooed my friends away and put me through an exhausting series of tests including another MRI, which again didn't turn up anything wrong. They ended up discharging me the next morning after giving me strict instructions—basically I had to take the rest of the week off and "really rest."

They put me in a wheelchair and pushed me outside. Lakeisha was waiting for me in Kevin's ancient station wagon—he was already on duty in Ocean City. The Percocet they'd given me had at least wrapped the hammers pounding on my skull in cotton, but made me muzzy. Wow. They'd taken me to the big hospital in Salisbury. She told me to rest while she drove me home, but as I was climbing out of the car on wobbly legs, she said, "This whole thing is about that girl, isn't it?"

"Wha-what girl?" I said.

She rolled her eyes. "Kevin told me you have a girlfriend, slick. You stayed down here for the summer because of her, didn't you? What do you two do, hang out on the beach and make goo-goo eyes at each other?"

"Sure, that's all Annie and I do." I clapped my hand over my mouth.

Lakeisha's eyes sparkled with mischievous curiosity. "So that's who Annie is! How old is she? Where does she go to school? Or does she work? I'll bet she's cute!"

"My head is killing me," I groaned, clapping my hand to my forehead and staggering away.

It wasn't an act. I walked over to the trailer door and tried to fit my key into the lock, but I missed by several inches and Lakeisha had to come help me. She all but tucked me in bed.

When I woke up, she was still there. Afternoon sunlight slanted in through the trailer's blinds. The air conditioning was cranked all the way up, and the old unit rattled like a pickup truck bouncing down a dirt road. The noise worried me less than the expense—I had cut back on running the thing to save money. I propped myself up on my elbows, mentally bracing for the headache to come roaring back. But there was only a dull throbbing—my lower back hurt worse.

"How are you feeling?" Lakeisha asked.

"Better. Yes, definitely better. Don't you have to get to work?"

She waved her hand dismissively. "Not for another hour. Are you still nauseated?"

I swallowed experimentally. "No. In fact, I'm starving. You didn't bring any food, did you?"

She reached over to the fridge—the trailer was small enough that she didn't even have to get up out of her chair—and grabbed a couple boxes of Chinese takeout and rice. "I got a nice mild chicken-and-veggie dish for you since I didn't know what you liked. You want me to nuke these for you?"

My stomach rumbled. "Nope, I'll eat it cold, thanks!"

"You're not seeing double, are you?"

I shook my head. "No, Mom. In fact, I'm feeling great. Tell Cropper I'll be back at work first thing in the morning!"

"Whoa, pardner." She put a cool hand on my arm. "You ain't a-goin' nowhere. Kevin would kill me if I let you out of bed. Not to mention your parents."

My heart sank. "You told them?"

She shook her head. "Hospital notified them. I didn't have nothin' to do with it. But Kevin ended up talking to both of them on the phone, and they both said they'll come see you if you want."

Which really means they're both too busy. "Nah, that's all right," I said. "I'll call them myself and tell them not to bother. Really, I'm fine!"

Lakeisha stared at me. "Are you sure you're not seeing

double? Why are you so anxious to get back to that stupid gatehouse?"

I wasn't. I needed to find out what had happened to Annie. But how? She could go as far as the bridge, but something strange had started happening as soon as we got in the car. So if she'd "survived," she would probably be back in Green Run. How could I get Lakeisha to drive me as close to there as possible tonight?

By sticking to the plausible, that's how. The stuff that had been in my pockets was on my bedside table, but my wallet was missing. "I think I dropped my wallet back on the island somewhere," I said. "Could you take me back there to look for it when you go to work?"

Lakeisha frowned. "Darren, I don't think you're well enough to go anywhere."

I put on my best pleading face. "I actually had money in it, for once," I lied.

She stood up, shaking her head. "If you insist. But we'd better get going now so I can bring you back here before my shift starts." That was fine by me.

Outside it was blazing hot and still. Cicadas whirred in the long grass, which I hadn't bothered to mow. I squinted at the sun, which was still blazing hot as it sank slowly toward the west. Lakeisha unlocked the car and climbed into the driver's seat, still shaking her head. "Darren, this is nuts," she said as she backed out of the gravel driveway and turned onto the Assateague road. "Why don't I just check for you if someone turned in a wallet?"

"I, uh, I think I may have hidden it under a bush near the roundabout where the road ends in the National Seashore. Hopefully, no one has taken it." The answer didn't make much sense, I knew. My headache was coming back. She handed me a bottle of water, hot from sitting in the car all morning. I gulped it down anyway.

"So how did you meet this girlfriend of yours?" Lakeisha asked as we drove onto the Verrazano Bridge.

"On the beach. I was out walking with my pH meter,

taking measurements for my class, and she was standing on top of a dune."

She wagged her finger at me. "You know you're supposed to keep off the dunes so you don't kill the grass."

"I told her that." Not that she could do the grass any harm. "She's local, and pretty sheltered."

"Hmph. Darren, are you sure you know what you're getting into?"

"It's okay! We haven't even kissed. At least, not really."

Before she could ask anything else embarrassing, we came up to the roundabout. My heart leaped. Annie stood there.

"Stop here," I said, my heart in mouth.

"Darren, she can't see me," Annie said as I got out of the car. I opened my mouth, then closed it. Lakeisha was staring at me from the car, waiting for me to find the wallet, or not, so she could drive me back home. How was I going to get rid of her?

I bent over and pretended to look under a bush. "It's not right here," I called out to her. "I think I'd better look around for a while."

"Let me help you," Lakeisha said, starting to get out of the car. Annie looked from one of us to the other, her forehead wrinkling at this charade.

"No, no!" I said, waving her off. "I think I might have dropped it in the back country somewhere. I'll have to look for a while. Just go… I'll call you if I need you." It took a lot more arguing, but eventually I got her to drive off.

I turned with relief to face Annie. "You're all right. Thank God."

"You mean I didn't disappear. No, don't feel guilty that you're glad about that. I—I'm also glad, for the first time in a hundred years."

I drank in the sight of her. She looked as if she had received a fresh dunking at the same time I had. "What are we going to do now?"

"I don't know, Darren. But it's clear you were wrong about my spirit being free to go where it will. I am limited to this place—perhaps my prison isn't as small as I thought, but I certainly cannot leave Assateague Island."

"It's something that happened to you here, on this island, in Green Run. Something connected to your death. You have to finish telling me your life story till the end. Leave nothing out!"

"Darren, I have no secrets from you. Any right I had to secrets died when I died myself. You know I used to hope that when you learned what a sinner I am that your infatuation would evaporate like sea spray, but now..." She broke off, frowning. "You don't look so well. The Negress was right—you shouldn't have come out here."

"Her name is Lakeisha," I said.

"Well, you should go home and rest. I will still be here tomorrow," she said, "and the day after that."

So I walked all the way back to the State Park gatehouse. Lakeisha's shift was just about to start, but she got Cropper to agree to stay on long enough for her to give me a ride home, though he grumbled about it, and she scolded me for not calling her to come out and get me.

On the way back home, Lakeisha suggested we stop at Island Market to pick up some fish cakes and other food. Jodie greeted me.

"Hey college boy, long time no see."

"Hi Jodie," I said.

"This your girlfriend?" she smiled, and the two women shared a chuckle. Jodie knew perfectly well Lakeisha and Kevin were a couple.

"He does have someone he's sweet on down here," Lakeisha said. Oh great, now I was going to have to lie to more people.

"Really?" Jodie said. "What's her name, hon?"

"Annie," I said.

"Annie who? If she's local I'll bet I know who she is."

I choked and gave her real name.

"Really?" Jodie said again. "That's downright peculiar. I thought my husband's family were the only Pearsons in this part of the shore. Where's she live?"

Now I was really in trouble. If I said Berlin or even Ocean City Jodie would probably know I was lying. But Salisbury's a good-sized town, so I said Annie lived there.

"Huh," Jodie said and rubbed her double chin. "I'll have to ask Bill if another branch of his family settled over there. I thought his little brother Norm was the only other Pearson left, and though he lives right here in Berlin they haven't spoken in ten years, since my in-laws died. Their great-great-grandfather William came here after the Civil War, you see, and far as I know all the Pearsons trace back to him."

14

"No, we never had any children, Darren. We'd been married barely more than a year when I passed." She paused. "I was pregnant, though."

It was four days later, a quiet Monday morning in early August. The drizzle kept so many tourists away Cropper had let me leave early, my first day back on the job. The kindness was disconcerting, coming from him. Lakeisha must have read him the riot act.

"I know that Will remarried," Annie said, staring out over the ocean. "I am glad of it. I caused him so much unhappiness, I can only hope he was able to be happy with someone else."

"But what about you? Were you happy with him?"

The question startled her. Perhaps women in her time didn't expect to be asked it. Or to ever ask it of themselves.

"I was as happy as I had any right to be."

"That's no answer."

"But it is the truth, Darren." She stroked my cheek with her intangible, glowing hand so that my face tingled. "I still saw Pa every day. I had the freedom of the woods and the beach, when I needed to be alone. What more could I have asked for?"

"Love?"

"I loved him, Darren. Don't give me that look! Yes, I did love him, and not merely from a sense of duty. He had always been so kind to me when Mama was dying, and after. You know what kindness means. You have it from your friends."

I nodded. Lakeisha and Kevin had checked in on me at home every day since the accident, often bringing me food over my protests. But their kindness was starting to become a little suffocating. I was sure that if I'd worked my full shift today Lakeisha would have physically prevented me from getting on my bike and riding away into the National Seashore to meet Annie.

"I am getting ahead of my story, Darren, but perhaps it is as well that you understand how much Will meant to me, to all of us, going back to the night when he saved Mama and me from the mob and continuing throughout the war. Sometimes he was able to come visit us when Pa couldn't, bringing Pa's pay packet and fresh seafood the men had caught in the long slow hours between battles.

"The most memorable of Will's visits was in the final summer of the war, when he brought Jimmy with him. We didn't know the war would be over in less than a year, of course; the news from the front was bad, there were even rumors of rebel raids in the countryside north of Baltimore, and we hadn't seen Pa in months. Mama seemed to have gotten better, however, or maybe she'd just gotten better at hiding her coughing. Some of the neighbors even complimented her on the roses in her cheeks.

"I forgot about my worries over Mama in the excitement of Jimmy's arrival. I was old enough to know that a young lady didn't just start talking to a strange boy— even though we were both but eight years old—so there was nothing I could do but stare at him, and he at me. He was very dark, darker than Violet, with a round face and shining eyes of a brown so deep they looked black, as if within the whites his eyes were all iris. He was wearing coveralls that were too big for him and homemade moccasins.

"'We found him during a reconnaissance near the town of Montross, Virginia,' Will explained to Mama. 'He'd been living in the woods there ever since his so-called master ran off. Can't tell how long.'

"'Miz Margaret, I don't want to cause no trouble,' Violet said softly. 'I can find a rooming house where I can stay with the boy.'

'Nonsense,' Mama said, 'you must stay here with the poor little mite.'

"A frown spread across Will's handsome face. 'I didn't think the boy was going to stay here,' he said. 'Is that really a good idea? Poor Jimmy, here, was forced to live off the land, the Lord knows how long—'"

"'But at present he is a sojourner in civilized life again,' Mama said, and smiled at Will and Violet's puzzlement. 'It is what Mr. Thoreau wrote at the beginning of his little book. Never mind. Thank you for your concern, Will, but I think we need have no fear of what Violet's little brother might do to us. It is rather he who should be afraid, given what the white race has done to him.' And that was the end of it. When Pa came home on leave toward the end of summer, he wholeheartedly approved Ma's decision. In fact, he took her in his arms and kissed her and said it gave him yet another reason to love her, though he had no need of more." A single tear rolled off Annie's cheek and fell sparkling into my palm. She needed a few moments before she could continue.

"By that time I had done my best to ruin poor Jimmy with my deviltry, but he was too soft and gentle a soul. He was horrified when he saw me throwing rocks at the carriages and begged me to stop. I laughed and called him a sissy, but that was the end of my rock-throwing days. Anyway school was about to start, and soon I had a new, unexpected responsibility. Jimmy couldn't go to school with me, of course—he had to be very careful even about venturing beyond our fence—and when I would come home with my arms full of books I thoughtlessly called him lucky not to have to suffer Mrs. Wintergreen's attentions, until Mama pulled me aside, looking angrier than I ever saw her, and asked me did I not think Jimmy would give anything to be able to go to school. I protested that school was a bore and a torment.

"Mama interrupted me. 'He can't read. They forbid slaves to read. Haven't you listened to anything Violet has told you over the years?'

"'Well, yes Mama, but—'

"'Then stop your complaining and do your homework so you can help Violet get dinner on the table!' Mama's face paled, she put her hand to her chest and began to cough. Lately even I could not help noticing she had taken a turn for the worse. I backed away, frightened, then fled upstairs where the dull verse I had to memorize for tomorrow morning's recitation—it was my turn in class—came as a welcome distraction. I did not notice until I came to the end of the poem that Jimmy was crouching in a corner, sucking his thumb and watching me.

"'Aren't you too big to be sucking your thumb?' I demanded, stalking over to him and pulling his hand from in front of his face. He just looked at me with his big dark eyes. I scowled at him. 'Is it true you can't read?' He nodded slowly. I crouched down beside him with my book in my hand and said, 'But it's easy! Here, this is a capital A. Can you say "A"?' And just like that, I started teaching him. It went slowly at first—I am afraid I was very impatient with him."

"You are always too hard on yourself," I said, rubbing the tear around in my palm. Somehow it had not dried up. Annie shook her head.

"I am honest, Darren. It is in the nature of the living to comfort themselves with illusions. Yes, even in your own time, which you think so cynical compared to mine. Nevertheless, you fool yourselves. Perhaps you must, to go on living. But death strips away the illusions."

"I refuse to believe you were a selfish monster. I know you were not," I said.

"Be that as it may, as autumn deepened into winter, Jimmy's reading began to improve. By Christmas he was able to read my discarded elementary primers by himself, sounding out the words and laughing with joy when Violet saw him and smiled. She even thanked me for 'learning him to read.'" Annie smiled at the memory, a smile that quickly faded. "I was glad of the distraction. Mama was in a bad way by then. She had lost a lot of weight, and couldn't eat even when Violet cooked her famous sweet potato pie. She made an effort, but it was obvious that eating caused her pain, from the sores inside her mouth. Her cheeks were sunken, and her eyes glittered horribly in their sockets." Annie closed her own eyes as she said this, and though she struggled not to cry, tears welled up along her eyelashes. Again I put my hand out as they rolled off her cheeks. With each droplet I caught, I told myself I was taking on some of her burden of sorrow to relieve her of it. And this strange physical connection brought us closer together.

"She spent most of the day in bed," Annie whispered. "Dr. Sherman came almost every day, but there was little enough he could do."

In my own time, of course, tuberculosis could be cured with a simple course of antibiotics. I shook my head at the waste of Annie's mother's life.

"The doctor could do nothing, though he billed my family right enough," Annie said. "I used to hear him speaking to Violet, he thought out of my earshot, but of course I strained to hear every word until I trembled with the effort. 'There is no doubt it is the later stages of consumption,' he said. 'The final crisis can't be far off now. Mrs. Wright may have terrible pains. There may be blood. You must try to protect the child from seeing such things.' Violet was crying quietly, and that frightened me even more than what the doctor was saying."

"How old were you?" I asked.

"This was just after Christmas, or perhaps early in the new year, 1865. I'd only turned eight in September. I must have gotten up from the knothole in the floor that served as my listening-post and gone outside. But I don't remember walking out the door. The next thing I remember I was huddled shivering in the hollow of a tree overlooking the carriage-road. It was getting dark, and I'd forgotten my coat. But I couldn't bear to go back home. Perhaps a child that age doesn't really understand what death is—indeed, I've come to understand that adults don't really know what it is, either. I knew that death abided in our house, though.

"Jimmy found me. 'Violet, she out looking for you,' he said. 'She calling your name over and over. Ain't you heard?' 'No, Jimmy,' I said, 'I haven't heard. I've been hiding all this time.' 'What for?' he asked. 'You ain't in trouble. Or you weren't. Your mama is worrying about you now, though. She tried to go out too, but Violet told her to stay in bed.'

"I was crying by now. Jimmy just looked at me with big dark eyes. He was small for his age, and since I'd been teaching him to read I'd gotten in the habit of thinking of him as if he were a little child. But we were the same age. He watched me while I cried. A grown-up would have looked away or told me to stop. Maybe he wanted to hug me but thought he'd best not—as young as we were there was that impossible gap between us, him being a Negro and I a white girl. When I was done he took my hand— Violet had made him mittens. I can feel the scratchy wool as if I was touching his hand now. And so he led me back to the house."

Annie fell silent for a moment, then said, "Jimmy was far better acquainted with grief than I was. Even I knew enough not to ask him about the older brother Violet had mentioned. Instead I tactlessly pestered Violet with my questions. But all she could do was shake her head and tell me God alone knew where Tom was. Jimmy told her he had run off long ago, at the very beginning of the war, and nobody knew what had happened to him—whether he made it to the Federal lines and freedom, or was captured and killed. None of us ever did learn his fate. At least, not by the time I passed."

"And their parents?" I asked.

Annie shook her head. "What do you think, Darren? Even Violet barely remembered her mother. Tom and Jimmy had a different father. In Virginia, you know, Colonel Greer's sort didn't use their slaves to raise cotton, and they didn't even care much about the tobacco their slaves grew for them. No, the main point was to use them to breed more slaves, and then sell away either the parents or the children, whichever would fetch the higher price in the Deep South. For the masters, there was as little sentiment involved as they would have felt breeding horses for stud. Less."

My stomach churned. It was one thing to read about slavery in a book, but something else entirely to know someone who had seen its effects firsthand.

At that moment, as if in response to Annie's remark about horses, we heard a pony nickering. She smiled. "Shall we see how our friends are getting on?" I didn't need to be asked twice. I got to my feet, ignoring the torrent of pins and needles in my legs, and followed her over the dunes and through the woods. Scotty's band was grazing at the edge of the salt marsh. Annie and I crouched and watched them. It was just like the day we met. The sun broke through the soft gray clouds that had been drizzling all morning and sent golden lances of light through the high branches of the loblolly pines. Annie talked in a low voice about the band—she had names for all of them— and I could see the colt Jamie had definitely grown bigger now and was cantering in wider and wider orbits around his mother. The air smelled fresh and clean after the rain, and the mosquitos were taking a break for once. I broke out the egg salad sandwich I had brought and Annie watched enviously as I ate it.

"Don't even think of putting it away, Darren," she said, as if sensing my guilt. "I draw almost as much pleasure from your enjoyment as I would if I could eat myself."

"I hope you can remember at least some of the joy life brought you."

"Yes. Even when Mama lay dying, there was pleasure in waiting for Pa to come home and take me in his arms. That he could do so even as Mama lay stricken in the next room, that he could laugh and call me his little Annie-fish, is a wonder to me when I think of it now. How strong he must have been to swallow his heartbreak for my sake!"

I turned to look at her. She was sitting with her hands clasped around her knees, watching the ponies, and she didn't glance my way. A gentle breeze was blowing from the marsh, but her hair didn't move. Instead, it looked wet again, while before the accident on the bridge it had seemed to be drying out. What did that mean? And why wasn't she looking at me? Did she not want me to see her cry again? But her eyes were dry.

"They sent me away when Mama lay on her deathbed. I went to stay with Will's family, so I missed Mama's last days, her death and the funeral. Doubtless it was meant as a kindness to me, but for years afterwards I secretly expected her to come back. Certainly I waited for her every day I stayed with the Pearsons. They lived within walking distance of our home, but it was a different world. Mr. Pearson was a banker, a portly man with graying sideburns who was never without his well-cut hounds' tooth jacket and his gold watch-chain, and Mrs. Pearson was a prim and proper lady whose mouth was always set as if she disapproved of me, though I can't recall her ever actually uttering a cross word. It would have been beneath her. She was always hosting meetings of the Baltimore Temperance League and sewing circles with her well-to-do friends to raise money for the troops in the field—but how different was their needlework from the industrious piecework Mama and Violet did to make money simply to live on! Their house was like a museum full of breakable china figurines and fine carpets that a child like me could ruin simply by looking at them.

"They were too genteel to say anything to an orphaned little girl, naturally. But I know they were relieved when I took to spending as much time as I could out of the house, in the evenings that were growing warmer and longer as spring approached. Sometimes I would play with Jimmy on the wooded hillside where I used to lie in wait to ambush the carriages, a time that seemed so distant now. I began to skip school and spend whole days wandering around back there, but I was never switched or even scolded for it. The Pearsons didn't care as long as I wiped my feet before coming in and didn't make trouble for them—which was probably another reason they didn't tell me Mama had passed: a wild little girl consumed by grief was more trouble than they needed. Perhaps they said to themselves the burden of telling me could be left to Pa, when he came home on leave. Meanwhile, for Mrs. Pearson I was another Good Deed she was doing, and a patriotic one to boot since Pa was off serving the country, like Will and his older brother Kent, who had been killed two years before at Vicksburg.

"There was only one duty they did demand I fulfill, but that was a hard one—I had to accompany them to church every Sunday morning. Mrs. Pearson would put on her hoop skirt and her white gloves, and she would insist I dress up in a miniature version. The gloves were the worst, for I dared not touch or play with anything lest they tear or become smudged with dirt. Even fidgeting dirtied the dratted things—stop grinning, Darren, you'll embarrass me. I had scant experience of church. My father considered himself a Transcendentalist, like Mr. Thoreau, and refused to set foot in any but 'the church of the woods, or the church of the seas,' as he put it. Mama was happy enough to follow his freethinking example, though for Daddo's sake she had me baptized at the Baltimore Basilica and took me there for Midnight Mass every Christmas Eve, excepting of course the last one before her death. I always found the great stone building and the cavernous space it contained chilly and forbidding, and the Pearsons' Episcopal Church scarcely less so, though I liked the stained-glass windows of their cathedral better, for the shifting, colorful patterns they made on the floor. If the Pearsons had any quarrel with the Almighty for taking their eldest son, they concealed it well. Certainly they weren't about to show their grief before a little girl like me, who would soon have enough of her own to fill her own heart."

15

The next day was Saturday. I called Cropper and let him know my head was still pounding, which was true, but instead of staying in bed I rode my bike aimlessly to be alone with my thoughts. But these went round and round in circles until I decided I needed distraction instead, and pedaled all the way north to Ocean City, miles from where I lived, for some old-fashioned boardwalk honky-tonk. As I maneuvered through streets crowded with families loudly enjoying themselves, an electronic whoop and a blast of noise almost made me lose me balance. I braked and looked around to see Kevin climbing out of his patrol car, grinning. "Let's see your license and registration, buddy."

"Very funny, Kevin. You almost made me fall off my bike and hit my head again."

"Yeah, well, you should be wearing a helmet. Actually, you shouldn't be out at all. Don't tell me you're back at work already."

"I was yesterday. Today I called in sick because my head was hurting."

"And went right out on the road? I should tell your boss on you. No, no, I'm just kidding, don't look so afraid. I got no use for that jerk Cropper. It's a shame Paul couldn't get you a job working with him."

"Paul?"

"Just how hard did you hit your head, man? Paul Truitt, the National Seashore ranger who had to come out and get you after you sprained your ankle that time. I was talking with him the other day when I drove out to pick up Keisha, and he reminded me that you're interested in the history of Green Run."

My pulse sped up. I nodded.

"Well, after I spoke to him I got to thinking about my great-grandmother Hattie, the one I told you about who's in Sunbeam Assisted Living up in Selbyville," he said. "If anyone would know about my great-whozewhatsis Jim, it would be her. She must be over a hundred years old. I can take you to see her this afternoon after I pick Keisha up, but you got to promise me you'll go home and lie down until then."

We had ourselves a deal, and as a low evening sun sent its orange rays over the flat fields of Delaware Kevin ushered me into the nursing home, which stank of piss and vomit brightly overlaid with lemon floor-wax and Lysol. Kevin had been exaggerating a bit about his great-grandmother's age. As soon as she had her teeth in she informed us she was going to be ninety-six in September. Her eyes were the milky blue-white of the blind.

"Whyfore a white boy like you is so interested in colored peoples that lived out on Assateague a hunnert and fi'tty years ago?" she asked drily.

How does she know I'm white if she's blind, I wondered stupidly. It was my accent and the way I spoke, of course. I gave my cover story about it being for a college history project.

"Huh. Ain't never was nothin' very historic about Green Run. Just a bunch of shacks out that ways with nothin' there but that ol' hotel and the Life-Saving Station."

"But didn't a relative of yours work in that hotel?"

A shrug of bony shoulders. "It was before my time, sonny. But yeah, they said my Uncle Jim was a cook there."

"Your uncle? Your father's brother?"

"My grandfather's brother. But he was gone long before I was born. Matter of fact, he was gone long 'fore my granddaddy came out here."

"Was his name Tom, your grandfather?"

"Now how do you know that?" Kevin was eyeing me curiously, too. What could I say? That it was a lucky guess? I mumbled something about having talked to a lot of people in the black neighborhood of Berlin and decided I'd better not prompt her with any more facts I had no credible way of knowing.

"They was born slaves in a run-down plantation outside a little dump of a town called Montross," she said. "But my granddaddy, he ran away when the Civil War started. Tore him up all his life that he left his little brother Jim behind, but what could you do? You had to take your chances to get to freedom if you could. He served with the colored troops in Mr. Grant's army out west somewheres. When the war was over he came back and hunted all up and down Virginny for Jim and their older sister, but he never could find them. He had about given up when someone told him they was out here."

"When was this?" I could hardly hear my own voice over the pounding of my heart.

"I'm not sure. Many years after the war, anyway. It weren't so simple for a colored man to come out this way, not back then. Colored folks stayed put, mostly. If they didn't they could get in bad trouble. I remember that lynching they had in Salisbury when I was a girl. They dragged that poor boy's burnt body around the streets outside our home. Makes me sick to think about it." She shook her head, and Kevin put a glass of water in hand, which she proceeded to drink noisily. I tried to catch my breath. Could something just as awful have happened to

103

Jim and Violet?

Hattie held the empty glass out and I took it and put it down carefully on the bedside table. My hands were shaking so badly I was afraid I'd drop it. Kevin watched me narrowly.

"My granddaddy had to work his way over on one of them boats they used to haul melons up to Baltimore in," Hattie said. "But eventually, so my daddy told me, he made it all the way to Spence Landing, only to learn his fambly was long gone and the hotel burned to the ground."

Burned to the ground? Then why had Ranger Paul told me it was later dismantled for the wood? "Were they killed in the fire, Jim and Violet?"

"No, they was gone before that. Nobody knew where. But how do you know the sister's name? Even I didn't know that!"

A friendly ghost told me. I don't remember how I explained myself. I only remember the curious looks Kevin kept giving me on the drive back home. "That's some research project you're doing," he said after a while.

I tried to shrug like Hattie had. Anyone who had lived that long—though Annie had been around much longer!—had to have some toughness worth emulating. Of course, I wasn't that tough, so I tried to fill in the obvious gap with words. I spoke of my love for Assateague, for the wild world of the sand and the forest and the bays, and said that the people who had lived here over the centuries were a part of it too and I wanted to know everything about them.

"Well," Kevin said when I finally ran out of breath for all this hot air, "I do wish you luck in what you're looking for, whatever it is. But I think you'd best be careful."

16

"I had no idea Tom came here looking for them. It must have happened long after I passed."

Annie looked ghastly. Ghastly: like a ghost, which is what she was, after all. Her hair was a tangled, knotted mess, her dress looked soaked, and all the color was gone from her face, except for a blue tinge to her lips and a vast, pale blue bruise on her left temple, which I'd never noticed before. If you saw a living person looking like that, you wouldn't think twice, you'd stuff them in the car and drive as fast as you could to the emergency room. But what could I do for Annie? I couldn't even touch her. My fingertips tingled with the frustrated desire to stroke the side of her face.

"I suppose you blame that on yourself, too," I said, "the fact that he never found them."

When she looked at me her green irises had gone so dark, like seaweed washed up after a storm, they looked almost black. Today there was an eerie harmony between her appearance and that of the sky, which was roiling with thick gray clouds. "I was a big part of the reason Pa came out here and built the hotel," she said. "He wanted to get me out of Baltimore after Mama's death. 'The freedom of the fresh salt air,' he'd say, smiling and ruffling my hair. 'A new start for both of us,' he'd say, and Will and Violet and Jimmy came along to help. It might never have happened, without me!"

"Annie, your presence in the world was not a crime!" Lightning flickered behind the clouds, and a light went on in my mind. "This is really about the burning of Wright's Ocean House, isn't it? You know that I know. But what is it I know? Did it even happen? Paul Truitt told me the building was taken apart and the lumber shipped back to the mainland after World War I. That was more than forty years after…" I superstitiously avoided saying "after your death." But Annie had no such compunctions.

"Will rebuilt it the second summer after I was gone," she said. "Six months after it burned, yes, Tom's granddaughter was right, after it burned to the ground."

My head started to whirl and I sat down in the sand just as fat drops of rain started to fall, each one like a miniature meteor strike kicking up a misshapen oval of darker gray granules. "It burned the winter after…"

"It burned three nights after Pa saw me," Annie said. The wind howled behind her, and I saw a spray of grit emerge out of her chest, because there was nothing there to block it. For a moment I could barely see her silhouette in the swirling chaos. Her voice rose above a rumble of thunder. "There was no one else in the hotel at the time. Andy and Betty Birch lived closest and came running when they saw the flames through the trees, but it was already too late. Pa may have dozed off and dropped his pipe… or he may have forgotten to clean the chimney, he was always falling behind on things like that after Violet and Jimmy left."

"And so his death is on your conscience too!" I had to shout to be heard over the pouring rain. "That's what this is all about, isn't it? That's why you insist you are a miserable sinner who deserves everything you have suffered."

"Come out of the rain, Darren." I realized her voice was coming from further away, moving behind the line of the dunes. I struggled to follow, pushing my way through the thorny underbrush, hardly feeling the sharp needles tearing into my hands and arms. Just as I stumbled onto the soft carpet of dead pine needles on the forest floor the world went white. I smelled ozone as a sound too enormous to hear lifted me up and threw me against something hard.

When I came to my first sensation was the taste of salt. Annie was leaning over me sobbing uncontrollably, and her tears were wetting my face and rolling into my mouth. I shook my head groggily and tried to figure out if the sky was really a lurid violet or if it was the afterimage of the lightning. Rain was still falling steadily but the loblolly boughs far above my head shielded me from the worst of it, and besides the storm was already passing.

"Annie," I said, reaching up to grab her by the shoulder. "Annie, I'm all right. Stop crying."

"Everyone I ever loved, I destroyed," she cried as I staggered to my feet and pulled her close. "I know you think, dear Darren, that I never meant to hurt anyone. But can't you see, it doesn't matter what I *intended*, what mattered were the *results* I always caused—" I stopped her abusing herself any more with a kiss. Her lips were dry and cracked and tasted of salt, but she kissed me hungrily back. Realization struck us both at the same moment. *I had touched her. I had kissed her. How was that possible? I must be dreaming...*

"Darren, what—" she gasped.

"Never mind," I said and pulled her in for another kiss.

She wriggled away. "Something is wrong..." She turned, her eyes widened and she pointed at a figure slumped against a tree. The figure was wearing a soaked T-shirt and jeans just like I had on, was bleeding from a long gash on its head, and was snoring loudly. He was a young man with shaggy brown hair and an oval face, the same one I saw in the mirror every morning, because of course he was me.

The snoring would have added a humorous touch to the surreal scene, except I remembered from a first-aid course that that kind of snoring could be a sign of respiratory distress. But there was nothing I could do about it—I'd taken that course way back in high school, the details had gotten kind of hazy, and besides I knew I would no more be able to touch my body to help it than Annie had been able to touch me before. I pitied it distantly, but the feeling was overwhelmed by the excitement of being able to be with Annie. And besides, the body I had been trapped in was ugly.

"You are not ugly, Darren. How could you even think such a thing?" Annie said. I didn't realize I had spoken aloud.

"Of course I am... was. Just look at that long nose, that funny widow's peak of dark hair. In a couple of years I would have gone bald... and with those pimples still on my cheeks!"

"Do not think that. You must not! You're not dead!"

"Annie, I don't care if I can be with you." I reached out to press her hand, but the sensation was gone from my fingers, and the salt tang was going out of the air.

Annie must have read the confusion on my face. "Oh, no! You're becoming like me. Already you can't smell, taste or feel anything. Oh Darren!"

But just then I felt a tug, followed by a rushing sensation. I tried to fight it, but it was like trying to fight the windblown sand at the height of the storm. It was all around me, overwhelming my consciousness. When I came to this time the darkness retreated only grudgingly, and it left a lot of pain behind, mainly in my head, which swelled fit to burst with every beat of my heart. My vision was doubled and blurry. Annie was crouching beside me, saying my name over and over. I tried to smile to show I was all right.

"Darren, you have to get help," she said. "Can you stand? Can you walk?" I tried to get to my feet, but couldn't keep my balance and tumbled in a heap on the soft, wet pine needles. The rain had stopped, but the tree branches were still shedding pure, bright drops of water. I stuck out my tongue, trying to drink some of it—I was incredibly thirsty. There were water bottles in my backpack, but that was on the other side of the dunes somewhere. It might as well have been back in my dorm in College Park, for all the good it was doing me.

"Don't worry, Annie," I said, my voice coming out in a croak. "The rangers patrol the beach all the time. Somebody is bound to come along and see my backpack and clothes on the beach and come to investigate."

"But it's going to be dark soon," Annie said. "They won't be out patrolling at night, after a storm that kept visitors away."

"Then I'll just have to hold on till morning," I said. "We'll have to spend the night together, without a chaperone for a proper young lady like you."

Annie looked shocked, then began to chuckle ruefully. "You're turning into quite a tease, Darren. I didn't think you had it in you."

"I'm full of surprises," I said, and began to cough, which made my headache worse. The raindrops from the trees were turning bright orange with the sunset. They were gorgeous, but I had to close my eyes against the blurring and doubling. "While we're waiting, tell me how your father decided to leave Baltimore after the war and build the Ocean House. It must have been exciting, right?"

17

Yes, it was very exciting. Mainly I was thrilled that I wouldn't have to go back to Mrs. Wintergreen's school and the endless tortures the boys there thought up for me. If Pa had instead decided I was to accompany him on our own ship sailing around the world, my happiness would have been complete, for I would have had him all to myself. But this was next best.

It wasn't only for my sake, of course, that he decided to leave Baltimore and build a hotel on what was then a remote island. I listened in as he talked the idea over with Will, whom he now treated as an equal, though Will always called him "Captain" or "sir."

"This wasn't what we fought for, Will," I remember him saying as he swirled a little brandy around in the bottom of his glass. He never became a heavy drinker, but before Mama's death I had never seen him drink at all. Will grunted something. "Yes, we could make a good living, you and I, piloting steamships back and forth across the Bay. The lines are all offering good money. Mobtown is growing! We could rake it in, retire early and enjoy ourselves. Meanwhile the rebels are in control of the Statehouse in Annapolis, and now that Mr. Lincoln is no longer around to put them in jail where they belong, no one cares enough to stop them taking the vote away from the Negroes. They'd put them back in chains if they could!"

"The war is over, sir," Will responded quietly. Jimmy and I were crouching wide-eyed by my trusty old spyhole. He trembled when Pa mentioned slavery and I put my hand on his shoulder, whispering as his big sister Violet had that Pa and Will would fight the slavers off themselves, if it came to that. "And I'll hide you," I added.

Pa sighed. "That it is, Will, but where is the peace? There is none for me here, I fear. Sometimes I've a mind to build myself a cabin like poor Mr. Thoreau and live in it."

"But what of Annie, Captain? She can't live in a cabin."

Now Jimmy was squeezing my hand and whispering reassurances to me! Of course I knew Pa would never forget about me and what I needed—was I not his "morning star," was I not even, as I had heard him say quietly to Will on another occasion, "the only reason I have to go on living now that Peg is gone"? Still, imagine my relief and excitement when Pa said, "Of course I've been thinking of her, Will. I know she is as unhappy here as I am. She misses Peg too, and it is not good for her to have to live in a house with such ghosts in it. Still, you are perfectly right, a cabin in the woods is no place to raise a young girl. But... did you know Thoreau also wrote about the sea, Will?"

Will made a neutral sound.

"Well, he did. In *Cape Cod*, as fine a description of the place as I have ever read, and I grew up there! But instead of going so far north, what if I were to find my way someplace nearer? Many's the time before the War that I ran a cargo of oysters from Chincoteague Island up to Philadelphia. They were good people—stayed loyal to the Union when the rest of the Eastern Shore of Virginia turned traitor—and just the other side of a narrow channel from there lies the most beautiful, wild, uninhabited island you have ever seen. It fronts on the ocean, this Assateague Island, but I used to pilot the oyster boats north from Chincoteague on its leeward side and out to sea through a narrow inlet at a place called Green Run. I loved looking at the forests and the unspoiled beaches—I even used to daydream what it would be like to live there with Peg and Annie."

"But how would you make your living? Solely through clamming?" Will sounded disbelieving, but I could think of nothing finer.

"Of course not," Pa said, and for a moment I was disappointed. "But suppose we were to open an inn there? No, hear me out. Have you not heard the men on the *Anne Marie* say many and many a time that they wished they could find some place far away from all war and trouble, a place they could rest and remember what the world was like before it was filled with pointless death and suffering?"

"Certainly I have, Captain. Men like Williams and Greene... all they could talk of was getting on the next train out West, out into the empty plains where no one has ever heard of Johnny Reb and they could farm in peace."

"Of course. But not all will be able to go out West who want to. Would not some wish to forget their sorrows and take the healthful air at the seaside?"

Will chuckled. "Not everyone has read your Mr. Thoreau, sir."

"No indeed." Pa was smiling. "But many who are not lucky enough to be able to meditate in their own cabin in the woods will sometimes wish to escape the overcrowding, noise and dirt of the city for the solitude and restful quiet of the seaside. What do you say, Will? Does it not sound like a wonderful adventure?"

I could contain myself no longer, and nor could Jimmy, who ran downstairs with me as I darted into the sitting room crying, "Yes, Pa, please, let's do it! I would love to be an innkeeper's daughter and live by the sea!"

"You are getting too big to climb on my lap, Annie!" Pa laughed as I threw my arms around his neck. "But yes. If I can get the help of a few stout young men like Master Will here, we shall be pioneers!"

"Oh please, Will, please do come!" I cried, jumping down from Pa's lap and running over to him.

"I always follow my captain's orders, pumpkin," Will said, smiling and ruffling my hair. Then he wagged his finger at me. "And so should you, and I believe it is past your bedtime, and you should not have been eavesdropping on us."

I was immediately contrite, and made ready to retreat to my room, even though Pa mumbled that Will was being too hard on me. But first, Pa had a question for Jimmy. "What do you think of the idea, young James?"

Jimmy looked surprised. "Me, sir? Wherever you go, I will follow. As long as my sister agrees."

"I have already spoken to Miss Violet," Pa said, smiling, and turning to Will, he added, "It may be up to your father, Will. If he can help me secure a loan—"

Will raised his eyebrows. "This is not suitable conversation to hold in front of a child and the help, surely, Captain." He glanced at Jimmy and me and we made ourselves scarce—he returning to the back room he shared with Violet while I went back upstairs. But not to bed, of course. Only to my spyhole. I peered through it at Will's face, stern lines radiating from the short, neatly trimmed black beard he had grown while in the service. As the saying goes, he had left as a boy but returned as a man—a man who seemed older than Pa despite the lack of gray in his beard.

"I think I can get my father to lend you the money, Captain," Will said, with less deference than he usually showed my father. He toyed with his glass and avoided looking Pa in the eye. "But I would avoid mentioning Thoreau to him, if I were you. Or going on about Negro equality. He certainly won't want to fund another Brook

Farm."

"I wasn't planning to discuss Transcendentalism with him, Will," Pa said a little stiffly.

"That would be best," Will said. He softened a little. "You must understand, we are an old Maryland family. My ancestor James Pearson was among the colonists at Kent Island. His son George was among the first to import slaves from Africa to work on his tobacco farm on the Eastern Shore. Our side of the family doesn't hold with slavery anymore, but we do not wish to be shamed for our history by a bunch of Boston busybodies."

"Then it is as well that I am a Truro man," Pa said.

I know what you are thinking, Darren, but remember it was Will who found Jimmy hiding in the woods—he was with a landing party Pa had sent out from the *Anne Marie II* to track down some rebels firing on the ship, but he interrupted this vital mission to rescue a runaway slave boy. And his relations with Jimmy and Violet over the years were never anything less than correct, though it is true they were never warm. Nor was he in the habit of using the terrible names for Negroes that were so common then. Most people would have said he was a great friend to the black man.

In any event, Will's father proved more than willing to arrange the loan for Pa, though he was not so happy to have his only surviving son head off into the wilderness rather than joining him at the bank. But he could not refuse Pa, who had brought Will through the war safely. Getting the money was only the beginning of the work, however, and all that winter and into the early spring Pa and Will were busy arranging a thousand details. They had no time to pay me any mind and I found I could skip school without getting in trouble. I spent the days playing with Jimmy in the woods above the carriage road, though sometimes he asked to stay home and read with me instead, although by this time he could read by himself as well as I could. Pa would come and go on his endless errands, and he always smiled when he saw the two of us huddled together in front of the fire, reading a novel by Walter Scott or Charles Dickens. Sometimes we'd take turns reading aloud to Violet, who couldn't read. She doted on us whenever Pa and Will could spare her, mixing us up special treats in the kitchen—fresh corn bread baked with peach preserves was a specialty. She treated Jimmy like a son, and he treated her like a mother, which was not surprising as she must have been fifteen years older than him. When I asked her once whether she was looking forward to moving out to the island she cocked her head and put her hands on her hips before replying, "And why wouldn't I be, Miss Annie? We'll get all the fresh crabs, clams, and oysters we can eat. The Captain says the fishing out there is a natural wonder of the world. I'll learn how to prepare bass and flounder every which way!"

"But won't you miss your friends here in Baltimore?"

"A little," she admitted, and then added as Pa had, "But there's too many ghosts here, Annie sweetheart." Her eyes were sad, but with the heartlessness of youth I was already forgetting Mama. Her image was fading in my mind when I tried to call it up. Pa could not have been so thoughtless, of course, but planning the hotel occupied all his attention and energy. He looked younger than I ever remembered seeing him before, and always smiled at me and ruffled my hair when he hurried by, rushing from one task to the next. Will too appeared excited by the adventure we were setting off on. "We shall be 'pioneers! O pioneers!' as Mr. Whitman writes, only to an eastern shore rather than a western one," he said, grinning so that I could not help but smile back.

And pioneers we truly were. Today one of your "cars" can carry you from Baltimore to Assateague Island in less than three hours, but back then it was a significant journey—it took us the better part of two days just to reach Spence Landing, on the other side of Chincoteague Bay from here. When the hour arrived it was a bright, cold day in early April, and all the church bells were striking nine when we set out in a carriage Pa had hired for the occasion. For once, the penny-pinching Yankee in him had given way to an irresistible desire for a grand gesture. Even I could not help imagining how thrilled Mama would have been if she had been with us. So it was for both of us that I waved gaily and blew kisses out the window to the people walking by, who couldn't have cared less.

"You're making a spectacle of yourself," Will scolded, but he couldn't help but smile.

As for Pa, he positively egged me on. "Let's show Mobtown our backsides!" he laughed. Violet and Jimmy were happy, too, but they avoided showing their faces.

I'd been to the port of Baltimore before, but this excitement was of another order, now that I myself was about to become an ocean voyager! Well, a Chesapeake Bay voyager, anyhow. It looked like an ocean to me, considering I couldn't see the other side, and the ferryboat we boarded looked sturdy enough to me for a trip across the Atlantic. The paddle-wheels alone looked as big across as our old property had been—I fancied the boat could have carried our future hotel with room to spare, if only Pa had had the money to pay for it!

We lined up with the pushing, shoving crowd to buy our tickets. Not everyone was going across the Chesapeake Bay to its eastern shore, as we were—in fact, more than half bought tickets for Annapolis, which Pa said we would reach in a couple easy hours of steaming along. The day grew warmer as we sailed. The shrieking seagulls were no match for the shrieks we children made running around the deck. Jimmy wasn't with us, though. He and Violet had to go belowdecks, along with a few other Negroes and a shipment of cattle. I'm embarrassed to say I was so excited I hardly noticed, though it took some of the brass out of Pa. He asked to speak with the captain about "this outrage" but was given the brush-off.

"It's all right, Captain, this boat moves just as fast for

those who sit below," Violet said wryly.

Pa shook his head. "The forbearance of your race is a wonder of the world, my dear."

"I'll see you in Queenstown, Jimmy!" I said. "Last one on the stagecoach is a rotten egg!" He grinned dutifully, but I quickly forgot about him, there was so much delicious trouble to get in. I was so bad a crewman threatened to pitch me over the railing, "skirts or no," but I just thumbed my nose at him as I scampered over the roof of the wheelhouse.

By the time we made landfall on the eastern shore of the bay the afternoon was well advanced, but Pa had memorized the stagecoach schedule and was confident we could get at least as far as Cambridge by nightfall. There was a more serious snag at this point, however, as the driver point-blank refused to let Violet and Jimmy ride.

"I ain't lettin' *them* in my coach," he drawled, narrowly missing Pa's boots with a brown jet of chewing tobacco.

"You show some respect, sir! This man is a captain in the United States Navy!" Will said, looking about ready to duel the driver.

"Violet and James Greer are my employees. I need them for my business," Pa insisted.

"Do tell. And what business is that? Y'all up to a little hanky-panky with this dusky gal?"

I watched wide-eyed as Will's hand twitched toward his holster—he'd insisted on going armed in what he called "the backwoods"—but he kept his voice steady as he said, "Watch your tongue around ladies and children, sir."

"Never mind, Captain, we'll make our own way," Violet said softly.

"What? But such a journey—"

"We've both been through worse," Jimmy broke in, sounding as old as his sister.

Pa shook his head in disbelief, and insisted that they at least take some money from him. "Perhaps the next stagecoach driver will remember who won the war," he growled. But it took them three extra days to get to Spence Landing, and Jimmy told me later they had to walk much of the way when they couldn't find a farm cart to hitch a ride in. It seemed that it was not as easy to escape Mobtown as Pa had hoped.

18

Spence Landing was a tiny village, almost as small as Green Run was to become, which is to say it was home to no more than twenty families who made their living fishing and crabbing. The population was more than doubled by the workmen Pa paid to come in from Salisbury thirty miles to the west, Pocomoke twenty miles to the south, and even a few from as far away as Chincoteague Island and southern Delaware. They lived in lean-to shacks that they threw up themselves overnight, while Pa, Will, and I boarded with a waterman named Andy Birch and his wife, Betty. They had no children as yet, so Mrs. Birch fussed over me and spoiled me silly. "The poor orphaned child," I heard her call me when she thought I couldn't hear. She seemed terribly motherly to me, but I suppose she must actually have been quite young, perhaps only eighteen or nineteen and married to Andy for just a year or two. She had straw-colored hair and the kind of strawberries-and-cream complexion that men went crazy for, and the sweet disposition to go with it, and I'm afraid I took endless advantage, managing to get out of the chores Mama or most any reasonable person would have expected me to do, or else I fobbed them off on poor Violet, who worked as hard as any man. I spent my days getting into trouble around the waterfront. Chincoteague Bay was as placid as a bath, if still a bit chilly so early in the spring, and Jimmy and I would go splashing around, although often we helped Andy and the other watermen about their work seeding oysters for harvest later in the season.

Early in May came a big day: our "pungy," the *Margaret Deirdre*, arrived at Spence Landing. The whole village and all the workers turned out to watch Pa and Will sail her up to the dock. Pa took off his captain's hat and made a sweeping bow, and everyone erupted in cheers. He and Will had gone down to Chincoteague three days before to take delivery of the boat, a type of schooner that the Eastern Shore was famous for. Her bright white sails flapped bravely in the brisk offshore breeze. I clapped my hands when I saw she had a vivid crimson stripe from bow to stern on both sides, a touch I had suggested. Red was my favorite color, as it had been Mama's. As two workmen tied her to the dock, Will leaped down, smiling, and took my hand with a little bow. "Miss Annie, may I have the pleasure of offering you a maiden cruise upon the *Margaret Deirdre*," he said.

"Why, yes you may, First Mate Pearson," I said with a curtsey—I had rushed to put my best dress on when Jimmy came running up to tell me he'd spotted a white sail on the southern horizon. It was lavender, I remember, with frilly white cuffs, and I even had my best, shiny black shoes on. I hesitated as I was about to step aboard, turned my head and saw Jimmy beaming at me from behind the little crowd. "Could Jimmy come too?" I asked. Will stiffened a little, but Pa said, "Why, of course! And Miss Violet, you must come with us, and see where we shall build the finest hotel in all Maryland!"

We had to tack against the wind, which kept trying to push us back across Chincoteague Bay. But as the sun neared the zenith the low, irregular blue line on the eastern horizon that was all I could see of Assateague from the mainland grew up in tall, dark green trees with an inviting carpet of bright green marsh grasses laid out before them, through which ran sparkling blue creeks. A gray-haired crewman warned me not to jump out of the boat to go play on the grass or in the salt creeks, which he called "guts," unless I didn't mind getting covered in smelly black marsh mud! "Which I don't think would suit that pretty dress you're wearing so well, miss," he said with a wink.

"Don't you go running out there, neither," Violet said, clamping her hand over Jimmy's arm just in time to stop him.

"We'll have a picnic on the beach," Pa promised, chuckling gently at the identical scowls on our faces. "It's just on the other side of those trees. We'll drop anchor in the inlet and I'll have the men put down a plank for you so you don't ruin your shoes."

Indeed, I hadn't noticed till now, but one of the marsh creeks was considerably wider than the others, and the water on it was choppier, with little whitecaps. There was a current running through it from the east, the direction of the sea, although the ocean itself was hidden behind a tall screen of trees.

"Will, what do you think? Far enough?" Pa asked Will.

Will nodded. "I think so, Captain. I wouldn't go much farther, it might be too shallow in there."

"Your first mate's right, Captain," said the gray-haired crewman, whose name was Mike Powers. "This-here inlet is so shallow it silts up all the time. Matter of fact, it was closed for six-seven years till that nor'easter we had last fall."

Pa nodded and gave the order to drop anchor and set a plank down—not just for me, as it turned out; the pungy already had a load of bricks in her hold for the hotel's foundations. But I was the first one down, striding boldly onto the patch of firm sand where the plank's lower end had been placed and calling out in my loudest voice, "I hereby claim this land for the United States of America and dub this place Wright's Point!" I heard laughter and applause behind me. Jimmy darted up, found a stick, and planted it in the sand, and I fished a red handkerchief out of my sleeve and tied it to the top, where it fluttered in the breeze.

As if that had been the signal to start work, Mr. Powers and the other workmen began trundling the bricks off the ship in wheelbarrows, while Violet lifted a heavy bag of cement as if it were nothing and carried it down to the chosen site. I was a little miffed at this proof that Pa and Will had scouted out the area long since, instead of letting Jimmy and me be the true explorers, but I quickly got over it when I heard a whinnying through the trees. "Pa, did you already bring horses here?"

He smiled down at me. "No, sweetheart, those are wild ponies that live all over the island. People say they've been here since an old-time Spanish galleon wrecked offshore and they got loose."

"Wow! Can I go look for them?"

"Okay, but be careful. Ponies bite and kick if they aren't trained." Before the words had left his mouth I had kicked off my shoes and set off running through the trees, with Jimmy in hot pursuit. Sure enough, we found a band of six or seven mares, a colt or two and a rangy old stallion in a clearing, drinking water from a little pond. I longed to stroke their heads but for once decided to do as I was told and keep a respectful distance. It was Jimmy who must have got a little devil in him, for he took a running jump, swung off a tree branch and dropped himself neatly on the back of a half-grown colt. I suppose it was natural to think of the little beast as scarcely more than a toy, since he was hardly any taller in the withers than I was myself. But Jimmy's foolishness caused instant chaos. The animal reared up and threw him, and the stallion, who had been eyeing us warily since we had appeared, galloped away over the dunes with his band close behind him.

I ran up to Jimmy, put my hands on my hips and,

imitating his sister's sternest tones, said, "What possessed you to do such a thing, Jimmy Greer?"

"My leg hurts," he said softly.

My annoyance vanished. I helped him to his feet and he leaned on me as we made our way back to the bayside. Pa gave me a spanking, one of the few times he ever did that, while Will examined Jimmy's leg.

"Luck was with you, it isn't broken," he said. "But Annie might have been trampled! How could you put her in danger like that?"

"I didn't mean to!" Jimmy wailed.

Violet looked mad enough to give him a hiding too, but relented when she saw how bruised up he was. "I reckon that'll learn you well enough," she snorted. I joined her, still sniffling from my own sore rear end, and helped her carry the picnic things out to the beach. As soon as we topped the line of dunes and I beheld the clean white beach stretching away into the hazy distance, I forgot my troubles, flung my burdens down and set off running with a shout. I hiked up my skirts as far as I could and squealed when the cold seawater foamed around my bare legs. A little of it splashed up under my skirts where my rump was still warm from Pa's spanking, and it felt good, although I'm sure it didn't do my best dress any good!

Luckily for me everybody was too happy about our picnic to mind that I'd run off to play without finishing my chores. Jimmy joined me and we splashed each other until a sharp word from Violet reminded me not to completely ruin my clothes. So I pretended to be a lady and started strolling along just beyond the reach of the breakers, turning right to follow the inlet where the waters made their rushing rustle through the dunes and beyond, into the forest and out to the bayside marsh. Mr. Powers saw me and smiled. "D'you see how the trees on either bank stretch their branches out to touch one another?" he said, taking my arm and pointing. I nodded. "Their reflection turns the water a dark green. That's why this inlet is called

Green Run."

"That would be a good name for the town," Pa said, overhearing.

"What town, Captain Wright?"

"Why, the flourishing town that will grow up around Wright's Ocean House! I can see it now. There will be a town hall, a post office, a schoolhouse—" he smiled at my pout—"a barbershop, a Transcendentalist Society—"

"I'm afraid you will be the sole member of that club, Captain," Will said with a grin.

"I shall be a member too!" I said loyally, though I still had only the vaguest idea of what Mr. Thoreau had been all about.

"Point is, this isn't New England, Captain," Will said. "And first of all, we have to get this hotel built."

"Exactly the point I was going to make, Will," said Pa. "Violet, would you get everyone settled and make sure each and every one has a glass of beer—lemonade for Annie and Jimmy—for I have an announcement to make."

When everyone was sitting on blankets, drinks in hand, Pa cleared his throat and said, "I want to thank you all for the hard work you've done so far. With such excellent workers, we shall soon have the finest inn south of the Mason-Dixon Line!"

"I heard you call it the finest hotel in Maryland just this morning, Pa!" I blurted out. There were chuckles, and Pa mussed my tangled, wet hair.

"So I did, my Annie fish! But my ambitions have only grown since then! I have a surprise for all of you," he said, reaching inside his jacket and pulling a piece of newspaper out of his inside pocket. He unfolded it carefully and held it up for all to see, but there was a stiff breeze and it nearly blew out of his hands.

"Better be careful with that, sir," Will said.

"What's it say, Captain Wright?" Mr. Powers asked. I learned later that he could not read.

"It is an advertisement in the *Baltimore Evening Sun* from

last week, just arrived with yesterday's mail. 'Come one, come all to the grand opening of Wright's Ocean House, on the beautiful sea isle of Assateague! Just in time for the Fourth of July holiday, to celebrate the return of peace and prosperity to our beloved nation, we shall be hosting an all-you-can-eat seafood feast, featuring the succulent blue crabs, oysters, and clams for which the Free State of Maryland is justly famed around the world.'"

"He's mad," I heard one of the workmen mutter. "We'll never be ready before September, at the soonest!"

"...for such low prices, rooms will not be available for long, so place a reservation through your nearest telegraph office today! Just two days' relaxing ferry and stagecoach ride from Baltimore or Washington City!' And so, my friends, enjoy the feast I have prepared for you, and then our work resumes!" Pa made another little bow. I applauded enthusiastically, followed a moment later by Jimmy, and then by the adults, who seemed more polite than enthusiastic.

We all worked harder than I could have imagined, loading, unloading, hauling, carrying, pouring cement, laying brick, sawing, hammering, glazing, rain or shine. I set to work with a will, to make Pa's dream come true. Blisters immediately broke out on my soft hands, but in time the skin on my palms and the pads of my fingers grew tough as a crab's shell. If nightfall found me on the mainland, I would fall onto the pile of worn-out burlap sacks I used for a bed at the Birches' home, too tired to undress myself, and if it were on the island, I slept on the ground under the open sky if the weather were fine, or under a crude canvas lean-to if not. But I had never been happier, for I was always at Pa's side, as he slowly emerged from out of the legend of him I had constructed in my mind all those years when he was away at war. Now I knew what his breath sounded like when it was ragged from strain, and the way he would press his lips together when lifting something heavy until the gray hairs of his

mustache met the gray hairs of his beard and all that could
be seen of his face was the skin around his eyes and nose. I
grew to love the ritual he made of filling and lighting his
pipe at mealtimes and the sweet scent of the tobacco,
which was carried away soon enough on the fresh sea
breeze.

The Fourth of July finally arrived, and it was everything
Pa had promised and then some. It is another of my most
treasured memories. Word had spread all along the
Maryland and Virginia Eastern Shore, and boatloads of
people arrived all day. The advertisement in the *Evening
Sun* had done its work, too, and there was quite a
delegation from my native city. They seemed like fine
upstanding people, too—I wondered where they had been
hiding when we were living there. The new dock at
Wright's Ocean House was a very busy port that day,
crowded with boats of all kinds and descriptions—so
many brilliant white sails in the bright sunlight, it looked as
if a flock of giant seagulls had come to roost. There was
even a little steam launch, the *Lucky Star* out of Norfolk,
which tooted and huffed like a tame dragon.

For five cents you could dig into the mountains of
fresh seafood Pa and his helpers had set out on long
wooden plank tables. There were also heaps of fresh
bread, which Betty Birch had led all the ladies of Spence
Landing in baking in a heroic all-night session, fresh-
roasted corn on the cob, bushelsful of peaches, and vats of
beer and lemonade. When it grew dark, Pa gave the signal
and the sky was suddenly full of whistling, exploding
rockets. I had never seen such fireworks, not even when
the news broke that Lee had surrendered. Pa put his arm
around my shoulders and together we looked up at the
whirling, sparkling colors. "This is a new beginning for us,
Annie fish," he said softly. "Tonight we have our first
guests, a minister and his family from Baltimore City, a
party of young ladies from Annapolis with their
chaperone..." He rattled off some names, not enough to

fill the twelve rooms that were all we had on the partially completed ground floor—the second floor wouldn't be ready until the autumn.

19

We weren't able to do much more than start on the second floor before the first hard frost set in and most of the workmen Pa had hired had to return to their families to prepare for winter. A few stayed behind with us to settle in the new village Pa envisioned, staying temporarily in the hotel rooms while they built their own homes from the ground up, using what little hardwood could be found in the forest mixed in among the loblolly pine. I was overjoyed that the Birches and Mr. Powers were among the settlers, and I know Pa was happy that I would have a substitute older sister. For himself, he gave no sign of ever wanting to marry again after my mother passed. Of course there were no unmarried women in Green Run, not even when the village was at its height—all the residents were families, except for Mr. Powers, who had lost his wife to yellow fever many years before. Pa had so much to do running the hotel, serving as the village's unofficial mayor, and keeping me out of trouble, that I doubt he ever had much time for loneliness.

We were all busy all the time that first year. After the Fourth, the din of hammering and sawing again became constant. Pa had ambitious plans for the hotel, which he'd sketched out himself and showed to me as well as to the workmen. The building was to surround three sides of a courtyard. Walking into the main entrance you'd find yourself in the lobby, with the kitchen reachable through a door behind the desk. To the right, another door was to open onto a bar, and to the left, a third door was to open onto a dance hall. In the wings behind the bar and dance hall the men's and women's privies were to be found, with storage areas surrounding them. At the very back of the left wing would be Pa's and my living quarters, while Will was to be allotted a room at the rear of the right wing. In a silent concession to the probable "color feeling" of the guests, Violet and Jimmy were to have their own separate little cottage on the far side of the courtyard. All twenty of the planned guest rooms were to be on the second floor— two large corner suites and the rest evenly divided between the main section and the wings.

The twelve ground-level guest rooms we had made ready for the grand opening were temporary only, and the partitions between them were accordingly flimsy. The whole original structure as it stood that summer was nothing more than the first story of the main section and the stubby beginnings of what were to become the two wings. It was probably just as well that there were no guests after the minister's family and the young ladies who had come for the Fourth departed a few days later, for even the most patient would have been driven to distraction by the constant racket.

I took to the woods and the beach as often as I could for a little quiet. Jimmy sometimes joined me, and our games were more peaceful than they had been back in Baltimore. We swam and climbed trees, mostly. By contrast, watching the wild ponies was usually a solitary occupation for me—Jimmy was understandably shy of them after his misadventure the first day. Back then the ponies were not used to being around people, since outside our new village the island was uninhabited and unreachable except by boat, so they shied away from me until one band—I think they may have been the ancestors of Scotty's band—grew accustomed to my watching them from a safe distance. Gradually as summer turned to fall I crept closer and began to be able to tell them apart. From there it was but a short step to naming them—the one pastime I had in life that I have persisted in through the long years since. The stallion was an ill-tempered old beast with a shaggy chestnut coat. I called him Jeb. Fortunately he was too lazy to bother much about me. My favorite was a piebald mare who showed such affection for her colt that I named her Peg, after my mother. Since the colt had a white star above his nose I named him Star. I was very upset when Jeb drove him out of the band the following spring.

The weather was mild that first winter, luckily for us, since the newly built, inadequately joined walls let in every damp breeze. We didn't get any snow at all until January, but when we did, oh, what a wonder it was for me and Jimmy! You may pity us, Darren, lacking twenty-first century amusements, but consider what it was like for two children to have a thirty-mile-long stretch of fresh, unbroken, eight-inch-deep snow all to ourselves to frolic in. Will made me a sled, and Jimmy and I took turns riding it down the snow-covered dunes and onto the beach. In the lee between two steep dunes we built ourselves a fantastical "snow house" modeled on Pa's plans for Wright's Ocean House, which drew praise from everyone who trekked out to see it, which was everyone except Violet, who said she was too busy for "children's foolishness." I suppose she was, too, having taken on the role of cook and laundress for the entire group. Pa kept telling her she didn't have to do all that work, but perhaps she believed it was the only way to appease those who would rather not have had the pure snowy beauty of the island spoiled by the presence of a pair of Negroes. You understand, nobody dared say anything around Pa and me, but I could sense the ill feeling in the air, like the cold heaviness before the snow started falling.

Evenings we would gather around the fireplace in the future lobby, Violet and Jimmy always hanging back in the outer half-darkness, and pass around warm mugs of apple cider (I got the unfermented kind) while Pa and Mr. Powers told tall tales about life on the sea. They had both worked on whaling boats as young men, but their paths had never crossed. I gasped when Pa told of how a mortally wounded Leviathan had thrashed around, threatening to smash his ship to matchwood with its mighty tail, or when Mr. Powers told of how he was once covered with bloody mist from a dying beast's blowhole. Of course I favored Pa's storytelling style, which was slow and deliberate, building up to a roaring climax, but Mr. Powers could certainly hold his own, telling stories just as amazing as Pa's in a quiet monotone you had to lean forward to hear. Sometimes Betty Birch would play the banjo, making Pa smile and say it was a pity the dance floor wasn't ready yet. The storytelling and music were grander when the Ocean House came into its own, of course, but I missed the intimacy of those early days.

Pa worried about the interruption in my schooling. He'd shipped over as many books as he could and made sure I applied myself to them, but it didn't take long until I'd exhausted his stock, so on one of his runs to the mainland, he gave the stagecoach driver a letter to mail off to his old teacher in Massachusetts. Several weeks later the driver returned with a package for Pa, which proved to be full of old exercise books in grammar, rhetoric, mathematics, and Latin. You may imagine that I was not pleased! The Latin in particular I could never make much of—*Gallia est omnis divisa in partes tres*, that's all I remember, and as far as I was concerned the Gauls could have all three parts of it. But Jimmy took to it as naturally as he took to sledding down those dunes. "What is he going to do with his Latin? Become a classics professor?" I heard

Mr. Birch scoff, and though he was an amiable man who was always kind to me, I liked him less for saying that. The truth was, learning gave Jimmy pleasure for its own sake, and I was more than happy to fob Caesar off on him.

For Pa the books were a temporary solution at best, no more satisfactory than the flimsy partitions between our room and the Birches' that left us privy to their intimate conversations. Yes, you're right and also very witty, Darren: my eavesdropping was an education in itself. But Pa wanted real schooling for me, and so when spring came and the work of building started up again full steam, I was not permitted to take part, for Pa had found a tutor for me. And that was how Pastor George Scarburgh, late of Salisbury, scion of a family with roots on the Eastern Shore going back more than two hundred years, came into my life. How and why he came to leave a flourishing church in that sizable town to move out to the edge of the world I never did quite manage to discover, though there were scandalous rumors. He was young, unmarried, and good-looking, with strong clean features, warm brown eyes, and a head of curly brown hair just beginning to recede around his temples. He was shorter than Pa but solidly built, and had no objection to wielding an ax or a saw, which of course was all to the good. He thought that I had been indulged terribly, which was true, and that I needed a firm guiding hand to bring me back onto a godly path after being exposed to my father's "atheism," as I overheard him telling Mr. Birch late one night. I immediately ran to Pa and reported this conversation to him, expecting that he would pack the pastor onto the next boat back to the mainland.

"No, Anne, I'm afraid you will have to continue your studies with the good pastor," Pa said, puffing away on his pipe.

I was determined not to be distracted by my pleasure at his calling me Anne, like a grown woman. "But Pa!" I said. "He called you an atheist and said he would break me of my heathenish ways!"

Pa chuckled. "I suspect he will have a difficult time doing that, Anne."

"But how could you hire such an ignorant backwoodsman to teach me, Pa? Mama would be appalled."

Pa took his pipe out of his mouth and frowned, and I feared I had gone too far. But he spoke calmly. "Anne, we have chosen to make our lives among these people, not among freethinkers in New England. That means we will have to try to fit in here, and people would certainly raise an eyebrow if our new village didn't have a church."

"If you care so much what 'people' think and say, Pa, how could you have married Mama? Surely your family didn't approve."

Pa's eyebrows drew together, but his anger vanished as fast as a flicker of heat lightning. "It is true they did not," he said quietly, "and that I was determined to follow my own way. And so you do not know your grandparents and uncles, Anne. It is best that you learn what the common way is, before you reject it for a lonely life such as mine." And he would not discuss it further.

So I continued my lessons with Pastor Scarburgh, if not joyfully then at least dutifully. After all, not everything he taught me was useless. Far from it. He was skilled at woodworking and, though he disapproved at first, eventually he let me help him as he built the beds along with the highboys and lowboys for our future guests— these were chests of drawers, the highboys taller than I was and the lowboys a head shorter. These were my favorite times with him, for he did not speak much except to guide me in sawing and carving so that I did not end up carving a chunk out of myself. The air would grow syrupy with the sweet, sharp scent of pine resin, and wood chips and sawdust would pile up around our feet.

My other lessons with him were not so much fun. Gone were the novels of Mr. Dickens, which the pastor considered to be dangerously racy—don't smile, Darren, it's really true. Instead he insisted I practice my reading on household instruction manuals that would prepare me for my future life as a helpmeet. But I couldn't knit to save my life and as for cookery, Violet was far better at it than I, so why, I wondered aloud, should I trouble myself? Pa just laughed when the pastor and I came to him with our competing complaints and told us to come to a meeting of the minds.

When the pastor's lessons proved too much, there was always the lure of the woods, the beach, and the marshes. Even on hot summer days when the mosquitos swarmed in clouds, or in the depths of winter when the marshes were rimmed with ice, it was a relief to escape his endless hectoring and shouting. Sometimes I was so sick of his voice that all human voices were loathsome to me, and I wouldn't even let Jimmy come with me. If I had known what lay in store for me, I might not have been so quick to spurn all company. But you know the pleasures of walking this island alone, Darren. The wind sighs through the high branches of the loblolly pine, and depending on your mood it seems either a close companion reflecting your own thoughts back to you, or a cool hand sweeping your fevered meditations away. There are so many different kinds of ducks, geese, swans, sandpipers, and other small birds that pass through in spring and fall or make Assateague their permanent home, that I never felt entirely alone in the world, even when I hadn't seen either a person or a pony for hours. Sometimes I'd come across a deer feasting on berries, and over time I learned how to approach them gradually and quietly enough not to scare them off. These were the native whitetail deer—the smaller sika deer were brought here long after my time as a mortal girl.

In those early years I learned to follow Star, the orphan colt who had been kicked out of his band, and I cheered as he started his own little band, first with one young mare I named Susie, then a second I named Daisy, and then two more, and another three, and before I knew it he had the biggest band north of Green Run Inlet! I was very possessive of them—I wouldn't tell anyone but Jimmy where to find them, and sometimes not even him, and I would sneak them apples and dried oats and anything else I could get away with.

I wished I could tame one of the ponies, preferably Star himself, but here my indulgent Pa was firm. "No, Annie, I'll not allow you to take the risk," he said.

I didn't miss the fact that he'd slipped back into calling me by my "baby name," and I stuck out my lower lip as if to acknowledge that he was right to do so. "I'll be careful!" I pleaded.

"No, Annie! I forbid it. And stop arguing with Pastor Scarburgh all the time. I hired him to teach you reading and practical skills, not to mold your character. Just smile and nod when he says something foolish. You may grumble about it to me afterward."

What could I do, what could I ever do, but agree to Pa's requests? He asked so little of me, but he deserved so much more than I could give. How many hours a day, after all, could Pastor Scarburgh really afford to spend on the impossible task of molding me from a tomboy into a compliant, "feminine" woman? How many more hours did I have to spend on chores like helping Violet wash my own clothes, or cooking when it was time to give the poor woman a break, or helping carry a few things here and there for the men who worked from first light till twilight building the hotel? Not so many, really. The rest of my time was mine to do with as I pleased. I only regret I did not spend more of it with my father.

20

Wright's Ocean House grew without much help from me. By the beginning of the third summer, the whole structure was complete, and all twenty guest rooms were ready for their occupants. The guests were slow to arrive, however. The previous year, only twelve rooms had been complete, including our own living quarters—mine and Pa's, and Will's—so to make room for our guests, we spent that summer roughing it in army surplus tents Pa was able to get hold of through his connections. And let me tell you, for the first time I really began to appreciate what all those poor men had suffered during the war. "Camping out" is fun when the weather is fair and you always have your nice, warm, dry house to return to, but it's a lot less fun when you have to do it rain or shine, on cold days as well as warm, and with lots of mosquitos and biting flies to keep you company! I complained so much that even Pa became cross with me, but luckily for me in August the trickle of guests thinned to nothing and Pa and I were able to move back into our Ocean House lodgings—Will stayed on in his tent without complaint.

One late September morning when the oaks and maples scattered among the pines were showing vivid crimson and orange, I overheard Will talking with Pa about the need to fill more rooms the following year.

"We cannot withstand another year like this one, Captain," he said.

"It takes time to build one's reputation in a business like this, Will!" Pa said, clapping him on the shoulder. I made sure I was well concealed in a thicket of brambles, biting my lip to keep from crying out at the thorns pricking my arms and legs. "I think we have done very well. That minister came back with his family for the second year in a row, and he's sure to talk with his parishioners about what a wonderful time he had, and then we shall have so many people clamoring to stay here that we'll have to start turning them away."

"Nevertheless, sir, we haven't made any money," Will said bluntly. I stiffened. Was Pa allowing him to see the books? It seemed that he must be.

"That will turn around, and quickly too!" Pa said. "I have already arranged to place advertisements in the *Evening Sun*, and also in the Philadelphia *Evening Bulletin*, inviting one and all to come stay in the twenty rooms we shall have ready for our opening in June."

"But to finish all that construction, you will need a new loan from my father, isn't that so, Captain?" Will said quietly. I clenched my fists.

"Well, yes, that is true. I have run through the original loan and the money our guests paid to stay with us. But your father surely understands that new businesses require investment—not just of money, but of time, patience, and hard work."

"Of course. Understanding such things is a banker's job. And when I go home I shall speak to him in favor of his writing you another loan." Will was going back to Baltimore? This was the first I had heard of it. But I had no time to think through what that meant—I was too busy being astonished and furious that he would dare shake his finger under Pa's nose! "But listen here, Captain," he was saying. "I know my father. And he will want to see some repayment on that loan starting in the coming year. You have your grand plans for a dance hall and a bar—"

"I've already ordered the bar, Will," Pa said. His voice sounded hoarse and a little too loud. "I have hopes it will come on the same ship that will take you back to Baltimore. It is to be a solid piece of mahogany, twenty feet long, two feet wide and no less than thirty inches thick—"

"And costing a pretty penny, too, I have no doubt, sir." Will had put his hands in his pockets and was speaking quietly, which added emphasis to his words. I found myself leaning forward. "I will speak to my father, I give you my word. For your sake and for Annie's. But for everybody's sake, be a little more frugal with your outlays so that the First Bank of Maryland may enjoy a return on its investment. Remember, sir, my father has his superiors to answer to, as well."

Will left when a boat put in at the dock three days later, a boat that was indeed carrying Pa's new bar, a slab of dark wood that looked big and solid enough to build a house out of. There were crates of fine whiskey to serve on it, too, and I thought I saw a look pass between Will and Pa, a look in which silver dollars jingled. Will climbed aboard and I did not see him again until the spring thaw had set in, but his mission must have been successful, for when he stepped ashore he seemed to float as if carried on the fresh onshore April breeze. He was wearing a new herringbone jacket and a sharp new hat, and his beard was trimmed close and fine. He spotted me first and came bounding up to grab me in his arms and swing me around. I squealed with delight as if I was still a little girl, but the grunt he made let me know that I was no longer that!

"How have you all managed over the winter, my little Annette?" he asked lightly.

I stamped my foot on the planks of the dock. "That's not my right name!"

"Should I call you Annie instead?"

"That's a baby name! And we managed just fine without you, Mister Pearson. The second floor is all but complete, and Susie gave birth yesterday morning."

He raised an eyebrow. "Susie? Who is that?"

I refrained from stamping again, lest I appear childish. "Star's first mare, of course! The one he really loves."

"Ah, your precious ponies." Will laughed and shook his head. "I see that you have not changed at all over the winter, Miss Anne, except that you are growing into a young woman."

"I could hardly grow into a young filly."

"And your tongue is as sharp as ever. I am sure Pastor Scarburgh is enjoying it more than ever."

"The reverend and I have come to an understanding. He will not attempt to make me into a lady, and I shall refrain from pulling the curly hairs out of his head."

"Well, that's all in order, then." He shouldered the heavy traveling bag he had come with and squinted up at the hotel—the sun was directly behind it. "The building is coming along nicely."

I scowled at him. "No thanks to you! We needed you over the winter. Why did you stay away so long?"

Will smiled and drawled, "Why, Miss Anne, I do believe you missed me!" He started walking up the slope in his easy, long-limbed pace, forcing me to scurry to keep up. As I danced along beside him I pelted him with a continual stream of commentary on everything that had happened in the past six months, right up to Mr. Birch turning his ankle while carrying one end of a large wooden beam for the nearly complete roof two days before, "which wouldn't have happened if you'd been here helping like you should have!"

"Anne, you have your mother's fire, but I assure you your wrath is misplaced," Will said, still smiling a little but looking me in the eye in a way that made me blush. "I have been about the business of Wright's Ocean House the entire time I was in Baltimore. I assure you it was always at the center of my thoughts. There is nothing I wish more than its success, for I know it would make you and your dear father happy." There was nothing I could say to that, and I stood rooted to the spot as he proceeded into the lobby, where Pa greeted him with a cry of joy and a hearty backslap. As I expected, they headed straight into the kitchen, which was empty at this time of day, and shut the door behind them.

I might have expected it, but I fumed silently. It was beneath my dignity, at twelve going on thirteen, to be spying on Pa all the time, so before the sun went down I cornered him down by the now-deserted bayside docks and asked him bluntly whether Will had persuaded his father to lend the money we needed. My father confirmed it, smiling a little at my impudence, and I cried out with joy and flung myself on him, embracing him around the neck. It meant his dream was really coming true! For once I was thinking little of myself, of what it would mean for me to grow up in such a remote place. If Pa was happy, that was the important thing.

I had no idea, then, that someday I might marry Will. The notion would have struck me as fantastic. To me, Will was the figure of towering strength who had rescued Mama and me from the rebel mob. He was Pa's stalwart comrade in arms, and he was also twelve years older than I. If I gave him the business when he stepped off the boat it was because his long absence had genuinely unsettled me, as if one of the pillars of the world had been knocked out and the earth was sliding beneath my feet. Years later, he told me that he had spent the previous winter and spring in Baltimore fending off suggestions from his parents that he court one or another young lady of society. "I knew even then that those delicate blossoms were not for me. I needed a young lady with guts, someone like your poor mother," he said with a half-smile. "Someone, in fact, like you."

If I did have courage I certainly needed it later that summer, just after a successful Fourth of July holiday, when we endured our first hurricane. Our annual seafood feast had brought us enough reservations to keep all twenty rooms filled through September. It is the way of things, is it not, that every gift Providence gives comes with its price? I remember how the old salt Mr. Powers looked at the sunset sky, sucked his lower lip, and warned us to expect "heavy weather," and we knew enough to take him seriously. Pa was most worried about the new glass in the lobby windows, and the men nailed up scrap wood to protect them against "the blow." I was sent running around on one errand after another the morning before Mr. Powers thought the storm would hit, but round about noon I found myself with nothing more to do and wandered out on the beach to watch the choppy waves rolling in. It was hard for a landlubber to tell how Mr. Powers had made his prediction, since the day was hot and still, with only a few high clouds darkening the blue. Jimmy joined me and we stared at the breakers, each of which reached a little higher than the one before, though it was low tide.

"You scared of the storm?" I asked him.

"The blow? Naw," he said, shaking his head. "We had one when I was little on the plantation. The master's house got smashed up and some of the slave cabins in the bottomlands was flooded, but didn't nobody get too bad hurt." Jimmy had kept up with his reading, grabbing each book I read as soon as I had finished it—Parson Scarburgh flat-out refused to have him in the room when he was tutoring me. Lucky Jimmy! In any case, he could certainly read and write at least as well as me, if not better, but he still talked much as he had when Will first brought him to our house in Baltimore—though he certainly talked a lot *more* than he had back then.

"Jimmy, what was it like back there? On the plantation, I mean."

He scowled and jammed his hands in the pockets of his homemade dungarees. The offshore breeze was picking up, and it blew back the mass of his thick black hair. "I don't like to think about it, Annie. I don't remember too much, anyhow."

"I'm sorry," I said. We were playmates, we enjoyed being children around each other. I really was sorry if I had upset him.

"It's all right," he said. "It warn't no fun, you can be sure of that. Some white man or lady was always yelling at you, telling you what to do. Even little kids that weren't hardly no bigger than me could tell me what to do, long as they were white, and they could beat me up if I didn't hop to it."

"Do you remember your brother Tom much?"

His face softened. "Tommy was bigger and stronger than me. He knowed how to do most everything better. When I got in trouble he always took the blame if he could. He got a lot of whippings I deserved." As if little Jimmy had ever deserved a whipping for not fulfilling a slavemaster's whims fast enough! I clenched my fists at the thought.

"He'll find you and Violet, Jimmy. If he's alive, he'll find you," I said. How cruel fate was, that when Tom finally did make his way to Green Run, I was dead and Violet and Jimmy were long gone. I am glad that you have become friends with one of Tom's descendants, Darren. Kevin is a good man. I hope he will be the one to find you here, when it gets light.

It was already getting dark when Jimmy and I left the beach a few minutes later. We were driven away by the wind, which was full of stinging particles of sand. On the dunes we met Violet, who was marching out with her face set in angry lines to fetch us. "Come on, you fool children," she snapped, grabbing each of us by the hand. "You want to be plumb blown away?" She had to raise her voice to be heard. As we ran through the woods there was a tremendous crack overhead, and a branch as thick as Will's leg crashed down right in front of us. And yet when we ran into the hotel, hardly a drop of rain had landed on us! That came later, when Pa and Will and I and most of the guests had huddled in the bar, which had no windows. Drinks were on the house, Pa announced, though he had sense enough to put the most expensive stuff, and the strongest, under lock and key in one of the storage rooms.

"I don't understand it, Captain," Will said, with an effort at joviality, though he practically had to shout to be heard over the rapid gunfire noise of the gale-driven rain striking the building. "I thought you Puritans were all temperance men!"

"You know me better than that, Will!" Pa said with a forced chuckle. "I am a follower of Mr. Thoreau! I march to the beat of my own drummer!"

"I'll drink to that," said one of the guests, a bewhiskered gentleman with a loosened cravat who looked like he'd already had quite enough. As for me, I was determined not to let a little wind and rain scare me. I saw a little girl and boy about five or six years old who were wide-eyed with fear clinging to their mother, so I led them in a singalong, changing some of the words to keep them interested. Even in the flickering lamplight I could see the mother eyeing me strangely as I introduced dolphins and blue crabs into "The Farmer in the Dell" and had them jump and scuttle over the cow and the pig. But the children loved it and were laughing and clapping along until the ominous creaking noises from the lobby turned into enormous groans and then the crash and splinter of shattering glass. The children had been sitting cross legged at my feet, and while their mother threw herself over the boy I threw myself over the girl. Something sharp was cutting into the back of my neck and there was a roaring that went on and on as wind and pelting rain blew into the lobby. I think I was screaming, my throat hurt as if I was screaming, but it was impossible to hear anything over the storm. The little girl lay motionless beneath me. There was some banging, wood against wood it sounded like. A man's voice cursed loudly. Abruptly the wind died down and I could hear people calling out to each other, a few crying in pain. Strong hands were pulling me up and away. My cheek brushed against a soft beard.

"Pa?" I asked hoarsely.

"No Annie, it's me, Will."

"Will, am I dying?"

"No, child. Your back is cut up, that's all. I've seen men hurt much worse who were back in battle the next day, it's nothing to worry about."

Was he calling me a brave warrior? I pressed myself against his neck and the soft comfort of his beard. Out of the corner of my eye I could see the reason the noise of the storm had dropped: he and Pa and the other men had yanked the bar loose and hauled it over to the entranceway to the lobby, piling stools and whatever other furniture they could find up against it to make a barricade. I thought of Odysseus and his sailing companions holding off the Cyclops. Poseidon certainly was as angry at us as he had been at them, I thought. I hoped Violet and Jimmy were all right in their little cabin. They wouldn't have dreamed of sheltering with us, especially since several of the guests were from Baltimore and Tidewater Virginia.

Luckily when the storm finally died down it turned out nobody had been killed. Violet, however, had a badly bruised leg—that falling tree branch had actually hit her, but we'd been in such a panicked flight she hadn't felt anything till later. But losing her for heavy work while she healed was a blow to Pa, who had to hire additional laborers to fix all the damage the storm had caused. He fretted, too, that word would get around that Wright's Ocean House had been destroyed by the hurricane, and in truth almost half the guest rooms were wrecked, leaving only eleven or twelve habitable for the rest of the season. He had to cancel some reservations and return the disappointed guests their money, which required him to spend two days traveling back and forth to Salisbury, where the nearest telegraph office was. He returned tired and disheartened, for another four parties had canceled of their own accord.

Little did we know the storm would be the making of the hotel, and it was on my account! I blush to tell you this, but it turned out that the father of the girl I had jumped on when the lobby windows came crashing down was a reporter for the *Evening Sun*, who had brought his family to the seaside because Pa had offered a special deal to the newspaper employees in return for a reduced advertising rate. Darren, I read the article that man wrote, and a more fantastic tale I never heard told! If you believed Miles Turner, I was "as strong as any man, yet with a fair innocence and grace that would put any society lady to shame."

I'm embarrassed to admit I reveled in being called the "Angel of Assateague." For years, right up until my death, people would come stay at Wright's Ocean House just to meet the "angel." Pa found that hugely amusing and made me the "desk manager," which meant that I signed the guests in, gave them their keys, and walked them to their rooms. To give Pastor Scarburgh his due, he immediately began teaching me copperplate handwriting, "a ladylike script to match the ladylike misimpression of you under which our poor visitors labor." Stop laughing so hard, Darren, you'll hurt yourself.

Jimmy, who was beginning to prefer being called Jim, was fascinated by the curlicues of fancy script I showed him and wanted me to teach him too. Like everything else except seafood and the few vegetables Violet and the Birches were beginning to grow, ink had to be shipped to the island, so we experimented with different wild berries until we made a concoction that would leave its mark. Naturally paper was in short supply, too, but when Pa learned what we were up to he put in an order for an extra ream and a beautiful new pen for Jim, a gift that left him speechless.

"Consider it my birthday present to you," Pa said.

"I don't even know when my birthday is, Captain," Jim pointed out.

"Then I have been the more remiss in not appointing a day to celebrate it. Wright's Ocean House would not exist without the work you and your sister have done," Pa said.

When the holidaymakers stopped coming with the first cold weather in late September, just after my birthday, Pa added up the accounts and discovered that he had just managed to break even, clearing only a few dollars that he could repay to the bank. I wondered whether Pa would have to speak to Will about that, but I was afraid to ask.

21

That winter was a hard one. Jim and I had little time for frolicking in the snow, our help was needed too badly around the hotel, as well as in people's cabins and the various outbuildings. When I did manage to escape out on my own I found tragedy striking Star's band. Two of the three new foals had frozen to death in a big blizzard before November was even out, and the thin forage had all the ponies moving sluggishly and huddling together for warmth. I was worried the last foal, whom I had named Sally after the one girl who was nice to me back at Mrs. Wintergreen's schoolhouse, would die too, so I lobbied Pa to build an enclosure where I could keep her and care for her.

Pa eyed me wearily as he crouched by the fire in the lobby, trying to warm his hands after another hard day chopping and hauling ice from the little pond that was still our main source of fresh water. "I can't spare anyone," he said shortly. "Annie, you're not a little girl anymore. I can't even spare you. Would you have Violet or Betty Birch take on extra work because you are too busy caring for an animal?"

"It won't be like that, Pa," I pleaded. "Jim will help me,

we can build a fence on the open side of the courtyard in two or three days. And once Sally is tamed and grown a little, she will do her share. She can be a plough horse in the spring when Andy Birch plants his corn."

Eventually I talked him into it. It was easier than I expected to lure Sally away from her mother, Susie, with the promise of food, and the mare was too weak with cold and hunger to do anything about it. Jim held her off by flicking a stout branch at her nose. "Don't worry, we will take good care of Sally," I said as Susie whinnied piteously. Sally's nostrils flared at the faint scent of dried apples, and I held one tiny piece out to her teasingly, letting her take it from my hand. "Careful," Jim said, "she'll bite you, Annie," but I was confident she would not; after all, hadn't she and the other members of her band all grown accustomed to me? Her lips were cold, rubbery, and faintly damp when they touched my hand, but I laughed with delight.

"That's right, girl," I said, "come with me and you'll always have enough to eat!" And I backed away from her, putting two or three yards between us before I dropped another piece in the old, crusty snow and let her amble up and eat it. Jim got between her and Susie, switching again with his stick to keep the mare away, while Sally walked into the trap we had laid for her. We fed her the rest of the apples and a cupful of dried oats while everyone gathered to watch.

Mr. Powers shook his head. "It's blamed foolishness. That's a wild pony, and if it wasn't so weak it wouldn't take none too kind to being cooped up like that."

"I think you've done a great thing, Annie!" Betty said, clapping her gloved hands together against the cold. There was a high color in her cheeks and her eyes sparkled. I looked into them and had to force myself not to wink— she'd confided in me the night before that she thought she was pregnant but hadn't wanted to tell "my Andy" until she could be sure.

"If you do manage to keep her, we'll have to move her someplace else come spring," Pa said, glancing at our ramshackle fence and raising his eyebrows. "I know you and Jim worked hard, Annie, but we can't have our guests looking at that eyesore."

"They won't have to look at it, Pa," I said. "All the windows of their rooms face the other way." This was mostly to give people a better view of the woods, the calm, tree-shaded waters of the inlet, and the brilliant white beach stretching down to the sea; but it was also, Pa told me once, "to keep those Baltimore and Virginia folks from giving us trouble about Violet and Jim's cabin."

Around the middle of March a thaw set in. Jim and I had been taking care of Sally all winter long, brushing her coat and talking to her in soothing voices as well as feeding her and cleaning up her dung. Mr. Powers softened enough to make a bridle and bit so I could at least walk her around the little enclosure. But as she gained strength, his prediction came true; she became more and more restless and started kicking holes in the fence we'd built. I had to tie her to one of the posts in the courtyard that Violet used to string her clotheslines, which did not please her.

"I can't have that nasty animal chewing up the good sheets and towels," she said. "You and your rapscallion friend better find someplace else for it."

"Rapscallion? You mean your little brother Jim who you love so much?" I asked.

"Rapscallion's too kind a word for him. Where's he been hiding all morning, anyway? You tell him he better get in here and peel them potatoes for Sunday dinner if he knows what's good for him," she said, shaking the huge wooden spoon she used to stir the soup kettle.

There were now nine or ten families living in the village, but every Sunday Pa insisted we all eat together, a practice I wouldn't have minded so much if it didn't involve Pastor Scarburgh giving the blessing. Invoking divine protection for our tiny settlement wasn't enough for him. He had to go on and on about the dangers that awaited us at every turn "if we fall away from You, O Lord," the fire everlasting that waited just below our feet to torment the unrepentant sinner. I wasn't the only one who wished the reverend would be a little less detailed about that, either—I overheard Mr. Powers complaining to Mr. Birch that those sermons "are enough to put a body off his chowder."

I decided I was honor bound to go warn Jim that his sister was on the warpath. "I hate peeling potatoes," he scowled as he sat in the shade of one of our favorite clearings, idly chucking pinecones into the marsh, where they hit the muddy water with a gloopy splash. "I always get my fingers cut up. And then if that ain't enough, Sally likes to chew on them! I say Violet can peel her own potatoes and you can take care of your own pony!"

That was a problem. I was going to need his help to build a new enclosure for Sally. I bit my lip, thinking fast. "Let's see," I said, taking a pinecone away from him and turning his right hand palm up. I ran the ball of my thumb along the line where his dark brown skin faded into the pink of his palm. Then I turned his the hand over, raised it to my lips and kissed it mockingly, mimicking the grave courtesy Andy Birch showed Betty in public. "Hmm. Doesn't look too bad to me. I think you're complaining about nothing."

He snatched his hand away. "What do you know about it! You ain't never peeled potatoes!"

"But I have fed Sally many times, and she never bites my fingers," I said. I started to wheedle him about how Sally was really his too, that we were both going to ride her equally once she'd been broken to the saddle (how to get Pa to pay for one was another question, but I was confident of my powers of persuasion over him). "I tell you what," I said when he still looked sullen, "I'll tell Violet I couldn't find you, but I'll peel the potatoes, if you scout out someplace new we can keep Sally."

"Really, you'll do that?"

"Really I will."

"Not just this once, but from now on?"

"Well—" He put his hands on his hips, and I had to strike a deal with him—we'd take turns on the potato peeling. How hard could it be, I thought?

Not hard at all with the sharp little knife Violet gave me, it turned out. And also not hard to peel the skin off three of my fingers.

"Give me that before you really hurt yourself, child!" Violet cried, snatching the knife away and throwing me a towel. "I can't have you bleeding in my soup."

"Can't you be a little more sympathetic?" My voice was muffled as I sucked on my bleeding fingers and tried not to cry.

"Not when it's your own fault, being so clumsy! Here, let me show you how to hold a knife so you don't turn your own fingers to ground beef." Jim got the best part of the deal after all, I thought ruefully. Between the two of us, Violet and I did get those potatoes peeled, though I am sure she did five for every one I finished, and without once injuring herself. I wondered jealously where Jim was off scouting—it was a beautiful day and here I was stuck in this damp, crowded kitchen.

The soup drew twice as much praise as usual that evening, when it became known that I had assisted Violet in preparing it. "A chef as well as a heroine!" Betty cried, to much applause, and I made a curtsey. Then I went off to join Jim where he squatted under a tree slurping his soup from a bowl. I think he did it deliberately to annoy the villagers who'd just as soon see no black faces on "their" island.

"Did you find a place for Sally?" I asked.

He nodded and pointed. "There's a bend in the crick back there," he said, meaning the inlet. "An oxbow bend, you know the one I mean?"

I nodded.

"Well, I checked and the water's pretty deep back there. We could build the same kind of fence we got here, across that neck of land, and Sally wouldn't be able to get out."

I frowned. "Sounds good, but how wide is that neck?"

"Probably no more than a couple of the bigger pines laid end to end."

"I don't know, Jim. It might be too much work for just the two of us."

"We can do it, if you can get your Pa to give us a week."

"Problem is, Pa won't be the one to give permission— he leaves all that up to Mr. Powers." At Jim's scowl I hastily added, "I'll work on him. He likes me."

It was true. He liked me so much, he volunteered to do the work with me, "so we'll be done in three days, and do the job much better than you could with your *boy*." I frowned at this, but he wagged his finger at me and said, "I can't understand why your Pa lets you run around with him all the time. It ain't good for you."

I tried to split the difference between standing up for Jim and offending Mr. Powers so much he withdrew his offer to help—or even forbade me to work on the project myself. "Violet and Jim have been with my family since before the war," I said. That was stretching the truth, and also making it sound as if we were their slavemasters! And it didn't do much to mollify Mr. Powers. "'Tain't right, I'm telling you," he said stubbornly. "A girl your age, gettin' big enough to marry off, nearly…"

I bit my tongue to keep from telling him to mind his own business. "Tomorrow morning, then, Mr. Powers?"

"Not morning. I need to work on the roof of the Ocean House. Maybe after lunch." Next day, I noticed he kept Jim with him, running back and forth fetching nails and shingles and whatnot, as if to keep an eye on him; and then in the afternoon he ordered Jim aboard the *Margaret Deirdre* for a supply run to Spence Landing. But he was as good as his word with me, Darren, and we did finish that enclosure for Sally before the week was out. The ground was clear and almost flat within it, except for a lone dead tree near the center, which I used as a hitching post. Later that year Pa relented, seeing how much I loved Sally, and how dutifully I cared for her, and built a small stables in a corner of the courtyard so I would have a place to keep her in bad weather.

That spring and summer the pastor had his hands full trying to keep me at my lessons, when all Jim and I wanted to do was tame Sally. We got thrown a few times, each of us, but never came away with anything worse than a few bruises. I really think she didn't want to hurt us. When Will returned from Baltimore and saw what I had been up to, he didn't scold me as I thought he would. Instead, on his next supply run to Salisbury he bought a saddle! I was overcome when he gave it to me.

He smiled when I fell all over myself thanking him. "I was already away when your birthday came last September. Consider it my much delayed present. Here, let me put it on this fearsome steed of yours." Like all the island ponies, Sally stood much shorter than an ordinary horse, and had a belly swollen from dining on salt grass. I'm afraid I had oversold her potential as a workhorse. She never was good for much more than pleasure rides for me and Jim.

That first year at least I did my best to keep my promise to let him ride as much as me. I was very selfless about it, too—every time Pastor Scarburgh called me for lessons or Pa to see to some guests, I told him he was free to ride old Sally. Which gave him little enough time with her, really, seeing that Violet and Mr. Powers needed his help more often than not. Still, he didn't begrudge me. "I think she likes you more than she likes me," he'd say ruefully.

"Aww, that's not true, Jim," I'd say. "You just have to be gentle with her, is all."

"I'm gentle as can be," he protested, and he was, too. But it was me she preferred for a canter down the beach in an early morning mist, or to step delicately through the salt marsh on a cool October evening when the first frosts had killed off the mosquitoes and biting flies. At best she only tolerated Jim until he outgrew her.

That year and the next business started to take off for the Ocean House. The dock was so crowded on nice summer days that if you squinted you might imagine you were back in Baltimore Harbor. Whether it was the tale of my so-called heroics, a tale that grew taller every summer with the return of the Turners and little Kate's increasingly embellished account of how I had saved her, or the rebuilt bar and dance hall which offered the finest entertainment east of Baltimore and north of Norfolk, with singers and fiddlers and trombone players Pa engaged for the busiest periods, or the natural charm and beauty of the island, it soon became unnecessary for Pa to advertise. But as quickly as he paid off the debts to Will's father, he incurred new debts for new expansions and embellishments. The Fourth of July parties were enough by themselves to wipe out his profits for half a year, but Pa couldn't resist the role of master of ceremonies.

Sometimes I tried to kid him about what a spendthrift he was becoming. "What would your thrifty Yankee ancestors have said, Pa?"

He'd frown, then say lightly, "Damn them, the self-righteous killjoys." The first few times he cursed like that, he chuckled at my shock, but eventually I grew hardened to his outbursts. I think, though, that he really was determined to rebel against his upbringing by stretching out a generous hand to the guests and the village he had founded. If Will's father got his money back a little more slowly as a result, well, it wasn't going to sink the First Bank of Maryland, which would only enjoy a handsomer reward in the end. "Life isn't about money—not the getting of it, not the hoarding of it, not even the spending of it," he told me more than once. "My family in New England, Annie—your family too, should you ever wish to seek them out—are losing their old religion and clinging to Mammon in its place." Sometimes I wonder if his judgment on them would have been so harsh, if only they could have accepted Mama. As it was, he saw Will and Violet and Jim, and the Birches and Mr. Powers and the other villagers, even the prickly pastor, as his adopted family—though all came second in his heart to me, of course. I tried to repay him by being a gracious hostess to the guests at the Ocean House, by doing my chores and biting my tongue in my lessons with the good pastor.

Now that Sally had been broken I rode her every chance I got, even in bad weather, which is how it happened that I spotted the shipwreck that was to change Green Run forever. It was a blustery day in late October, six weeks or so after my thirteenth birthday. Clouds had been rolling in all day from the ocean, but I was determined to get in one last ride before the weather really set in and I had to hunker down with Pa in the boarded-up hotel. To my surprise I saw a steamship laboring among the billowing whitecaps that flashed against the rapidly darkening water. I reined in Sally and covered my eyes against the blowing sand, peering through my fingers at the huge vessel. It was coming from the south, which meant it was probably the regular Norfolk-to-Philadelphia cargo run, the *SS Walter Scott*, though it was running hours late and should never have sailed at all in the rising gale. As I watched it swayed from side to side, its huge paddle wheel vanishing in a shower of spray, then reappearing, until the whole craft settled on its side with a tremendous roar, kicking up a wave that tore up the beach and into the inlet, reaching out for me. I wheeled Sally around and urged her back home as quickly as her short legs would carry us. By the time I got to the hotel the rain was coming down in hard, cold gusts. Will ran out, his mouth open to berate me, as well he might have, but he closed it again in a hurry when I told him what was happening. Without a word he shoved me inside and ran off to round up Pa, Mr.

Powers, Mr. Birch, Jim, the pastor and every other male on the island.

I huddled under the bar with Betty, my hands around my knees. It was like the hurricane had returned, only this time there were no men around to raise a barricade if the storm smashed in the lobby windows again.

"I do hope they won't risk the *Margaret Deirdre*," Betty said softly as she rocked her little son Caleb back and forth in her arms. "That pungy ain't built for weather like this!"

"I hope they won't risk themselves," I added. Betty threw me a look, and I said, "I wish the men on that ship no harm, but what happens if one of our men is lost?"

After a miserable, cold, dark hour of waiting, during which Caleb mercifully stopped crying and fell asleep, there was a racket out front, and Will and Jim burst into the lobby carrying a half-drowned sailor between them. Pa was next, carrying a girl about my age, and the others were close behind with several other shipwreck victims. Luckily some of them at least were able to stand on their own two feet and help as we tried to make the injured comfortable. Will was the closest thing to a doctor we had in our little colony. I daresay that with his experience in the war, he treated the survivors as well as they could have expected this side of Baltimore. But the toll was grim. The man Will and Jim had saved died in the night, while I sat up and held the hand of the girl, whose name was Mabel and who kept crying for her father. In the morning his body was found washed up on the beach, along with four other passengers and three of the crew. The captain had been sitting drinking Pa's brandy all night—so much for heroic myth—and the first mate was missing. Pa was furious, partly at the captain, who wouldn't stop justifying himself, but mostly at the pointless waste of the whole disaster.

"To have such loss of life on a modern ship like that is inexcusable," I heard him saying to Will, while I knelt and tried to comfort the sobbing Mabel. "Nobody need have died at all, if we'd had proper equipment to save them!"

"The government was planning to build more life-saving stations and lighthouses out here before the war," Will replied. "Maybe now that there's been loss of life, they'll actually do it. This whole stretch of coast is notoriously dangerous."

In the meantime we had to reopen the guest rooms for the survivors of the wreck of the *Water Scott* until the weather cleared enough for Pa to take them to the mainland on the *Margaret Deirdre*. The Birches took in the orphaned girl. I felt an instinctive kinship with Mabel and wanted her to stay with us, but Pa shook his head and said it wouldn't look right. Once again he'd disappointed me.

"I thought you didn't care a fig for social convention, Pa."

He raised a busy gray eyebrow where a typical father would have reached for his belt. "Being the 'mayor' of Green Run binds me rather more than it frees me, Annie," he said. "I'm not the master of my own little cabin by the shores of Walden Pond, with only the loons and the muskrats to dispute with me."

I was full enough of vinegar to ask Pa, "What was the point of coming out here and building Wright's Ocean House, but to be your own man?"

He flushed, but his voice came out low and even. "Despite everything, Annie, you've led a sheltered life. A child always thinks its parents enjoy complete freedom, but my darling, you're old enough to know that isn't true. If you disapprove of the way I lead my life, I invite you to find a husband just as bold and determined as you, and together you can defy society to your heart's content." A year before I would have broken down in tears with shame, or anyway with the desire to get back in Pa's good graces, but as it was I flounced out of our little apartment, pushed my way through the storage room and out into the empty dance hall, where I wasted the next hour doing clumsy reels and imagining I was in the arms of a strong and understanding man such as Pa had sarcastically suggested for me.

Perhaps that is a cute picture in your imagination, Darren, but I was perfectly awful to everybody around me, not just that night, but all through that winter. I do not know how Pa and Violet tolerated me. I even pity the pastor, when I think of what I put him through. Jim and I no longer enjoyed our innocent games of hide and seek in the woods or sledding down the dunes after a snowfall; he must have been wary of the raging monster I had become, and really, who could blame him? Perhaps I would have pretended better to being a civilized young lady had Will wintered with us for once, but his journeys to Baltimore had become firmly established as an annual ritual, and jealousy gripped me when I imagined the smooth and stylish debutantes his parents were no doubt setting him up with. His return with the first mild weather of April brought me no relief, even though there was no debutante on his arm, for Pa set off on a journey of his own as soon as his faithful second was there to take command.

"If you are going to Washington City, I am coming with you," I said to Pa.

"I'm sorry, Annie fish, but you cannot," he said firmly. "I shall be seeking audiences with Congressmen and other government officials to plead for a life-saving station here at our little inlet, and even grown women are not welcome at such meetings."

"Betty could chaperone me. Oh, please, Pa, I want to see the capital!"

He shook his head. "Annie, it cannot be done. I need you here to help her and Violet redecorate the lobby in time for our summer visitors. Will brought back with him from Baltimore the December issue of the *Saturday Evening Post*, which has an excellently illustrated article on the latest in hotel furnishings in New York and—"

"Nothing could possibly bore me more than sewing and hanging curtains. If you force me to do it, I may set fire to them."

"You are not making a great case for your mature womanhood to accompany me to Washington," Pa said drily. Stop laughing so hard, Darren, you'll hurt yourself! Are you still seeing double? It's starting to get light... Oh, when will the rangers come and find you?

I did not, as I have said, get my way, but I did not carry out my threats of arson. Instead I waited till the morning after Pa's departure, when I saddled up Sally and packed some leftover bread, dried fruit, a bottle of water, and a fishhook on a good strong piece of cord. We forded the inlet at a shallow spot fifty yards seaward of her corral, and rode as far away from Green Run as I could get. The day started out cool, but warmed as I rode on to the south. Back then there was nothing man-made on the island for fifteen miles from our inlet to the southernmost tip, where a new lighthouse stood. That suited me just fine.

I carried with me two rough pieces of canvas, enough to make a lean-to shelter with a ground cloth underneath it, and flint so I could build a campfire. For the first couple of hours I headed steadily down the beach. As the sun blazed higher overhead I took Sally under the trees into a cool clearing with a white sandy floor of old dunes. There I shared a drink with her from a pond not much bigger than the dance floor in the Ocean House—I'd brought water with me but wanted to save it for an emergency. After tethering Sally to a tree I wandered over to the bayside marsh, kicked off my boots and started feeling around with my bare feet for clams for my supper. My haul wasn't very impressive, but it was more than enough to satisfy me. Then I went back to Sally, fed her some dried apples—which had remained her favorite food—and dozed away most of the afternoon, waking toward sunset to pitch my makeshift tent and collect wood to bake my clams.

I stayed there for three days. Sometimes I thought with childish glee that Will and the others must be out looking for me, but other times I thought that no one was bothering at all, that they didn't care whether I'd drowned or a tree had fallen on me. Mostly, though, I enjoyed the quiet. No one spoke to me but the wind. *Maybe I should just stay out here,* I thought as I gazed at the stars at night through the gaps in the pine trees. Men like Mr. Powers often went off on their own to hunt and fish. Why couldn't I do the same?

Of course this idyll couldn't last. It was Jim who found me, when the sun was about halfway down the afternoon sky on the third day. At least he didn't scold me. "They all going crazy looking for you," he said.

I shrugged. "Let them. Want some of the bass I caught yesterday?" It wasn't completely cooked, but Jim didn't seem to mind. I sat and watched him eat. He was growing up a short man, shorter than his sister, but with a powerful torso and arms from all the fetch-and-carry work white folks made him do. I noticed these things more because I hadn't spent much time with him in the better part of a year, long enough for his face to lose most of its childishness and take on the wariness about the eyes black men had around white people. That caution was less evident now that we were alone, but he did not know what to say to me, and it was mutual.

When he was done eating he stood up and said, "Thanks. I'd better start back or I'll never make it before dark. You coming?"

I sighed and stood up too, noticing as if for the first time that I was slightly taller than him. "Guess I'd better, or Will'll run off to Salisbury to telegraph Pa, and then the whole entire navy will be out looking for me. Want to ride?"

He looked down at his canvas sandals, which were too small for his feet and pretty raggedy, besides. It was all the answer I needed. We took turns riding and walking—there was no way Sally could have carried us both at the same time—but when we came within two or three miles of the inlet, the sun poking reddish orange rays from behind the dunes, he dismounted and said, "Guess I'd better go on ahead." I nodded. There was no need to say anything more. If we were seen together, far from getting credit for finding me, he would—well, without Pa around, almost anything might happen.

That didn't mean I didn't owe him thanks, though. "I'm glad you came to get me," I said, putting my hand on his arm. He nodded but wouldn't look me in the eye. What was this about? We'd known each other since Baltimore, for heaven's sake. I'd taught him to read. Out of exasperation more than anything else, I grabbed him by the chin and turned up his head until he had to look at me—then I planted a kiss that landed on his nose. His eyes went as round as the sand dollars I loved to collect, and he let out a little gasp. Then he turned on his heels and ran as if something terrible was after him.

I never did find out what he told folks about why he was running, or even if he had to explain at all, thanks to the uproar that began the moment Betty saw me riding Sally up the beach and let out a scream—But Darren, I hear something out on the beach. Can't you hear it? It sounds like a car! Can you stand? Can you walk? We have to get their attention!

22

The Park Service 4X4 stopped dead in its tracks and Paul Truitt leaped out the moment I staggered out from behind the dunes—although I only learned later that it was him; at the time my rescuer was no more than a blurred silhouette against a bright smear of dawn sky. Now that Annie was gone my back was on fire and the pounding in my head was swelling to fill the whole world. I started to pitch face-first in the sand, but Paul caught me and lifted me up. I heard him speaking, asking me something. Even moving my lips was agony and my voice came out in a croak. "Make sure they don't beat Annie for running away," I think I said before blacking out. When I woke my field of vision was full of crisp, bright whiteness. *Must've snowed overnight,* I thought woozily. *I hope they let Annie and Jim go sledding.* Then the sun broke through an even gray cloud cover, shining right in my eyes. I groaned.

"Yep, looks like a concussion, all right," a voice said. "The second one this summer for this kid!" The pain was still there somewhere, but it was muffled by those gray clouds. I tried to ask if they'd sent Captain Wright a telegram asking him to come back from Washington, but they must have thought I was delirious. They wouldn't let me sleep, though, for fear I might go into a coma. Eventually my head cleared, and I saw Kevin frowning down at me. "Man, you are a mess," he said.

"Where am I?"

"Peninsula Regional Medical Center in Salisbury again. Hey, give me some money to buy you a lottery ticket."

"What? Why?"

"Because you got hit by lightning—well, grazed, anyhow—and all you've got to show for it is a concussion, a ruptured eardrum, a gouge in your right leg, and a lightly char-grilled back that is going to make one hell of an interesting network of scars to show your girlfriend."

"I have to go find her," I said, trying to sit up.

"Hey man," he said, gently pushing on my chest, "you're not going anywhere for a while. Your parents are on the way."

Kevin raised an eyebrow at me when I groaned, but he hadn't lived through their divorce. But when they got there in their separate cars, Mom and Dad were on their best behavior, so much so that I hoped to wheedle another car for myself out of them. I struck out on that score, though, and my nurse gave me a good scolding when I asked how soon I could be discharged. "You're a burn and concussion patient, Mr. Trachtenberg, or have you forgotten?"

The doctor said the same thing to me the next morning. He kept blinking and shaking his head. "You've suffered major trauma, Darren. I don't understand why you wouldn't want to rest and heal. I mean, it would be different if there was someone to take care of you at home."

Annie's all I need, I thought. But it was true that I'd barely been out of bed yet. There was a long gash down my right leg that made walking difficult. Lakeisha was appalled when she came with Kevin later that day and I said I wanted to go back to work.

"Are you out of your mind, Darren? You get hit by

lightning and the first thing you can think of is you miss that damn gatehouse?"

"Please don't swear," I said, which earned me a puzzled look. "I'm worried Cropper won't hold my job open if I stay here too long."

"Honey, you are in no shape. I don't want to hear any more about it. You just lie here, watch TV, and get better."

"Do you need anything from home?" Kevin asked. "I've got to drive by there anyway later."

"No, that's really all right. It's the job I'm worried about," I said. "I tried calling Bob earlier but he wasn't answering his phone."

"Probably out on beach patrol," Lakeisha said, a little too quickly. "So where's this girlfriend of yours? How come she ain't here holding your hand?"

"Why is everyone so curious about that? It's family stuff, she can't get away." Inspiration hit me. "Her father just had a stroke."

"Wow. Okay. It's just that you two spend so much time together. I mean, you told the nurses you were with her when the lightning hit you," Lakeisha said.

I did? When did I say that? Must have been right after I was brought in, when I was still pretty out of it. Kevin was watching my confused face keenly. "Are you sure you're gonna be all right when they discharge you? I don't want you sitting around that trailer all alone," he said.

"What is this, my mom fails to be a stereotypical Jewish mother, so my black friends have to step in? I'll be fine," I said, irritably swiping at my eyes with the back of my sleeve. What was I crying for? Now I'd never get rid of them. I couldn't play the I'm-not-feeling-well-please-leave-me-alone card, it'd be too obvious. But how to change the subject? "Kevin, have you been back to see Hattie since we visited her?"

"How's that? Uh, no, actually. Why?"

"I wanted to ask her some more questions about Wright's Ocean House. She told me the place burned down, but Paul Truitt told me it was around till after World War One, when they dismantled it and shipped the lumber back to the mainland. They couldn't have done that if there was nothing there but ashes. I wonder if she knows anything about when and how it was rebuilt."

Kevin rubbed his chin. "I guess I can ask her, but what are the chances she'll know? She must have been born around the time the hotel was being knocked down for good."

Good point, and what did I expect to find out, anyway? I just had a nagging sense it might be important. Lakeisha put her elbows on her knees and her chin in her hands and gave me a long look. "Darren, I don't know what you're involved in, but you sure are getting banged up an awful lot. What is all this about, really?"

I looked from her to Kevin and back again. Could I actually tell them? They were such nice people, but I was afraid if I said anything to them about ghosts, they'd think I'd lost my mind. I might actually be in danger of a psychiatric commitment, if I "confessed" to a cop!

That was the thought that decided me. "Oh, don't worry about me," I said, leaning back against my pillow with a nervous chuckle. "Accident-Prone Darren, that's me! I'll just have to be more careful from now on." But when they finally left, I started brooding. Assuming that I wasn't delusional, was there something about being around Annie that was putting me in danger? Were the living not supposed to be on such intimate terms with the dead, and was some force trying to correct this, by killing me if need be? It was an irrational thought, but it made a kind of intuitive sense.

I knew, though, that even if I had proof of this terrifying notion, I could never stop trying to see Annie, to be with her, to ease her suffering and bring her peace. *And if I die as a result,* a voice in my heart whispered, *won't we be reunited forever, then?*

23

I was finally discharged from the hospital after two weeks as an inpatient that included rehab to help me walk again on my injured right leg. Hobbling up and down the hospital corridors for two hours each day, with a nurse's aide by my side to catch me if I fell, was a torture dreamed up especially for me by the same unknown demons who were keeping Annie in her twilight state. But I kept on, for her sake. I kept on even though my suspicions about Cropper were confirmed when he told me curtly by phone that there was no job waiting for me when I got out.

"I need someone to man that gatehouse every day, Darren, and you've been gone for almost two weeks. Anyway, don't you have to be back in College Park next week? I assumed you'd be giving me notice by now." Telling him that I'd arranged to take the semester off made no difference. "You don't want to be sitting in that gatehouse when the Labor Day crowds come in, anyway, trust me."

Wasn't it against the law to fire someone for being in the hospital, I wondered? Later I found out that you had to have worked at a place for at least a year for that law to apply. But later would have been too late, anyhow. I started to plead with him, but he said he had to go take care of an emergency on the beach and hung up on me.

So now I didn't even have a job. But I didn't care. I was getting closer to saving Annie. She had told me the story of her life up to age thirteen or fourteen, right? It was obvious that her "sin" involved Jim, but the point wasn't solving a mystery; I had to get her to see she was no sinner, to free her from the terrible burden of guilt that she'd carried for a century and a half, and I couldn't work on that until I saw her again. Of course I also wanted to see her again for my own sake.

But I began to despair before I even pedaled onto the tree-lined road leading to Assateague. My right leg hurt so much, I knew I'd never be able to make it to the roundabout at the end of the road, much less all those miles on foot over the sand. Of course I was also breaking my promise to Kevin and Lakeisha, who had brought the bike back home for me. "You won't go anywhere on it but the supermarket until you're really healed, right, Darren?" Lakeisha had said, gripping the handlebars as if she meant to snatch it away if I refused to promise. Annie would have thought it dishonorable, but I gave my word.

But it's no use, I thought as I labored up the slope of the Verrazano Bridge. I was biting my tongue hard to keep from screaming with pain. It was a muggy late August morning, and the cars were backed up on the bridge. If I collapsed I would have a crowd to deal with, and I didn't want that. So I gritted my teeth and pushed myself over the highest point, so I could coast on the downslope. It was all flat ground after that, and with just a little more effort, maybe I could make it as far as the State Park gatehouse and get help. If I was in luck, Lakeisha would be there instead of Bob or some stranger. It was obviously going to be a long time before I'd be well enough to make it Green Run on my own and find Annie again. But I knew she'd be waiting for me.

Sailing down the slope onto the island with the cool

wind in my face, I saw something bright gleaming up ahead and to the right, on a narrow sand embankment that stretched out from the island proper into the bay. A small band of wild ponies milled around the shining object, which was probably a hubcap from a passing car or a broken side mirror. Whatever it was, it was awfully bright with reflected sunlight...

I almost lost my balance. It was Annie, shining painfully bright as she had that time I tried to take her off the island! She was standing in the midst of the band of ponies, her green eyes glowing as she looked at me. Even her drab brown dress was lit up from within. I coasted to a stop a few yards from the stallion, who eyed me warily—what had Annie called him—Scotty, that was it!

"Don't worry, Scotty boy, I'm not going to hurt you," I murmured.

Annie walked toward me, tears streaming down her face but vanishing before they could reach the sand. "You're all right, Darren!"

"You came all this way to see me!"

"No, you are the one who made such a terrible effort—so much pain—but why, Darren? I would have waited for you."

"I didn't want you to be lonely." I hesitated. "That moment we were together, *really* together, when I was out of my body... I'd do anything to hold you again like that..."

"You must never, never, never!" Annie cried, her eyes two green flames with a midnight darkness at their centers. "Promise me, Darren, promise me or I swear I'll never show myself to you again!"

My breath caught in my throat and I couldn't speak.

"Swear to me, Darren! You must swear you will never harm yourself."

"I swear it," I said. "It was only my loneliness talking... I could never do anything like that, I'm too afraid of pain."

"You don't know what would happen to you, if you

died," Annie said. "It's crazy to assume you would become a—" her voice caught "—a ghost like me. Perhaps those who haven't sinned as I did go straight to heaven—or perhaps they vanish, and their souls are at rest. I know nothing about it, Darren. I know nothing but my own experience."

"Your experience," I said. "You must finish telling me about your life. There must be some clue in your story as to why you ended up as you did. And don't keep telling me it was some sin of yours. I will never believe it. I refuse to believe in a God who could wreak such a terrible vengeance. And for what? Because you kissed Jim—"

"Stop, Darren! You must stop. You understand nothing yet. I shall tell you all, and when I am done, you will want nothing more to do with me."

"How can you say that?" A thought welled up inside me. "These ponies. Scotty's band. I've only ever seen them with you at Green Run. They don't normally roam far from there, do they?"

"What?" She gazed at me with those glowing green eyes. Just a few yards away the cars were creeping toward the State Park and the National Seashore. Somebody had a window open, and loud rap music vibrated in the air. I barely heard it. I was in another world with Annie and the ponies, who were milling around acting strangely, at least to my untrained eye.

"You're right," she said after a long pause. "They never go more than a mile or so from the campsite. See Jamie, over there?" She smiled a little. Relief and joy surged through me, at the thought that something was giving her pleasure. "I bet you don't even recognize him, he's grown so much this summer from eating the soft salt-marsh hay below my tombstone. It's his favorite place… it's the whole band's favorite place…"

"So why would they have come here, Annie?" I asked gently. "We're a good twelve or fifteen miles away from their home range! They've had to walk through the territory of God knows how many other bands just to get here. That could mean trouble for Scotty, fights with other stallions who may be younger and stronger than him." I leaned forward. "But he led his band here, and they followed him, because they were all following *you*."

She shook her head, tears still flooding from her closed eyes. I reached out with my right hand and caught a fat drop, bringing it to my lips and tasting the salt. "I will take away your sorrow for you, if I can," I whispered. "If you let me. So tell me, Annie. What terrible sin do you imagine you committed, when you walked the Earth a century and a half ago?"

Annie sat down and hugged her knees to her chest. Her gestures were so intensely human I'd long ago trained myself to shove to the back of my mind the fact that she hadn't been a living person since before my great-great-grandparents were born. But with the eerie glow she gave off now, it was impossible to ignore that fact. Still, I sat down beside her, consciously rejecting the infinite distance that lay between us, even though she was close enough to touch.

"Yes, Darren, you've sensed the heart of the matter," she said, staring in the direction of the idling traffic although I'm sure she didn't really see it. "Even at the beginning, as young as we were, the extreme care Jim and I had to take to conceal what we were doing from everyone else brought a sense of shame to our love. And that was before I became engaged to Will, after which every passing moment added to my burden of sin.

"But for a long while after that snatched first kiss, Jim and I did everything we could to avoid one another. It was easy enough in the first days after my return, when Pa was still away and Betty took upon herself the burden of mothering me. Andy gave me the sound thrashing I deserved, and Betty said I was not to wander off on my own at all, not to ride Sally and not to bathe in the sea, until my father got back and decided what to do with me.

'But that could take months!' I cried. 'So be it,' she said, 'next time you will think twice before you run off into the wilderness and drive us all half mad with worry.' It was in fact early May before Pa returned; when he did he allowed as how I had been punished enough, but he did not reprove Betty as I hoped.

"Meanwhile Jim had taken advantage of my punishment to take Sally out whenever he could escape from the endless round of drudge-work people expected of him. Later in the summer, he told me that he'd found 'some really beautiful places' on those rides. 'There's a clearing a couple miles north on the island with a pond in the middle, a lot like the place where I found you that time,' he said. 'We could take a walk up there sometime...'

"'And do what?' I responded as rudely as I could. 'Play hide-and-seek? We're not babies anymore, Jim.'

"'Of course not, but it just looked like a nice place for a picnic...'

"'I'm too busy!' The gratefulness I'd felt toward him for 'rescuing' me had changed to resentment. I knew it wasn't fair, but when I thought of him I thought of the switching Andy had given me and of the springtime weeks I'd spent with nothing to do but look after the Birch babies and study with the pastor.

"Everything else was going swimmingly that summer. Pa had returned from Washington in triumph, having learned that no fewer than four life-saving stations were to be built along the length of the island—and our little village, the only oceanfront settlement for many miles in either direction, was sure to be the location of one of them. With his naval experience, Will at once sent a letter of application to be its commander. 'I will be involved in any rescue in any event,' he said to Pa with a smile, 'why should I not be paid for it?' Pa laughed and told him not to hold his breath. 'General Grant is a great man and a great president, but not all the people around him are up to his caliber. It may take a while yet for the men in Washington to get themselves organized.'

"'Let us hope it does not take more shipwrecks,' I said, remembering Mabel's poor father with a shudder.

"'It may require exactly that,' Pa said. 'If they don't move fast enough, I'll pay to build a station myself! I don't want Will or Mr. Powers or Mr. Birch or anybody else putting their lives at risk again because they don't have the right boats and tools.'

"'That could get expensive, Captain,' Will said. 'Let me write my father and see what he can do.'

"But nothing happened before the season ended and our summer guests departed. In the still, idle time before the weather turned and we had to start preparing for winter, I took to wandering the back country again, sometimes with Sally and sometimes on foot. I found the glade Jim had described, and it was as beautiful as he had said. I had kicked off my shoes and was sunning myself there one lazy afternoon in early September when I heard a rustling in the underbrush. I thought it was probably a deer and didn't bother opening my eyes until a shadow fell on me.

"Jim wasn't one for practical jokes or sneaking up on people, but he must have thought I was sleeping, because instead of speaking he sat down on a fallen log and simply watched me. I was only pretending to sleep, though, and as he watched me I watched him through slitted eyelids. He was dressed in worn dungarees and a dark blue shirt of good, strong, woven cotton that Violet kept clean and in good repair for him no matter how hard he worked—and he worked very hard. I was wearing a green summer dress, the skirts hiked up high on my thighs for my ramble through the forest—a state of undress that would have been considered scandalous even without any male eyes to see me. You might imagine, Darren, that living as we did in the wilderness I could dress and behave as I pleased, but nothing could have been further from the truth. The island might be vast, but our village was tiny, and everyone knew everything about what everyone else was up to, or so they thought. I wouldn't have embarrassed Pa for the world, and that's what I would have done if I'd dressed in the 'wanton' way I would have preferred, which is to say, as comfortably as a boy might wish to dress in the back country.

"In any case, I was growing tired of my little game of pretend with Jim and was about to open my eyes and tell him I knew he was there, when he turned and drew something out of his pocket. It was a neatly folded rectangle of paper covered on both sides with his careful, slanting handwriting. He stuffed it into one of my shoes, and stole away quietly into the woods. Of course I sat up immediately, unfolded the letter and read it.

"His writing was so different from the way he spoke, even I would have doubted he'd penned the letter if I hadn't seen him leave it himself. But he'd learned from all the books I'd given him to read over the years, so he wrote in the high style of our day." Annie closed her eyes, and I knew from what she'd described of the strange workings of her memory that she was seeing the letter before her inner eye, right down to the wrinkles in the paper and the accidental blots of bluish ink where Jim had pressed too hard.

"My dearest Annie," she began, quoting him, "You have been the kindliest angel to me ever since I arrived at your door, a friendless orphan. Anyone else in your place would have despised an ignorant escaped slave such as me, but you treated me just as you would have a guest born of the same high station in life as you." Annie paused and snickered. "Poor Jim, imagining the Wrights to be gentry!" Then her expression grew wistful and infinitely far away again as she recited the rest of the letter from memory. "In time you treated me as more than just a welcome guest. You became my instructor, and you became my friend. As my teacher, you gave me the same books you were learning from, so that I could learn as quickly and as well as you; and as my friend, you taught me how to be an innocent, playful child, a privilege never granted to a Negro slave. And in the fullness of time, I have grown—" Annie paused and gulped—"I have grown to love you."

Annie and I sat in silence for a while. I asked, "What did you do then?"

She sighed. "I was little more than a child myself. My fourteenth birthday was still a month away! I was scared, more than you can imagine, but thrilled too—but the two emotions were inseparable, a tangle like a thicket of brambles. The prudent thing to do would have been to destroy the letter immediately, to burn it to ashes or dunk it in the sea until all the ink ran. I couldn't bear to do that. Instead I hid it in my blouse, and when Pa was out I secreted it in a gap in the floorboards under my bed where I had been hiding childish treasures like my precious sand dollars. But as for Jim himself, I avoided him like the cholera. Every day, as soon as my lessons with Pastor Scarburgh were over, I ran to Sally's enclosure and rode her hard, as far as she would go, sometimes even as far as the clearing where I'd camped out the time I ran away. I volunteered to help with little Cal and newborn Addie Birch so much that Betty joked she might as well let me be their mother. At the Sunday clambakes I took care to stay as far away from Jim as possible, though I could hardly avoid noticing the haunted, pleading glances he threw me with his dark eyes. Those looks only hardened my resolve to avoid him, for his own good as well as mine.

"He finally cornered me the night of my birthday. Pa had been making a bigger and bigger occasion of it as the years went by, inviting everyone in town to a party in the lobby of the Ocean House and even unlocking the bar, which was closed up that late in the year. I found the attention embarrassing and slipped away into the night. The air was mild, with a gentle offshore breeze, and the stars crowded thick overhead—I stuck to the beach as I walked so that I could look at them without having to worry about turning my ankle on a hidden root or stumbling into a bramble bush. I knew how to pick out the constellations, but it amused me more to imagine my own. 'That's Little Nell,' I'd say aloud, for Dickens remained a favorite of mine, whatever the pastor said; or 'That's Horace, the Horseshoe Crab.'"

"Doesn't sound very imaginative to me," I chuckled, thinking of how common on Assateague are the huge shells of these creatures, which are shaped like an ancient warrior's helmet. Annie pretended to swat me on the arm; I felt that now-familiar tingle, stronger than ever.

"Eventually I tired of walking and turned toward the dunes and the forest behind them," she resumed after a moment. "These woods held no terrors for me, I'd walked them all and in any case they were no more than a couple hundred yards wide from east to west. I soon found myself by the pond where Jim had left me his first love letter. The starlight made everything look unreal, so for a second I thought I was imagining that he was sitting there, on the same fallen log as before, with his head in his arms. But he looked up at the sound of my footsteps. His eyes shone as he spoke my name. 'I have offended you. I am sorry.'

"'How could you be so stupid?' I blurted. Coming upon him so suddenly gave me no chance to think over what I should say to him, so I spoke from the heart. 'The trouble you could get in... You know Mr. Powers hates Negroes, he would love an excuse to get you and Violet off the island, or hurt you!'

"Jim puffed out his chest. 'A lynch mob, in Green Run? The Captain and Will would never allow it!'

"'You still put yourself in danger, Jim. Why did you do that?'

"He stared at me. 'Why? I said why in my letter. It ain't honorable not to confess such a love!'

"I shut my eyes and the salt-laden breeze caressed my eyelids. The balmy night, the fragrant forest, my earnest, sweet friend with his idea of love molded by books and the reality of his love shaped by the small kindnesses I had shown him, after such a brutal childhood... it was dizzying. My throat spasmed as I thought of the disaster in which this must end. Shakespeare, too, was part of my education with the pastor, though he used Thomas Bowdler's tame edition. Naturally the reverend thought Romeo and Juliet too racy to be suitable reading for a young girl, even with Mr. Bowdler's editing, but of course that had made the play all the more interesting to me. The resemblance to the predicament I found myself in was too obvious to ignore. But unlike the lovers of Verona, there was nowhere we could run, even had we the means, where our relations would not be considered unnatural in the extreme. All this and more passed through my mind in an instant... before he put his arms around me and pressed his lips to mine."

Annie bit her lip and stared at the highway, now deserted and shimmering with noonday heat. "All I had to do was push him away, as gently as I could, so as not to hurt his feelings. But I didn't. I returned his kiss, and that, Darren, was the first of the sins for which I am forever punished. Because I knew what must happen to us, and I paid no heed."

24

My right leg throbbed with pain as I labored over the bridge. There was sweet relief on the downslope onto the mainland, but soon enough I'd have to start pedaling again, and I didn't know if I could make it. So I turned into the Island Market parking lot, staggered up the steps and slumped over the counter by the cash register.

"That you, Darren hon? What's the matter? Here, sit down," Jodie said, dragging her own padded stool out from the other side of the counter. She brought me a bottled lemonade and wouldn't let me pay. Over my protests, she rolled up my pant leg and had a look at my bad leg, whistling respectfully at the scar. "You shouldn't be riding a bike around on a leg like that, you know? You're sure temptin' fate, after what you've been through!"

"You're not the only one saying so," I said, cold sweat joining heat sweat on my face.

"What-for you out riding to the island, anyhow? I know that stinker Cropper gave your job away," she said.

Over the summer I'd gotten used to the way everyone knew everything about everyone else in this part of the shore. I sighed and said I had gone to meet my girlfriend.

"How come she couldn't come to you? Never mind,

ain't my business. But I ain't letting you go back out there to ride home in this heat. That *is* my business, 'cause if you die on the road people are gonna say it was something you ate here."

That made me laugh, but it ended in choking and sputtering. Jodie put her hands on her hips and shook her head in a motherly sort of way. "Now, why don't you go in back and rest, I'm gonna have the supper rush to deal with pretty soon, and when you're feeling better we can talk." I was hardly in a position to refuse. She fixed me up with a few old padded chairs that had the stuffing leaking out of them, but might as well have been a grand hotel suite, and she even brought my bike inside. I was asleep before she was done wheeling it in.

I woke to Jodie gently shaking my shoulder. She told me she was closing up and offered me a ride home in her old 4X4, "we can throw the bike in back." I didn't even bother pretending to protest at the offer. It was less than a ten-minute drive back to my trailer, but by the time we got there I already had a new job, "just till Labor Day, you understand, I'll have to talk to Bill and see if we can afford to keep you on after that. We're only open weekends after the middle of the month, and we close for the winter in late October." It was only mid-August. She was giving me the gift of at least three more weeks with Annie!

But it still left me with the problem that I couldn't get to Assateague under my own power. Jodie said she could pick me up every morning. It was too far to walk from the store to the island, so I devised my own rehabilitation program, getting up early in the mornings and biking a little further each day to get my strength back. After work, I was too tired and my injured leg hurt too much.

Jodie let me sit on the stool and work the register most of the day, waving off my offers to help her and Bill unload the milk and soft-drink pallets. "You're doin' just fine there, hon," she'd say with a smile. Bill was a soft-spoken, heavyset man with blonde hair running to gray and an alarmingly red face even when he was at rest. But when I said maybe he should let me help him with some of the heavier items, he told me gruffly to mind my own business.

I was dying to have a real talk with Bill, who was a direct descendant of Annie's husband, but I held back out of shyness. Most of what I would have wanted to ask him came out in Jodie's chatter anyway—I was beginning to suspect she'd really hired me for the company more than the help, though she claimed she'd been overwhelmed before. Bill was busy most of the day with their "chicken house," a long, low structure that stank to high heaven and yielded, so Jodie said, barely enough income to make it worth keeping up.

"He loves them birds, though. Don't ask me why. I always say, if he's so fond of 'em, he should advertise the meat and eggs as free-range organic for all them tree-huggers, but he says it's too much darn trouble gettin' the right certificates."

"Were all his family chicken farmers?"

"His daddy and grandpa were. You'll have to ask him 'bout anyone further back. They been livin' on that farm of ours west of Berlin more than a hunnert years, I believe." Will's father would have been very unhappy at his descendants' falling so low in the world, even if Bill did own his own business—two businesses in fact, the store and the chicken farm. I scraped up the courage to ask Jodie if I could come out and see their place, but she mumbled something about it not being fit for company.

Meanwhile Kevin had some bad news when he stopped in for a Coke late one afternoon after dropping Lakeisha off: Hattie had passed away. "I'm sorry, I never did get to ask her your question about the rebuilding of Wright's Ocean House."

"Never mind," I said.

He eyed me curiously. "Listen, Darren, if Green Run is so important to you, why don't we take a ride out there

Sunday afternoon, you and me and Lakeisha? If you can spare him, that is," he added to Jodie, who smiled and said Bill could help her out then, all he did otherwise on Sundays was nap.

"But to get to Green Run, you need an all-wheel drive car to go over the sand," I said. My heart was pounding so loudly I could barely hear my own voice.

"I've got a 4X4 I bought at an auction last year. We'll make a picnic of it, the four of us." He chuckled at my blank look. "Won't Annie want to come too?"

"She's, uh, she'll be away visiting family this weekend." I hoped he bought the excuse.

I worried all week about what would happen, though at the same time I couldn't wait because I was missing Annie terribly and was beginning to be afraid she might just fade away in my absence. Between these obsessive thoughts and the pain in my leg I barely got any sleep. I'd started working the grill as well as the register, but when Jodie saw me starting to nod off over the hot surface she said I could go back to just ringing people up. The hospital had given me prescription painkillers and I took to watching the clock, willing the hands to move so I could take another pill, though they made me drowsy and worsened my recurring nightmares. In the worst of these I watched helplessly from atop a dune as Annie turned her back on me and walked slowly away down the beach, the glare of the hard summer sky shining ever more strongly through her until till she dissolved in a sea mist. There was no reassurance to be had when I woke alone in the dark in my trailer, with nothing but the air conditioner rattling away to keep me company—I had given up on trying to save electricity, after my accidents. I couldn't go for a walk in the quiet of the small hours thanks to the pain in my leg, but sometimes I dragged a white plastic chair out to the front step and sat looking at the stars through the branches of the oak tree, and I'd brood about how useless all the science I was studying was to the situation I found myself in. Reason itself was failing me. Long afterwards I read something the seventeenth century French mathematician and religious philosopher Blaise Pascal had written: "The last proceeding of reason is to recognize that there is an infinity of things which are beyond it. It is but feeble if it does not see so far as to know this. But if natural things are beyond it, what will be said of supernatural?"

The days passed in their lumbering, humidity-drugged way, and Sunday morning found me more alert than I'd been all week—the prospect of seeing Annie must have helped me sleep better than I had since the accident. Jodie said I looked "chipper" and I assured her that I was better.

I forgot all my troubles when Kevin came to get me. "Is that really you?" I demanded.

He scowled and clutched the lapels of his sober, dark sport jacket as Jodie pointed at him and laughed. "Lakeisha made me get dressed up for church," he said. His trousers were pressed and his shoes were black and shiny.

"Honey, you ain't gonna wear all that out to the beach, are you?" Jodie chuckled.

"Not if I can change in your storeroom." But when he came out, all he'd done was take off the jacket, roll up his sleeves and exchange the socks and shoes for foam clogs almost as beat-up as mine. Jodie shook her head as I rang up two 2-liter bottles of Coke for him.

"You sure you'll be all right on your own here, Jodie?" I asked.

She waved me off. "Go enjoy yourself. You've earned it."

Lakeisha was behind the wheel when Kevin and I walked out to the car. She chuckled affectionately at the sight of us, but of course she looked like a million bucks in the one-piece yellow bathing suit she must have had on under the lavender churchgoing suit hanging up in the back seat. The day was hot and still, and in the back seat, even with the air conditioning cranked all the way up, I was soon sweating and trying to resist the urge to scratch the scar on my leg.

While Kevin was bleeding the tires for the drive over the sand, Lakeisha said, "We heard from your parents that you're taking a semester off."

"That's right." When she shook her head I hastily added, "But it's only one semester. I'm going to transfer to Salisbury or UMES after that. I already filled in applications online." I'd had to drag myself over to the library in Berlin to do it, but I'd gotten it done. "It's better for me to study down here on the shore, where I can really do my field work," I added, keeping my alibi intact.

"You must be really sweet on this girl, Annie," Kevin said easily, closing the car door behind him. So much for the alibi.

It's not an interrogation, it's not a test, I said to myself. *This is just the way people talk to each other.* "Yeah, she's great," I said cautiously.

"So, what's she look like?" Lakeisha asked. "I mean, tall, short, blonde, black hair, what?"

"She's about my height, long brown hair, amazing green eyes..." Lakeisha elbowed Kevin and nodded meaningfully.

"Singing my praises, Darren?" a voice said through the car window.

I bumped my head on the ceiling. Lakeisha slowed to a stop and she and Kevin turned to stare at me. Annie was grinning through the window as I rubbed my head.

"Don't," I started to say to Annie, then stopped myself. "I'm fine. Just bumped my head, is all."

"I'm sorry, Darren," Annie said, but she didn't sound very sorry. "I hope I didn't embarrass you too much." I grunted, and Kevin asked again if I was sure I was all right.

"I think we're in the right place, anyhow," Lakeisha said, pointing.

I nodded, grateful for the change of subject. "Yes, there's the sign for the campsite. The foundations of the hotel are just a hundred yards or so further on, in a grassy clearing near the marsh."

"It's good to have such a knowledgeable guide," Kevin said, unbuckling his seatbelt and opening the door. "Are you sure you'll be okay walking all that way, with all those brambles underfoot?"

"I've been here so many times, I know the way around the worst thickets," I assured him.

"So these are your friends. You're lucky to know such nice people," Annie said, smiling as she watched Kevin unload the picnic things, his back to her. Lakeisha got out and took my arm to help me down. Then Kevin turned around, holding a cooler and a duffel bag, and Annie's eyes widened. She let out a gasp.

"Annie," I said and stopped.

Lakeisha raised an eyebrow. "What about her?"

Dammit. "Nothing," I said. I moved my lips silently, asking her what was the matter.

"It's him," she whispered. "It's him, to the life!" *She must mean Jim,* I thought. She started walking alongside Kevin as he plodded along with his burdens. She reached out and stroked his face, but he kept going obliviously. A tiny pain pierced my heart. "He's a little taller, his eyes are a little farther apart," she murmured, "his nose is a little broader, too, and of course he's a few years older but... I'd know him anywhere."

"Darren," Lakeisha said. She had stopped walking, and since she was still holding my right arm, I was forced to stop. "Darren, what's the matter?" Kevin, who was about a dozen paces ahead of us, stopped at the edge of the forest and turned around, frowning. Annie danced around, staying face to face with him. From where I was standing, or rather leaning against Lakeisha, I could only see the top of Kevin's head over Annie's head.

I shut my eyes against the unreality of the scene and forced myself to say, "Nothing. Just a bit of a headache."

"Maybe this wasn't such a good idea," Lakeisha said, grasping my wrist as if to take my pulse.

"No, really, I'm fine. Just let me rest here for a minute. You go ahead and help Kevin set everything up."

After I'd talked Lakeisha into leaving me behind, I turned to Annie and said, "What's this about? Kevin isn't even Jim's direct descendent, he's his great-great-grand-nephew or something."

"I know, Darren," she said. "But the resemblance isn't only physical. For want of a better word, it's spiritual."

"What does that mean?"

"I can't explain it. It's like an extra sense I have. How would you explain vision to someone who is born blind? Words are so inexact... Kevin is kind, as you are kind, as Jim was kind; but sad and wounded within, as Jim was from slavery. Oh, Darren, please don't be jealous!"

"I'm not jealous!"

Annie bit her lip. "I'm really sorry, Darren."

I shut my eyes against the bright sunlight. "No, I understand. You and Jim were girlfriend and boyfriend for a long time, weren't you?"

"We didn't use those words in my time. If you mean, were we lovers, no, we never went beyond passionate kissing and such." I opened my eyes again, but she was avoiding my gaze. "The wonder is that we managed to keep it a secret until my death. A secret from Pa, and Will, and everyone in the village, that is. Not from the Almighty."

"Annie, I won't believe that a wrathful God condemns you for adultery. You weren't married or even engaged to Will when you were 'passionately kissing' poor Jim. And you cannot believe the slaveholders' filthy lies, that God ordained the separation of the races!"

"No, of course not. And I was faithful in the flesh to Will, after we married. But not in the spirit, and what is God, and what is my wretched condition, but a matter of the spirit? I am punished for who I was, and for what I did, the deeds of the heart as much as the deeds of the body."

How I wished I could hold her hand! But all I had were words. "It is impossible that your punishment is to live alone forever, because I am here now, and I love you!"

She shook her head, her eyes downcast. "Perhaps I am shown a glimpse of what love is like only so that it can be snatched away again. Perhaps you are also to be condemned for a sin, the sin of loving a dead sinner in eternal torment! Those 'accidents' that keep happening to you must be warnings, to which I add my own for the last time—leave me, Darren, before you share my fate!" For an answer I reached out my hand, caught a crystal teardrop as it fell toward the ground, brought it to my mouth and swallowed it.

Just then Lakeisha appeared from behind a dune. "Feeling any better, Darren?"

"Much," I said, forcing a smile as I stood up and dusted sand off my pants. "Let's go have that picnic."

Annie followed us down a narrow, twisting trail of sand that led down to the site where Wright's Ocean House once stood. It looked different in the daylight than it had on the moonlit night when I'd last been there with Annie—smaller and less mysterious. The bricks were half-hidden in weeds. It was hard to imagine the whole little world Annie had described to me.

As I stood leaning on a stick, Lakeisha took the duffel bag from Kevin, took out some blankets and spread them on a bare patch of sand shaded by the spreading branches of a red maple. I sat down on it gratefully as she and Kevin offered me food, but it was water I craved the most, and I downed a two-liter bottle without stopping for breath. Kevin and Lakeisha also sat and drank water while Annie watched, I thought, with a touch of envy.

"This doesn't look like a good spot for a hotel," Lakeisha said, glancing at the salt marsh. The mosquitoes were out in force, and we quickly sprayed ourselves with a bottle she passed around.

"It didn't look like this in my time," Annie said,

sweeping her arm out over the marsh. "This was all open water then. When the inlet silted over, reeds started growing here, and gradually it all filled in." I relayed her remark to Kevin and Lakeisha as a hypothetical ("maybe the marsh wasn't here when the hotel was built...")

Kevin nodded. "These barrier islands change a lot over time, but they look permanent, as if they've always been like this," he said. "That's what Paul and the other rangers tell me, anyhow. In a place like Ocean City, of course, no one wants the landscape moving around, so the bulldozers dump tons of sand after every hurricane, and the beach is 'restored' for the tourists, until the next storm hits."

While Lakeisha broke out the tuna and egg salad sandwiches, peaches and plums, I hobbled around, exploring. On closer examination the horseshoe arrangement of the foundations was easy enough to make out, and I made my way to the end of the left arm, where Annie had once lived with her father. I saw nothing unusual there, until I stooped over to peer at the gaps between the bricks—the mortar that had once held them together had mostly eroded away. But there was something white stuck in one of the gaps—the pure, bleached, bone-white color seashells fade to after being left out in the sun for too long. I carefully dislodged it and saw that it was not a single object, but two uneven halves of what had once been a round, flat thing a couple of inches across. I brought the broken edges together and stretched my hand out wordlessly to Annie so she could see the reassembled sand dollar. Later I glued it carefully together and put it on my night stand, beside my radio. It is on my night stand still, after all these years.

"Huh. Wonder what that's doing here," Kevin said, giving me a start as he looked at the broken sand dollar in my outstretched hand. "You usually only see those on the beach. Well, ready to eat?" I nodded and accompanied him back over to the picnic blankets. We were all quiet for a while as we ate. The wind sighed through the maple tree branches and the water lapped in a nearby gut. When a blackbird cawed we all jumped a little, then smiled. Annie stood atop a low heap of bricks that might once have been a fireplace and stared out over the marsh, her arms folded. I wished I could give her a hug.

"So Darren, why are you so interested in this place?" Kevin asked, dabbing his mouth with a napkin.

I shrugged. "Why is anyone interested in a ghost town? People once lived here and now they're gone."

"Yeah, but there's not even anything to see but these old bricks," he said, absent-mindedly kicking one. It broke in half when his foot touched it.

Annie turned, her eyes flashing. "Tell him to leave it alone, Darren!"

"Please don't do that!" I said. Kevin looked at me. "I mean, the Park Service probably has rules against disturbing the site."

"Well, you're probably right," he said, picking up the broken halves of the brick and setting them back where he had found them. Then he looked at them and did a double take. "It looks a bit singed around the edges, this brick."

"Really?" Lakeisha and I crowded in for a look. Even Annie peered over. Kevin was right: the faded orange of the brick was stained ash-gray along one side.

He stood up, then bent over and started carefully examining a line of bricks that might once have marked an outer wall. "If you look over here, you can see these bricks look different from the ones over there," he said, pointing. "Those reddish ones don't seem to have gone through a fire like the orangey ones did. Guess whoever rebuilt the hotel took the opportunity to enlarge it."

Annie was nodding. "I heard Will say that there were so many summer guests it was a pity Pa had not thought to expand the place before he died. But I know he would have, had he lived... he would have done it for me... and without me, any joy Will had in the rebuilt hotel's success must have been ashes in his mouth."

"Must have been?" What a strange way of putting it, I thought. *Maybe Will wasn't quite the plaster saint Annie's been making him out to be.* I wished I could ask her about it, but I had no more chances to talk to her alone for the rest of the picnic. She was still standing there, a lonely, faintly translucent silhouette against the blindingly bright afternoon sky, when Kevin and Lakeisha and I packed up and walked back to our air-conditioned lives.

25

I had reached a turning point: From the day of the picnic on I found I had the strength to bike from the trailer to Island Market, and from there over the bridge onto Assateague once my working day was over. Annie waited for me faithfully every day, whatever the weather—of course, rain was no concern of hers, and I shrugged it off as I learned to shrug off the ache in my leg. We were so close to solving the mysteries of Annie's life and afterlife, I was determined not to slow our progress, even if I ended up with a permanent limp (which in fact happened). The answer was going to wash away her sense of guilt for good, I just knew it.

"Perhaps I never really loved him," Annie said, gazing out over the bay, where a pair of waterskiers made a jarring backdrop for our conversation.

"Who? Will? Surely that doesn't matter now, Annie, so long after your death, and his." How easily I had come to accept the fact that she wasn't really alive, that death was a part of who she was, perhaps because the strong glow she gave off here, so far from her usual haunting grounds, was impossible to ignore. Death was a familiar thing to me now, or so I imagined; I was half in love with the ease of it.

She shook her head. "I don't mean Will. I'm speaking of Jim."

I recoiled. "What? I saw your fascination with Kevin when you thought he looked like Jim... the way you followed him around, the way you studied his face."

She sighed. "Sometimes I forget how young you really are, Darren. I died before I had a chance to mature, but all the time I've spent alone has given me a certain pale imitation of wisdom. Of course I was fascinated to see a living person who so much resembles someone I knew in life. My reaction might not have been very different if I'd seen a double of my father... Jim was always the pursuer, and I was always the pursued. Perhaps it is always like that in love. I don't know. All I do know is that I was a vain and silly girl, and flattered to be the object of such devotion."

"Always you insist on thinking the worst of yourself."

"He left me love letters when it was impossible for us to meet, which was often the case. As I said, you might think that Assateague in its wild state offered limitless freedom, but our world was restricted to the village and its immediate surroundings. In winter and other times of bad weather, especially, it was impossible for us to slip away. He tried his hand at poetry, even, but there I think was one of the few realms where he lacked talent—

Where you walk, the woods are touched with song
When you are near, I can do no wrong
From the world our love must be secret
But for owl, and deer, and snowy egret.'"

She smiled, a smile that quickly faded. "I saved them all, all his letters and notes and bad poetry, and hid them all in that same gap under the boards in my room, until it was full and I had to find another gap, doubling my risk of discovery."

"Did you write him back?"

"Of course, but usually only with short notes agreeing

to meet and suggesting a time and place. There was a certain hollow in a sassafras tree, well above the tallest villager's reach—you had to climb to it. This was our telegraph station. But as far as everyone else could see, we were growing out of our childish friendship. We stopped walking the beach together where others could see us, and we never went sledding in the winter again. It was a frustrating paradox, but the more our secret romance bloomed, the less we saw of each other.

"One unpleasant result of the seeming end of my friendship with Jim was that Pastor Scarburgh noticed and was delighted. At the end of my lessons one day he said, 'I am glad to see my teachings have had an effect, and you are becoming a proper young lady.' But then he... he... Oh, Darren, this is so embarrassing, even a century and a half later! ... he said, 'I wish the privilege of continuing your education all your life.'

"I hoped against hope that I was wrong about what was coming next. 'But how will you do that, pastor?' I asked, feigning innocence. 'Surely a great religious leader like you will have important pulpits waiting for him, while I will remain a poor innkeeper's daughter.' No, don't laugh, Darren... please don't laugh, you're making me laugh too! Anyway, I don't think I sounded quite so sarcastic when I said it... But if I did, he was quite oblivious to it. He went down on one knee and proposed, 'so that you might have the benefit of my moral instruction as your husband.' Well, I saw at once that an ironical response would go quite unheard by this dunderhead, so I told him bluntly that I did not wish to receive moral instruction of any kind from a man who had dishonored the daughters of half of Salisbury's Baptists! I was only repeating what Betty had whispered to me—perhaps with a little exaggeration for effect—but he grew purple in the face and I thought he was going to strike me. I darted out of the way as he hurled such curses at me as would have made the old salt Mike Powers shrivel up and die! Naturally, I ran straight to Pa and swore to him that I would tolerate no more teaching from Pastor Scarburgh, and if he forced me to take any more lessons from him I would swim back to the mainland and run away! I give Pa his due, he did not embarrass me by asking me what had happened, though he did say mildly I would have to continue accompanying him to the church services the pastor conducted in the Birches' cabin, 'to keep tongues from wagging.' Though they must have wagged all the harder, thanks to all the hellfire sermons the good reverend preached about scarlet women, while looking straight at me! The joke, of course, is that he was right about my terrible fate.

"Through all this melodrama, I kept letting Jim put himself in terrible danger by continuing to see him in secret. If we had been discovered, there would have been a huge scandal for Pa and me. I expect he'd have had to sell the hotel and take me back to Baltimore. But as for Jim…" She let the prospect of his lynching remain unspoken. "That is why I say I didn't really love him, Darren: if I had, I would never have let him endanger his life for the sake of an occasional stolen kiss in a secluded clearing."

I shook my head. "Most people in my time wouldn't agree, Annie. If you and Jim snatched forbidden fruit for yourselves, that only means you showed courage in love— both of you!"

"You're wrong, Darren. There was nothing to admire in my behavior. Perhaps I was only able to fully appreciate how selfish I was in life after I died and became this *thing* I am now, this *thing* that can choose nothing, do nothing and affect nobody."

"But you know that isn't true." I stood up and encircled the place where her shoulders seemed to be with my arms. I didn't care at all how odd the gesture must have looked to the cars flowing landward over the sunset bridge. "I choose to love you for who you are. You have chosen to love me, even though it's impossible. No *thing* could do that."

"What you say doesn't make sense, Darren." But she was smiling and ducking her head like, well, like a nineteenth-century lady. I offered her my arm, she pretended to take it, and we strolled into the woods. Her hair, I suddenly noticed, looked completely dry for the first time since I had met her. It was long, straight, and light brown, and I longed to run my hands through it. Her brown dress—she had told me it was a "calico traveling dress"—looked dry, even freshly pressed, without fading or tears anywhere. How could that be? Until now the dress had looked muddy and torn. Like her hair, it seemed to have changed, "improved" somehow, in the time I had known her.

Instead of smiling and thanking me when I complimented her appearance, she grew thoughtful. "It is your doing," she said quietly. "I think you have become more aware of me—not just the romantic idea of me, a tragic ghost girl who died too young, but of who I actually am. Or was."

She stopped walking, stood facing me and lifted her arms. The sleeves of her dress rode up, as naturally as they would on anyone else. Her skin was pale white. "It was winter when I passed," she said quietly, watching me notice her skin. Then she lifted her arms a little higher, and rested her hands on my shoulders. That is, not her hands themselves, which had no material existence, but the strange tingling force field that surrounded her. I shut my eyes and imagined that I was really feeling her touch. It wasn't such a stretch.

"Jim loved me, Darren," Annie said. Her voice seemed to come from next to my right ear, and I shivered, imagining the electric tingle in the tiny hairs there was her breath moving them as the wind moved the treetops. "He loved me, but his love was a boy's love. We never had a chance to learn if it could have become the love of a man for a woman. And besides, as I said, I don't know if what I felt for him was really love. Yes, Darren, I will give myself my due, I will admit that I did *believe* I was in love; but that is not the same thing, and if you do not understand the difference I will only say again that you are very young. A very young man." She sighed, and this time I am sure a minuscule air current tickled my ear. Could her will, the will of a bodiless spirit, really move the world of matter? Or was it my own spirit, and that alone, that responded to her? I will never know.

I opened my eyes and looked into hers. "Yes, Darren, I am saying that your love is a man's love," she said. "You are wrong that being 'just a student' means you are still a boy. The difference is real, though words fail to explain it. I have existed for such a long time, though not in life, and have observed much of men's lives from my unique vantage point. There are some who pile up a great number of years, and never reach maturity, and some who achieve it while they are still very young."

She took a step back, taking her hands off my shoulders, and cast her eyes down at the sandy ground. "There was a man once who truly loved me, though I could not return his love. Perhaps I had not matured enough; perhaps, if I had had enough time, I would have. But my sins caught up with me first."

"Will," I said. It was not a question.

She nodded. "I must have known he had always loved me. Still I was surprised when he asked for my hand, on my seventeenth birthday! I longed to ask him to wait, perhaps for a year, but he had got down on his knee in the middle of my birthday party, in front of Pa and the Birches and Mr. Powers and everybody, right there in the hotel lobby—and I couldn't embarrass him by saying no. At least Jim wasn't there—he and Violet had stopped coming to village gatherings, knowing they were unwelcome."

I asked a stupid question. "If you didn't want to marry Will, why didn't you just refuse him? Your father would have supported you."

Annie gazed at me a long time. "Darren, have you not understood me at all?" she said softly. "There was no question of my not marrying him! I had loved him since the night he saved Mama and me from a fiery death at the hands of the mob. He was the support of our family, as much as Pa. He was my hero, my model in all things. When I reproached myself for not studying hard enough, for shirking my duties in the hotel, it was always to him my thoughts turned—to Will, the ever-faithful soldier. If anything, I suspected that he had not asked for my hand already because I was too far beneath him. I had already disappointed him so many times. I have told you how I burned with jealousy every time he journeyed to his parents' home, dreading as I did that one of the refined and beautiful ladies of Baltimore society would turn his head.

"Now that he had declared his intentions openly—and obviously, only after getting Pa's blessing first—I felt more certain than ever that I was unworthy of him. Whatever it was I was up to in the woods with Jim—and I dared not reflect too deeply on my own shameful conduct—I knew I had to break it off before I could presume to stand at Will's side as his fiancé. But in my selfish childishness, I was enjoying myself too much, though I told myself that it was Jim's heart I wanted to spare. But how could I possibly give him the news without breaking his heart?"

26

"You can't sacrifice your future for me, Darren," Annie said the next time I saw her. Jamie was cropping grass at her feet and she reached up and patted him on the nose. He spread his nostrils as if he could feel her.

"It's not a sacrifice. All I want is to be with you."

"But that's not enough," she said softly.

"Yes it is! It's all I need!"

"No, it isn't, Darren. You have to have a life besides coming out here and talking to the empty air. And we have a problem," she looked away, "a problem of the body. The fact that I don't have one, and you are a young man..."

"I don't care about that!" I shouted, jumping to my feet. Traffic was backed up leaving the island, and I saw a man with his elbow sticking out the window of his car look at me curiously. I sat back down and spoke quietly. "I don't care about that, Annie. I never had a girlfriend anyway, so it's not like I'm missing something I had before."

"But you will, Darren. All the boys and men I knew in life had strong desires. The lengths Jim would go to, to be alone with me the summer before Will proposed to me... He waited eagerly for thunderstorms, for nobody went out in such weather. At such times, we would make up excuses so we could be alone together almost within sight of the village! That we might be struck by lightning didn't much concern him, or me, for that matter."

"Did he find out right away that Will had proposed to you?"

"Of course." She looked down as if fascinated by Jamie's hooves. "I found a curt note from him: 'Meet me in the reed marsh.' He meant a spot about half a mile south of the village where a forest of reeds grew eight feet tall, with soft brownish tops as thick as young tree trunks. As I entered I felt as if my blood was draining away with every step I took, though the mosquitos were already dying down for the season.

"'Will has asked for your hand. You must accept,' Jim said abruptly, when I had pushed my way through the reeds and found him standing there with his shoulders drooping, but a stubborn gleam in his eye. As always he was wearing his blue cotton shirt and a weathered pair of dungarees. I took his hand in mine and massaged the pads of his fingers, which were as callused from work as those of a man three times his age. I thought of his skill with languages, of the poems he wrote me that displayed a vocabulary the late Mr. Lincoln might have envied. If not for the accident of his skin color he might have been a brilliant young scholar at Harvard or Princeton.

"I pulled away from him. 'So you are like all the others, telling me of my duty! Well, I have already given him my hand, damn you!' I cried with a violent gesture. I cut myself on the sharp reeds, but it didn't even hurt.

"He seemed unruffled. 'I always knew this day would come—hoped it would come, for your sake. Will reveres your father, and he loves you. His situation—'

"'God damn his situation!' I enjoyed making Jim flinch with such language. 'I am too young to marry!'

"'But you ain't—you aren't, Annie. If Will warn't a good man, I would tell you to run. But he is—he is the best of men. Sober, hard-working, loyal—'

"'Then let him marry someone better than me!'

"'There is no one better than you, Annie.' You see, Darren, he had so much in common with you. He had a large heart, a quick mind, and he was utterly devoted to me. He took my bleeding hand, blotted away the blood with his shirt tail, and looked me in the eye. 'You will be very happy with Will, Annie. You will not have to hide in a swamp, with dishonor at your heels.'

"I was very unfair to him at that moment. *If I am already dishonored,* I thought, *why not go further and break my word to Will?* 'You said you loved me, Jim, in all those letters and poems. Didn't you mean it?' He was silent, so I pressed what I thought was my advantage. 'The weather will still be fair for weeks yet, Jim. We could run away to the woods far down the island, and live by fishing and crabbing and clamming, as I did that time you found me. We could take a boat and make for one of the islands south of here in Virginia, places even more remote than Assateague. They'd never find us!'

"Jim squeezed his eyes shut for a moment, but then he looked me in the eye, shaking his head. 'It is a daydream, Annie. Could you really leave your father behind? I know I could not bear to lose Violet again.'

"But I was determined to be just as stubborn as him, and so I flung my arms around him, with floods of tears that a man far more mature than he was might have found it impossible to withstand. And poor Jim was hardly more than a boy. He, he told me he would think on my plan."

I was silent for a time. The landward traffic had thinned out with the end of the sunset. It was quiet except for the gentle lapping of the wavelets on the bay and the calls of the seagulls. Overhead, the stars were beginning to come out. A shooting star, perhaps a straggler from the Perseids earlier in the month, blazed white above us and was gone. "You must have really loved Jim," I said finally, "to have fought so hard for him."

Annie's face and eyes were brighter than the starlight, brighter than a full moon would have been. "Why won't you believe me, Darren? I had no understanding of love. I was only reluctant to give up one toy for another. Real love was what Jim had for me, and if I'd been as strong as he was, I would never have put him in danger in the first place by seeing him in secret, let alone by carrying on the affair for so long. He was right, too, that my idea of running away to a distant island was a child's fantasy. As selfish as I was, I could never have hurt Pa like that."

"Then why did you marry Will in the end? Were you in danger of being found out?"

Annie's gaze had grown distant again. "News from home came for Will... terrible news. There was a bank panic... do you know what those were?"

"We still have them," I said drily.

"Yes. Well, this one was something to do with railroads. I never did understand all the details. But Will's father's bank, the First Bank of Maryland, was heavily invested in one of the transcontinentals. Shortly after my birthday, Will began to get increasingly worrying letters from home. The mail reached us by boat from Spence Landing along with the rest of our supplies. Normally, it took more than a week to get a letter from Baltimore, but it was a telegram Mr. Powers handed Will as soon as he stepped down from the *Margaret Deirdre* that bright morning in early October. Will's hand began to tremble as he read it, and the paper made a snapping sound like a flag in the wind.

"'Captain, I,' he stammered, stopped, and swallowed. Pa, Mr. Powers, and I stared at him.

'What is it, Will?' Pa asked gently.

'I shall have to pack my things and return to Baltimore at once. Please be so kind as to ready the boat to sail back to Spence Landing,' Will said.

'But you are already booked for passage on the *Hesperus* to Norfolk on Friday—' Pa began.

"'I cannot wait!' I was stunned that he had interrupted Pa, a thing I had never seen him do. Without even waiting for a response, he turned and ran up the hill to the hotel.

'Even in battle, I never saw him like this,' Pa murmured. 'Especially in battle! What could be the matter?'

"That's when I noticed that he had dropped the telegram in his flight. It lay half crumpled in the gap between the edge of the dock and the grassy bank behind it. Pa saw it at the same time I did. 'No, Annie, we haven't the right,' he began, but I wasn't listening to him. I had smoothed out the paper and was reading the scrawl of the telegraph clerk. It was addressed to Will, all right, from a Sergeant Thomas Wilkins of the Baltimore Police. With many misspellings it said: 'Your help kindly requested in settling affairs of Mr. and Mrs. Jeremiah Pearson, dead of gunshot wounds Thursday last. Note in his hand says he was in despair due to his bank's failure.' I handed the accursed thing to Pa without a word and followed Will up the hill.

"Until that day I had never been in his private rooms. They were spotlessly neat, or rather they looked as if they were usually that way, although now shirts, pants, and other clothes were scattered over the sharply creased blanket as he hauled a wooden trunk out of a corner. He was talking to himself, too low for me to make out the words. His hair and eyes were wild. I said his name twice and he did not react. It was as if I was a ghost, ha! On the third try he looked at me.

"'Will, I am sorry,' I said. He stared at me blankly. So I decided to be clear. 'We shall have Pastor Scarburgh marry us at once,' I said, 'so that I may accompany you back to Baltimore, to settle your parents' affairs.' He dropped the clothes he was holding into the trunk and sat very slowly on the bed. 'I have not,' he said faintly, cleared his throat and began again. 'I did not, that is, I would not hold you to blame if you broke your promise to me now. The man I was, when I asked for your hand three weeks ago, I am no longer.'

"I thought of what Jim had said to me then. 'Do you mean your *situation*? Because I don't care about that.'

"'My *situation*, yes, of course. I was the son of a prosperous banker. Now I am the son of a bankrupt, and a suicide.' He choked out the last word. I sat down beside him and held his hands, which were cold and clammy.

'You are the man of your deeds, not of your father's wealth, Will,' I said. 'You are the man who saved a helpless woman and child from a mob, when you were as young as I am now. You are the man who saved my father's life in the war, and the man who has saved strangers from sinking ships in terrible storms.'

"He stared at our intertwined hands, then into my eyes. 'I would not have you marry me on account of my being a hero,' he said, 'because I am not one. Still less to take my hand now out of *pity…*'

"'I take your hand now because I choose to,' I assured him. Who was playing at being a hero now? Of course we embraced. We were married before we left Green Run that afternoon. But I slipped away right after the impromptu ceremony out on the docks, pleading that there was something I had forgotten in my room. Instead I ran to the sassafras 'telegraph' and slipped a folded piece of paper into the familiar hole, with a scrawl I hoped Jim would be able to read: 'I will always love you. Please forgive me for doing your bidding.'"

Night had fallen in earnest when Annie stopped speaking. The tide was coming in, and the bay water lapped at our toes—or at least, at my toes. The stars were thick in the clear night sky and gave the illusion of nearness. I played idly with a piece of driftwood, drawing slow circles in the damp sand. Annie was a beacon almost bright enough to read by. "Is it still there?" I asked.

"Is what still there, Darren?"

"The sassafras tree where you and Jim left messages for

each other."

"It fell in a storm long ago. Nothing abides, Darren."
We were quiet for a long time after that.

27

"You are so quiet today, Darren."

I was quiet every day, compared to Jodie. Of course I didn't say that. I didn't really mind her chatter. It was good to listen with at least part of my mind to things happening now, on the light surface of the present, instead of brooding all the time over the dark entanglements of a past that could never be changed. I went on brooding anyway, of course. Maybe Jodie's talk of yard sales and ornery chickens helped lubricate my mental wheels. But the thoughts that resulted were not happy or useful ones. The whole reason I'd talked Annie into telling me her life story was my idea that if we knew *why* she had become a ghost, she would stop being one. But what then? Would she fade away, or go on to some higher realm where I could not even sense her, much less talk with her? Or did I expect, on the contrary, that when the mystery was solved, she would rise bodily from her grave and become a living, breathing woman I could embrace? I did not like to admit even to myself that I harbored this impossible wish.

My doubts and questions only multiplied, but all I could think to do was borrow more and more books from the library and hope that one of them might provide a clue. I started bringing my reading with me to the Island Market, for the slow afternoon hours when hardly anyone came in. Inevitably Jodie saw what I was reading and asked matter-of-factly if I was interested in the occult.

"Oh no, well, not much," I muttered, reddening. "I'm just researching local history, you know, as a hobby along with my marine biology courses. Are there a lot of ghost stories in this part of the shore?"

"Oh, lots," she said cheerfully, and started to tell me some long involved tale about pirate treasure supposedly buried somewhere on or near Assateague and all the horrifying things that had happened to people who went looking for it. I didn't listen very closely, until she said something about a boat full of treasure hunters that sank in a storm, "and everyone drowned except for one guy who was saved by volunteers from the Green Run Life-Saving Station."

"Green Run Life-Saving Station? When was this?"

"Oh, a long time ago. More than a hunnert years. There ain't no Coast Guard station there now, of course, it was closed decades ago."

"I know that," I said. "But back then, back when this rescue happened, was Bill's ancestor one of the rescuers?"

"Most likely yes, if it really happened. He was head of the station. Bill's named after him, you know—my husband is actually William Pearson the Fifth. Sounds like we should be living in a big ol' mansion 'stead of in a falling-down old place next to a chicken house, don't it?" she chuckled.

I thought again about Bill. Whatever Annie's Will had really looked like, my mental picture of him was certainly very different from that of a balding, overweight, middle-aged guy who spoke in a slow drawl when he had to speak at all. But he was the closest living link I had to the man Annie had once loved. I still hadn't talked to him much.

"Bill would really be the one to ask," Jodie said as if reading my thoughts. "I guess I can fix things up enough to have you over our place for dinner sometime. Maybe after the Labor Day rush is done, say the following Tuesday?"

When I told Annie about this invitation she marveled at how easily we'd made the arrangement. "My age was too formal. There must be some ideal middle point, but where is it? Life has so little of perfection about it."

"Except for loving you," I said.

"Darren, you must know by now how flawed I was."

"I know you were human. Could I have loved you if you were a pure angel?"

"Oh, I was very far from that!"

I shifted position to look her full in the face. "What is this great sin you keep harping on, Annie? That you kept on loving Jim after you were married to Will?"

She looked at her lap. The cloth of her skirt was still despite the stiff breeze. "That is the heart of the matter, yes."

I almost smiled. "Then you must at least stop reproaching yourself that Jim loved you truly, but you did not love him back! Anyway, you weren't ever actually unfaithful to Will, were you?"

She looked up at me, her green eyes shining with that uncanny light. "I could never—even if I'd been tempted, and I was in my sinful thoughts, we never had a chance—"

I wished I could grab her hands. "Then where is the sin?"

She pressed her hands over her heart. "Here, Darren. Here is where my sin was, where all the sins that matter are."

"But you loved Will, too. Truly loved him."

She looked away. Scotty's band was grazing a little way off. "Yes, I did," she whispered.

"You traveled to Baltimore with him when he had to bury his parents."

"Of course."

"What was that like?" I was hoping to draw her out on

everything she had done to comfort and help Will, so she would have to admit she hadn't been entirely selfish.

"But I did so little."

I tried to make my tone stern. "Annie, you promised never to lie to me!"

"And I'm not, Darren. I did my duty as his wife, but no more."

"Meaning what? What more should you have done? What did you actually do?"

"I held his hand through the long journey back to the city," she said. "When we arrived in Baltimore we found that his parents had already been buried, though he had to arrange to pay the funeral home and the cemetery. And that, it turned out, was the sort of thing he had to do all winter long: talk to people his father had owed money to, sign papers, visit banks and lawyers' offices. He wouldn't even let me cook him his meals; he said no wife of his was going to engage in such drudgery, and kept on his father's cook and maid, though there was hardly any money to pay them. I told him there was no need for this, he knew well that I was no stranger to hard work from all the years I had spent helping build and run the Ocean House, but he wouldn't hear of it. Perhaps he felt that now that we were in town and he had to settle his father's affairs, he had to keep up appearances—that his family's reputation had been blackened enough as it was."

"You say perhaps he felt that," I said. "Why 'perhaps'?"

"Will was a man of his time," she said, "and would never talk about what he was feeling. When I caught him in an unguarded moment and I saw how much sadness was in his eyes I longed to tell him that he could mourn, that he could cry around me, that I would not think him any less a man. But my courage failed me. Lately I had begun weeping anew for poor Mama whenever I saw anything that reminded me of her. It could be something obvious, like the pungy Pa had named after her, or something that would not have made sense to anyone else, like the fall of a sunbeam at certain angle that made me think of Mama sitting sewing when the morning light came in strong through the sitting room windows. Whatever set me off, I hid my tears from Will, who had enough of his own to shed—although it was the awful deaths of his parents that had released the grief hiding in my heart."

"It doesn't sound like he was much of a husband," I said.

"He was good to me, Darren. I do believe he simply wanted to shield me from his sorrow. He wouldn't even let me accompany him to the cemetery when he went to inspect the gravestones he had ordered. It was I who wasn't a good wife to him."

"But he didn't make you happy," I said. "If he had, you wouldn't have yearned for Jim and then tormented yourself for feeling that way."

She gazed off into the distance, clearly not listening to my lame attempts to make her feel better. "There was a brief moment when I thought things might change for the better," she whispered. I had to lean closer to hear her over the rush of the last land-bound cars leaving the island as the dusk deepened. "Will had concluded the last of his business in Baltimore, and he said he was eager to return to Green Run and put 'the ghosts of this house' behind him. How strange, those are the words he used! The house itself had already been sold to help cover his father's debts. But it was February, and a terrible cold spell had set in. The Chesapeake Bay was so choked with ice, no ferries could sail. So we had to wait for the weather to change. There was nothing for us to do, nowhere for us to turn but to each other. And still," Annie choked, "still he would give me no more than a chaste kiss on the cheek! Did he sense that my heart was corrupt?"

"He was still mourning for his parents," I said gently. "It must have been hard for him, being back in that house."

But she wasn't listening. "After six days of this, I could

take no more. I walked out in the cold early one morning, hardly bothering to put a coat on first. I paid a coachman to take me to the cemetery where Mama lay buried. But once there, I wandered among the tombstones—so many there were, from the war—and could not find hers." She sighed. "Perhaps it didn't matter. Mama led a good life, and her spirit would not have been found skulking around her grave like mine does now.

"The weather didn't break until early March, but how good it was to be out on the open salt water of the Chesapeake Bay, going home," Annie said. "Will seemed relieved, if not exactly happy. When we arrived in Spence Landing, Pa was waiting for us dockside. He embraced me and shook Will's hand vigorously. But Will looked at his shoes as he said, 'I am sorry, Captain.'

"'Sorry for what, Will?'

"'I thought there would be some money left over from my father's estate, but I had barely enough pocket change to pay for our passage back here. In fact I had to write some promissory notes to his creditors.'

"'Don't worry, Will. Remember, the last two years have been so good to us I managed to pay off our bank debt in full last summer. What's a few more small loans to repay?'

"'They're not so small, Captain,' Will said, still not meeting Pa's eye.

"'You'll tell me the details later, Will,' Pa said, glancing at me. Irritation flashed through me—I was not a child any more, I was a married woman, and yet here was Pa conniving with Will to preserve my so-called innocence!

"But the day was too crisp and bright for me to hold onto my resentment long. I squeezed Will's hand as we climbed the hill to Ocean House, where everyone in Green Run had turned out to welcome us home. The little crowd set to whooping and cheering, led by Mr. Powers, when they caught their first glimpse of us. Though our hands were separated by the thickness of his glove and mine, I felt a tiny thrill at Will's return pressure.

"Mr. Powers stepped forward. 'Welcome back to the handsome couple,' he said with a deep bow. 'It is my pleasure to welcome you to your new home!'

"'New home? What new home?' I blurted out. Instead of bothering with explanations, Mr. Powers put one arm around my waist and the other around Will's shoulders and guided us to the other side of the hill, through the trees and past the Birches' and the Joneses' cabins, to a spot that had been a meadow of brilliant green salt-marsh hay whose deep purple flowers were just starting to fade when we left the previous fall. Now it was the site of a handsome new cabin. Will and I walked into it hand in hand, lost in wonder like a couple of children in a fairy tale. The logs that made up the walls were not the common loblolly pine of the island but solid oak that must have taken lots of time and hard work to find, chop down, and haul to the site. The walls were plastered solidly, while the roof was thatched with tough salt-marsh cordgrass that would keep us dry in even the fiercest summer downpour or nor'easter. Inside, the cabin boasted a sitting room with a brick fireplace and a woven rug dyed a warm maroon. There were two handsome rocking chairs, while the bedroom boasted a large four-poster bed with a homemade quilt that all the women and girls had doubtless labored over. There were two highboys and two lowboys, and not of rough wood either but polished to a shine. The kitchen was furnished with a roomy pantry and a large cast-iron stove. There was even an empty room off to the side 'for your little ones when they come,' Betty whispered to me with a wink.

"Will was too overwhelmed to speak, so it fell to me to say how grateful we were for the wonderful gift the whole village had made for us. 'It is nothing but what is due the handsome hero and the beautiful angel of Green Run,' Mr. Powers said to applause. 'I must give the boy Jim his due, he worked harder than anybody building the house and its furniture.' Betty added that the carpet and linens were

Violet's work.

'Where are they?' I asked, relieved that I could thank both of them and not just Jim.

"'Gone, both of them, more than a month ago,' Andy Birch said. 'As soon as your house was ready, they just lit out.'

"'Did they say where? Or why?' I hoped my voice didn't betray anything.

There were shrugs all around. No one seemed to care much, although I couldn't see Pa's face. 'They really were hard workers though,' Mr. Birch added. 'Even if their being here did upset some of our guests.'

"I was hardly listening. For the first time in my life, I was the one suffering from my own selfish actions. If only I had repented then!"

"Did you ever find out where they went?" I asked.

Annie shook her head. "If their brother Tom couldn't find them when he came looking after my death, it must have been far away. Despite the railroad, distances were much longer then, Darren. And for a pair of Negroes to disappear wasn't so difficult, for who would come looking for them?" She paused, staring at the peaceful twilight sky.

"He left me one last message, though," Annie said. "I was out walking later that spring when I chanced to pass near the 'telegraph' sassafras. I looked up idly, not expecting to see anything there, but there was something brown shoved deep in the hole where we used to put our notes to each other. After looking around to make sure no one was watching, I hiked my skirts and climbed carefully up. Not carefully enough though," she smiled ruefully, "the skirts ripped, and that was my good Sunday dress, too! Truth to tell I had slipped away from one of Pastor Scarburgh's sermons. The brown object was a large, crudely made leather case—it looked like it had been stitched together out of scraps, or perhaps from a pair of discarded shoes. Concealed within it was a single piece of paper on which Jim had written his farewell to me. 'I entreat you again, Annie, to make a good life with Will,' he wrote. 'Think no more of me and my childish verses. Our love was doomed from the start.' And more, much more of the same—even when I was still alive and not cursed with perfect recall of all my sins, I committed every word to memory. But greedy wretch that I was, I could not bear to part with this physical relic, and so I hid it in a gap in the floorboards of my new home. This time, however, I had to create the hiding place myself by deliberately chipping away at the wood with a knife—Jim had built the cabin too perfectly. To compound my vanity, I removed all his old letters from my old room at the hotel and stored them in the leather case too."

"That sounds risky," I said. "How could you be sure Will would not find it?"

She smiled wryly. "I made the gap in the corner behind the pantry. Whatever else Will was, he was no cook. Anyway, on my eighteenth birthday, I made an effort to leave my sin behind by burning the leather case and all its contents in the stove. Not that my motives were pure, even then: the case had begun bulging and I feared that Will might glimpse it someday."

"Why do you say it 'had begun bulging,' Annie?"

She bowed her head. "I have sworn to withhold nothing from you, Darren. As the weeks of that spring and summer passed and Will remained distant even though we shared the same table and the same bed, I started writing Jim letters. Letters I could never send, of course; letters that I would never have sent, even had I known where to find him. I confessed in them the love I thought I still cherished for him, but that was really just an excuse to pour out my grief at my inability to make Will happy."

"But where is the sin in that, Annie?" I said in exasperation. "If you wrote of what was in your heart and hid it away so no one would ever see it, who were you hurting?"

"I should have found the strength I needed, Darren,"

she said. "I was not friendless. I had Betty to confide in, and I did not shrink from doing so. She was full of practical advice for me—with two toddlers to raise and her belly already swelling with a third pregnancy, how could she not know the ways of women with men? Her advice was good, too—it was thanks to her that my marriage to Will was not a 'white' one," she said, as I turned red and looked futilely around for a rock I could crawl under. "But Will still felt like a stranger to me, the hero on a pedestal I could never hope to climb. And the distance between us only grew that summer. Pa had made good on his promise to build and furnish a life-saving station where the inlet met the sea. It was little more than a storage shed for the tackle Will and the other men needed to deal with an emergency at sea, with a boat lashed up alongside that could be pushed into the surf in seconds when it was needed. The next year, after I drowned, we finally got a real U.S. Life-Saving Service station there—and don't think I didn't appreciate the irony! But with the basic equipment my father had paid for, Will, Mike Powers, Andy Birch, Horace Jones, and a handful of other villagers—and even on one occasion a hotel guest!—had managed to save more than two dozen victims of three shipwrecks the previous year, the final year of my life. Betty and I took to organizing clambakes every time our men came back bigger heroes than the time before. Will said he didn't like a fuss made over him, but those were the only times I saw him smile. Certainly he never seemed happy when we were alone together."

"And me—do I make you happy?" I blurted.

It was full dark by now. If not for the light Annie gave off, so far from her grave, I could not have seen the yearning and confusion written on her face.

28

As Annie's tale reached the last months of her life I began to wish she would slow down in the telling, as if that would prevent her death. No matter what she said, she hadn't done anything to deserve dying so young, and I refused to believe in an angry God who would make her suffer as a ghost for more than one hundred years for any of the supposed sins she had committed. Maybe she hadn't been happy being married to Will, but he was a good man she had respected if not loved, and she was living near her father and in the midst of the wild beauty of Assateague Island, so it didn't sound as if she had been exactly unhappy, either.

"I am sure if I'd lived to have the baby, it would have drawn Will and me closer together," she said. It was the Friday before Labor Day weekend, and since Jodie needed me at the store I'd only been able to ride out to the island long after dark. I was so tired that Annie's words seemed even more dreamlike than usual, as I looked at the still, dark waters of the bay through half-closed eyes.

Then what she'd just said hit me and I sat up. "Oh, that's right. You mentioned you were pregnant when you died."

"Yes. I told Will on my birthday, but he wasn't as excited as I'd hoped he'd be. So I took Sally out for a ride. That's what I'd been doing all year when it got to be too much at home with Will. I always felt guilty about it, since I should have been staying with him, but I just could not stop myself. Seeing the waves crash onto the sand, watching the colorful ducks paddle through the tidal creeks and the hawks soaring high overhead, racing the other island ponies as they splashed through the surf on a hot summer day… these things restored my soul."

Which implied of course that her soul needed restoring after she spent too much time with her husband. But she denied he had been depressed—that he had suffered from "melancholia," as they said back then.

"Will could be happy, just not around me. He was always at his best when he was helping other people, whether it was something as small as toting heavy luggage from the docks—he wasn't too proud to be a porter, which was a good thing since Jim had done this job practically all by himself the previous two summers—or as important as saving a drowning man from a storm."

My eyes filled with tears at the mention of drowning. "But he couldn't save you."

"No. It happened too fast." Suddenly Annie's tone shifted to the drily factual, as if her own death was something she'd read about in the newspaper. "That storm came up out of nowhere. I'd gone with him to Spence Run in one of the smaller catboats—he said he was expecting a telegram from Baltimore and I was afraid it would be more bad news. I didn't want him to be alone when he opened it. But the stagecoach driver said there hadn't been anything on the Friday coach from Salisbury—this was the next day, Saturday, December 12, 1874. I was watching Will carefully, but I couldn't tell whether he was frustrated or relieved. All he said was we ought to be getting back, he didn't like the look of the sky.

"The day had started out sunny, but quickly clouded

over. It was spitting rain as we climbed back on the boat, and a brisk breeze had started up. But I wasn't worried at all about the five-knot run across Chincoteague Bay to Green Run, when both the mainland and the island would be in sight the entire time. Why should I worry, with such an experienced sailor at the helm of our little catboat!" She shook her head. "You would think, having seen all those shipwrecks, that I would have learned to be humble before the power of the sea. Or at least that I would have learned to swim."

"You never learned to swim?"

"Pa always said the water was 'too dangerous for my precious little girl,'" she said. "And I could never be bothered trying to learn on my own. I was too busy playing the fool."

"Just tell me what happened, Annie."

Her voice remained steady and calm as she told the tale of her own death. "No sooner had we pulled away from the dock than the wind began to pick up. I still wasn't worried, but I began to feel queasy. Betty had been saying for months how she envied me for hardly ever getting morning sickness, but now it was all catching up with me as I clung to the rail and heaved up everything I had eaten all day. No sooner had I finished retching than Will called for help with the sail, which was flapping dangerously in the wind. I knew little about seamanship but I followed his instructions and pulled on the rigging with fingers that were beginning to go numb. Although it was noon the gray sky overhead darkened until it was almost black, the wind rose to a wail, and the boat began to rock violently. I was thrown against the rail and fumbled desperately for it, grabbing onto it with all my strength to avoid being flung into the water. Will was shouting something, I couldn't understand what, and now I did begin to feel fear. I even began to pray, promising too late to leave off my sinful ways and do God's will if only He would spare my life. I even promised never to walk out on one of Pastor

Scarburgh's sermons again! Then the jibboom swung around and hit me on the back of head, and I knew no more."

I waited for Annie to continue. The gaudy band of sunset sky to the west turned blurry as my eyes filled with tears, which I tried to blink away—if she could be stoical, why couldn't I? I saw her brightly lit hand in front of me, close enough to kiss. As I had done so many times for her, she was reaching out to catch my tears. I should have found it astonishing that she could do that—that with nothing but her ghostly hand to stop them, my tears weren't reaching the ground. But even if it was a miracle, it was never going to bring her back to life, so what good was it?

"What happened then?" I asked, struggling to keep my voice as steady as hers.

"I woke up on the dock under the hotel, seemingly unhurt, though I couldn't remember how I'd got there— surely not by swimming? But I stopped thinking about myself when I saw what was going on out on the water. The storm had passed, and the water was filled with the bobbing lights of boats out searching for someone. I jumped to my feet, scared that Will might have fallen overboard too and drowned! But then I saw him on our wrecked catboat, and Pa coming in behind him on the *Margaret Deirdre*, holding something in his arms— something big... He turned to speak to Will and I saw my own face, blue around the lips, with a huge bruise at the temple. And then I understood my fate."

I closed my eyes. It was dark by now, and anyway my eyes hurt from crying.

"I have already told you how I attended my own funeral," Annie said. "Pa was leaning against Will for support. Poor Will, losing his parents and then me, and even so he was strong enough to hold Pa up! Andy Birch and Mike Powers were my pallbearers, and everyone was crying except Will and Pastor Scarburgh, who had to conduct the service."

We sat in silence for a long while. When she spoke again, her voice was almost too soft to hear. "Now you understand why I am condemned to wander the earth, an unquiet spirit."

"But I still love you," I said, opening my eyes and trying to focus on her brightly shining form, "and I always will."

"All right then," she said. "There is one more terrible thing on my conscience. Something that happened after I was already dead and buried. You must hear the tale so that you understand why it's dangerous to be around me."

"Whatever you tell me, I won't leave you."

A meteor streaked across the sky, hissing, casting an unearthly green light on Annie's face. "A year had passed since my death. It was three days since I had appeared to Pa, in a dream as he thought. It was still bitterly cold—not that I could feel it, but I could see how people walked around with their breath steaming in front of them, shivering under their heaviest coats. I was sitting next to my grave, on top of the hill. The tombstone was still only a few months old—Will had put it in place himself, on what would have been my nineteenth birthday, shortly after it was delivered to the island. I was impressed that he had gone to the expense. The shipwreck victims and the Joneses' little daughter Winnie, who had perished from scarlet fever, only had wooden crosses. Sometimes I'd trace the letters of my name with my fingertips, imagining I could feel the cold, grainy stone.

"The night was clear, with a waning moon low in the west, and all the world was quiet except for the murmur of the ocean waves at my back. I don't sleep, but sometimes I go into a state that might be called a trance, in a living person. Since I have no way of keeping track of time I can't be sure, but it seems to me that years have sometimes gone by for me in this way."

I shivered, trying to imagine that.

Annie resumed her tale. "The first I knew anything was wrong was when a fast-moving dark cloud began to block the moon. But it wasn't a cloud, it was a thick streamer of smoke rising from the hotel. In the winter, no one stayed there except for Pa and a young couple he had hired, who lived in Will's old room. I heard confused shouting from that side of the hotel, and I saw two figures running. Suddenly, without any sense of movement, I found myself standing in the lobby where I had made Pa cry three nights ago. He was sitting in his rocking chair, his head thrown back and to the left, his mouth open. An empty bottle and his pipe lay at his feet. There were flames everywhere! I—" She stopped and tried to compose herself to continue. I reached out to touch her arm, felt that familiar tingle of repulsion.

"The flames were coloring everything bright orange. I tried to grab his shoulder to shake him awake, but of course I couldn't get a grip. There were shouts from outside. Someone tried to open the door but fell back with a cry of pain—the doorknob must have been burning hot to the touch. I could hear Will's voice as he rallied the other men who served with him in the new, official Life-Saving Station. If anyone could save Pa, it would be him. There came a tremendous booming as if God Himself was knocking at the door, which splintered inward. The log the men had used as a battering ram fell to the floor. Will charged through first, even though the fire roared up with renewed energy from the fresh air. He saw Pa at once, grabbed him under his arms and dragged him out into the sand that served as a natural firebreak. I followed them out. In the garish, flickering light I could see that Pa's lips looked dark in his pale face, just as mine had a year before, after I drowned." Annie swallowed hard. "I will confess to you, Darren, I was still as selfish as I had been in life, for when I saw Pa lying there like that my first thought was not to hope that he might somehow still be alive, but that his spirit might be standing nearby as mine had been, that I might no longer be alone!"

"That's not such a strange wish, Annie. Anyway your wish didn't kill him."

"But seeing me three nights before plainly did. Pa hardly ever drank, yet he had drunk himself into a stupor while holding a lit pipe. I am responsible for his death!"

All could do was tell her over and over again that I loved her. I hope I made some impression.

29

I was disappointed that Annie's tale of her death hadn't yielded the epiphany she hoped for, but also more than a little relieved, for what if this "epiphany" had meant that her ghost evaporated? It was a selfish thought, but if I spent the rest of my life the way I was living now, spending time with her every day, I would be more than happy. I didn't care that there would never be anything physical between us; I told myself our love was stronger and deeper than that. There was so much we still had to learn about each other. She told me about some of the things she had seen over the century and more she had spent as a disembodied observer, some funny, some tragic. The rebuilt Ocean House had flourished more than ever after Will rebuilt it, she told me. But he'd hired Andy and Betty Birch to run it, while he moved away. "The memories must have been too painful for him here," she said sadly. "I never saw him again, after about 1876."

"He can't have moved far," I said. "His descendants still live here on the shore."

She smiled at the thought. "A whole tribe of Wills, imagine that! Andy and Betty did a great job running the hotel for him. Most people assumed they were the owners.

But business began to fall off as Ocean City grew, and after the turn of the century the place was half-abandoned. The village dwindled away until it was just the families of the Life-Saving Station staff. The inlet silted up. And in time the Life-Saving Station closed down, too, and there was nothing left. They shipped the lumber from the hotel and the cabins back to the mainland. Mischief makers stole all the wooden crosses in the cemetery, even Winnie Birch's. They'd have stolen mine if they could have carried it away. Nothing abides."

A chill strolled down my back.

Assateague had not remained the isolated wild island it had been during Annie's lifetime—it was only three or four hours' drive from Washington and Baltimore after the Chesapeake Bay Bridge opened in 1952—and Annie saw a lot over the years, though always at a remove. She told me of a great sea battle she had witnessed between "ships so big they looked like enormous metal monsters"—and I read later how German U-boats had sunk American ships within sight of the island during World War II. Years after that, she wandered to the northern edge of her range and watched as bulldozers flattened the forest to pave a road and build houses and marinas for a planned seaside housing development, which was flooded out in a huge nor'easter, the "Ash Wednesday Storm" of 1962.

"What did you think about that?" I asked. "I mean, here they were cutting down the trees and bulldozing the marsh…"

"And scaring off the ponies. Yes. Part of me hated them for it. I wished all those stories about ghosts that could frighten people to death with their very appearance were true! Or even better, that I could wreck their powerful machines. But I could do nothing but watch."

"And the other part of you…?"

"Was tired of being all alone, Darren." She closed her eyes and leaned back, propping herself up on her elbows. Such a natural, human gesture, and yet there was that eerie glow she cast all around her, which seemed all the brighter on an overcast night like this. "If a town had grown up here, and I could have passed among crowds of people going about their business, living their lives, perhaps I would have been a bit less lonely. But I would have missed the ponies, and the peace of the wind passing through the trees."

"Wasn't there ever anyone else who could see you and talk to you? Apart from your father, and Addie Birch, and me."

"A few over the years. Just isolated conversations here and there... enough to remind me of what it was like being human. But, Darren, I'm sure you don't want to hear every detail of my century here uselessly watching the people and the ponies, envying every lowly sika deer and muskrat for its ability to take part in the world."

"But I do. I want to know everything about you. I want to know every pain you suffered, every moment of isolation you experienced." If I was wrong that hearing about her life and death would free her, maybe taking on every bit of her suffering would do the trick.

But she was shaking her head. "No. I've been talking about myself all summer. I want to know about you, Darren."

I tried to laugh, but it came out all strangled. "Me? What do you want to know about me for? There's nothing interesting about me."

"I don't agree, Darren. What is it about you that makes you able to sense me?" Those green eyes bored past my every defense. "Are you in mourning, like Pa? An innocent, like Addie Birch? Or lonely, like those few over the years who could see me?"

Or perhaps all three at the same time? I squirmed, and seeing my discomfort, Annie proposed we walk along the beach. A break in the clouds over the ocean let a little moonlight through, enough to see our way and cast a shimmering pallor over the sand. Something was moving out there—many somethings—and I started to laugh when I figured out what they were. "Ghost crabs," I explained. The funny three-inch-long scampering creatures can blend right in with the sand, even in full daylight, as long as they stay still.

Annie smiled again and made as if to put her hand in mine. "Come on, Darren," she coaxed, "I've told you my every secret. What about yours?" I stammered that I didn't have any secrets. Or none worth knowing. She raised her hand and put her finger over my lips, which tingled in response. "I know it is hard for you. Don't speak."

"But if I don't speak, how will I—? Oh!"

Vivid but disconnected images of my past flashed before my inner eye. Two little girls making fun of me in day care. A gang of bigger boys stuffing me in a trash can and holding down the lid while I howled and slammed against the mold-stinking sides. Sitting around a campfire enviously watching all the other boys with their arms around girls. On and on, a dismal slide show of loneliness and self-pity.

I sat down in the sand, too dizzy to take another step. Finally the mental images faded and I dropped my head, exhausted. I might have fallen asleep like that if Annie hadn't quietly spoken my name.

I looked up at her. "You saw my memories, didn't you?"

Annie nodded wordlessly.

"Why did you want to see them? You have only seen what a shallow person I am... so full of self-pity and self-righteousness... I always thought I was better than everyone else, ha! I never knew what real suffering was. Or real greatness of soul."

"And you think that's what you see in me, Darren?"

"You know the answer to that."

"I think the real greatness of soul is in you, Darren. Who else but you could cherish and love a ghost like me with no hope of ever regaining living flesh? You worry about the world burning in the smoke of coal fires, you're a scientist with a measuring rule, but you never forget to care for the people who are close to you. Why do you think Kevin and Lakeisha, and Ranger Paul and Jodie and Bill, follow you everywhere to make sure you take care of yourself?" She leaned closer until her face filled my field of vision. "Because you're worth caring about. That's why, Darren."

30

"Can I get you a pillow, Darren?"

I raised my head from where I had put it down next to the cash register for just a second. "I'm sorry, Jodie."

She chuckled. "It's all right. We've been slammed all day till now." It was four-thirty Monday afternoon, the first time in the whole holiday weekend that there hadn't been a line of people clamoring for my attention, or kids running around knocking things off the shelves, or a frantic need to restock the milk or the sodas or the pretzels or the beach umbrellas.

"Wasn't this busy last year," Jodie said. "We're out of water."

I jumped guiltily. "Sorry, I'll just go bring some."

"No, I mean we're really out of water. All those flats are empty. And flashlight batteries and toilet paper too."

I goggled at her. "Huh?"

"Don't you listen to the TV or the radio, kid?"

I shook my head. "Don't have a TV. And I'm always too tired to bother with the radio when I get home." Which was not surprising, considering I kept getting home after midnight. Jodie didn't care for the ads on the local radio stations, so she put her own mix CDs of Eighties pop songs on the store's sound system. If I had to listen to Billy Joel's "An Innocent Man" one more time I might do something so that I'd no longer be one myself.

"It's that storm down in the Bahamas. Hurricane Norma. They don't know where it's going to hit yet, we might only get some extra rain, but it's already a Category 2 and it's definitely headed up the coast."

"Oh. Um, when?"

"Forecasters say they won't know till later in the week. We should still be good to have you over for dinner Tuesday night. We'll be having crabs, and I know how you love my crab cake sandwiches."

I started to say that would be great when a thought struck me. Shellfish aren't kosher, but I hadn't grown up following all those rules. Hell, I really had enjoyed Jodie's crab cake sandwiches just a few weeks ago. The *El Malei Rachamim* prayer had brought Annie back to me, though, and I was planning to go to High Holiday services at the Ocean Pines synagogue, "Temple Bat Yam," later in September. All this was a bit too much to explain, so I said, "Actually, I'm trying out vegetarianism, I guess, but I'm not going to be upset or anything if you guys have crabs. I just won't eat them." Jodie started chattering about what else she was going to serve and I forgot about the conversation until I got home late that night. As usual I flopped down on the bed without even taking my clothes off—there was enough sand on those sheets to build a whole new barrier island—but then I remembered what Jodie had said and tuned in the news station. Norma had already killed a dozen people in the Bahamas and the U.S. Virgin Islands, but they still didn't know where it was going to make landfall in the continental U.S.—it could be anywhere from the Outer Banks to Connecticut, like with Hurricane Sandy several years ago. I decided not to worry about it. It wasn't as if Annie could be hurt by a storm.

Within an hour of opening the store the next morning, Jodie said we might as well close up. Only a trickle of customers was coming in off the beach. "People must've started back early to beat the storm. We should start getting ready here, too," she said.

"Is Norma really going to hit us?"

She shrugged. "Your guess is as good as mine or the National Weather Service's, I guess. Last I heard over the car radio, landfall is supposed to be between Cape May, New Jersey and Cape Charles, down at the southern tip of the Delmarva Peninsula. And Norma's been upgraded to a Category 3. Ocean water's warmer than usual or something." This was back before they had to add Category 6 to the Saffir-Simpson Hurricane Wind Scale, when we started getting those two-hundred-mile-an-hour-plus storms barreling up the coast. Norma was actually the first of these monsters.

I hung a CLOSED sign on the door at ten o'clock and started hauling things around and putting up storm shutters over all the windows. Bill stopped by a little after noon to help; he said he'd been busy getting ready at home. The biggest problem was the chickens. "Got to move them all up to higher ground," he explained. "I ain't half finished with that." I wondered where he could even find higher ground within a hundred miles—the whole of Delmarva is as flat as eastern Kansas.

"I could help," I said.

Jodie smiled and shook her head. "Thanks, Darren, but if you ain't never been around chickens it ain't worth your time and trouble."

"I could use his help 'round the house, though," Bill said. "Been so busy with those dratted birds I ain't even had time to put up shutters on the living room windows."

"Would you mind, Darren?" Jodie asked. "I could get started cooking dinner early, and you'll have extra time to chat with Bill about Green Run and the old days."

"You can stay with us during the storm, if you like," Bill added. "I hear you live in a trailer."

"I couldn't impose," I said.

"No imposition. We've got plenty of room," Jodie said. And so they did, though the house turned out to be so run-down I wondered how much safer than the trailer it really was. We drove there with my bike in the back of the Pearsons' battered 4X4—they offered to put it inside, where they said it would certainly be safer than in its usual place locked to the oak tree outside my trailer.

The Pearsons' farmhouse was in the countryside west of Berlin. We drove along potholed roads through flat, featureless farmland. Eventually the pavement gave out entirely and we were riding on a dirt road. We pulled up in a cloud of dust at a two-story house with the steeply angled dormer windows typical of older Eastern Shore homes. The frame was visibly sagging, and the white paint was peeling away in strips. Off to the right was a long, low structure, unmistakable by its smell as a chicken house, though the relatively subdued cackling testified to Bill's success in evacuating most of the birds. This structure was twenty or thirty yards away across a stubbled field from where I stood, but even at that distance I could see the screens on it were as rusted and ill-fitting in their frames as the ones on the farmhouse itself.

"We're saving all the profits from the store to knock the house down completely and have a new one built," Jodie said in answer to my unspoken question. "Unfortunately we had a lot of money put away in one of them mutual funds tied to the stock market, and we lost our shirts in '08."

Inside everything looked run down, from the liver-colored carpet to the chipped wooden coffee table. The ceiling bulged alarmingly downward in the middle. "You get that in houses this old," Jodie explained, seeing me glance upward. "This one was built around 1900. They settle, that's all. Ain't nothin' you can do about it but knock 'em down and start over."

"The storm shutters are out in the shed," Bill said. "Want to come out back with me?" I nodded and we got to work. I kept looking at him as we covered the windows over with heavy wooden slats that were just as beat up as everything else. It was hard to believe that he was Will's direct descendant and namesake. He was strong enough, but he had a gut and a receding hairline. Well, maybe Will had looked like that too when he hit middle age.

Jodie brought us glasses of lemonade as we took a break and turned on the TV to a local channel for the latest updates on the storm, which was charging almost due north in a frightening display of garish false color on the screen. The outer bands of clouds were already passing over the Outer Banks, the forecaster said. "Norma is a large, dangerous storm, and we advise everyone to take it seriously. A mandatory evacuation order has just been issued for Ocean City and surrounding low-lying areas..."

Bill and Jodie peered anxiously at the screen and then began to argue over whether the map of the area to be evacuated included their house. It clearly did include the area east of Berlin where my trailer was, and I got out my cell phone and called Kevin to let him know I had already left so he wouldn't waste time checking on me. Lakeisha picked up. "Kev's out knocking on people's doors telling them they have to leave," she told me. "I've got the car all packed up, I'm going to go stay with relatives in Annapolis, but Kev unfortunately has to stay on duty. Want me to pick you up on the way out of town?"

"No, I'm staying with Jodie and her husband west of Berlin. I think we'll be okay," I said, glancing over at them. Bill had insisted on "riding it out" and Jodie was going along with him, though she wasn't too happy about it.

"I know this place is a falling-down old heap of junk, but it's been in my family forever. Maybe you'd be better off going with your friend," Bill explained apologetically as we nailed up the last of the shutters. It was already raining, and a stiff breeze had started to blow from the north, which at least kept us upwind of the chicken house.

"No, if you think we're safe here, I'd like to stay," I

229

said. I was getting hungry from the cooking smells wafting from the kitchen, but mostly I wanted to hear whatever he could tell me about the first William Pearson.

Jodie apologized that the only vegetarian meal she'd been able to whip up was a baked potato and a green salad, but I didn't care, even though it meant I had to watch them eating their way through four large blue crabs, covering the battered old dining room table with broken bits of shell and greasy napkins.

"So, Jodie tells me you're interested in the abandoned village that used to be at Green Run," Bill said finally, as he leaned back in his chair with an open can of beer. "What's so interesting about that old place? Ain't even nothing to see out there."

"I know," I said, nodding. "But I love Assateague. I want to find out all I can about the island's history. Besides, wasn't the first William Pearson a Civil War veteran? I love all that history."

"He was, at that." Bill sounded surprised. "How did you know?"

My cover stories were getting smoother. "I wrote a paper for my history class last year about the Potomac Flotilla and I saw his name in the Navy archives. Didn't he serve on a ship called the *Anne Marie*?"

"Why, yes he did. That's quite a memory you've got. I think there's a picture of him in his Navy uniform in a trunk I've got in the attic, along with a lot of other stuff of his. If you help me carry it down, we can have a look."

I practically tipped my chair over in my eagerness to accompany him upstairs, but just as he was pulling down the trapdoor to the attic, which had a rickety-looking set of wooden steps attached to it, the lights went out. He cursed, then apologized. "Jodie hon, the power's already out," he yelled. "Can you get the candles?" He fumbled around in the darkness of his bedroom until he found a flashlight. I waited in the hall, the thump of my heartbeat in my ears not quite loud enough to drown out the rising moan of the wind.

"There it is," he grunted. "Oh damn, the batteries are dead. You'd think I'd've thought to replace them before the storm... hang on, let me look..."

"You two all right up there?" Jodie called. "Maybe this ain't such a good night to go foolin' around in that attic, Bill."

"It's all right, I know where that trunk is. Might as well check it out tonight, it ain't like we can sit around watching TV!" he called back. He'd found another flashlight that gave off a weak, orangish beam. "Good enough. Let's go."

The attic was as full of dusty junk as you'd expect in a century-old house. I followed Bill up and stared at the looming dark shapes lying everywhere. But he was right, he did know where the ancient wooden trunk containing Will's memorabilia was. Unfortunately, it was under an upside-down old chest of drawers—*must be what Annie calls a "highboy,"* I thought—and was surrounded by several untidy stacks of old newspapers and magazines. I kept sneezing from the dust as I helped Bill move all that stuff aside. "Ain't been up here in years," he said apologetically.

Once we got the trunk over to the trapdoor I offered to take the bottom end, but Bill wouldn't hear of it. "Jodie told me you got a bum leg from being struck by lightning, so don't worry, I can manage it." Together we slid the trunk as near to the hole as we could, and Bill started down. "Okay, lower away," he said.

"Are you sure?"

"It's all right, I tell you! Let's just do it." Moving as slowly as I could, I tipped the trunk into the hole. Bill grunted as he caught it. "Okay, grab the other end," he panted. I did and started down myself, feeling guilty at how little weight I was bearing. It was just starting to seem like we would make it without incident when I put my foot—the good left foot—on a weak rung, which creaked and suddenly splintered. I gasped and let go of the trunk, scrabbling around wildly for purchase on the ladder so I wouldn't fall on top of Bill, who said "oof" and began to swear loudly. The trunk tumbled down and hit the floor of the hallway with a loud thump.

"You two all right up there?" Jodie called, starting up the stairs from the living room.

Bill said he was fine except for a chipped fingernail. I said I was too, though my hands were torn up from splinters. Jodie clucked and fussed over us, rummaging around in the bathroom cabinet for Band-Aids®. I waited impatiently. If my hands hadn't been bleeding, I would have ignored the pain and set about prying the trunk open with my fingernails. But there was a rusted padlock Bill didn't have the key for, and it took him several minutes of looking through his bedroom drawers before he found a screwdriver to break it open.

"Language, Bill!" Jodie said.

"Sorry," he muttered. "Now, let's just see…" He jiggled the blade of the screwdriver in the keyhole while Jodie put some candles in holders on the floor so he could see what he was doing. Outside the wind had risen to a constant shriek. It sounded like some enormous engine was overheating, and we had to shout to make ourselves heard. Bill shouted even louder when the screwdriver slipped and he cut himself in the hand. Jodie bit her lip and refrained from scolding him again for swearing as she bandaged him up again. I glared in frustration at the trunk, a massive wooden thing two feet high and more than three feet on a side, with black iron brackets at the corners.

"Now will you two just leave it alone until we get the power back!" Jodie said. But I picked up the screwdriver—the head was still slick with Bill's blood—wiped it off and began jiggling it around. "Men," Jodie sighed and rolled her eyes. Finally the lock split apart with a squeal of angry metal.

As I opened the lid, something dark, soft, and powdery brushed against my face. A lot of somethings! I yelped, first in fear and then in disgust as I realized I was being assaulted by moths. "Well, look at this," Bill exclaimed, holding a mass of yellowish rags up to the candlelight. "It's the old boy's Navy dress uniform! Or it was, before the moths got into it." The cloth was so badly rotted we kept finding shreds of it as all three of us started going through the items in the trunk. A lot of dull yellow brass buttons were scattered around that Jodie said would look very pretty if they were polished up. Outside the wind howled and howled. A loose shutter somewhere started banging against the side of the house.

There were a lot of knickknacks in that trunk, random souvenirs from a whole lifetime. A plaque of appreciation for 25 years of service in the Salisbury Volunteer Fire Department, dated September 18, 1901. A framed black-and-white picture of the firemen posing stiffly for the camera before a horse-drawn firewagon. "That's him," Bill said, pointing to a man in the middle who stood ramrod straight and taller than all but one of his fellows. His mustache and hair were gray, almost white, but I could see he was still a handsome man. We found some family pictures that were hardly less formal, though Will was a younger man in some of them. I smiled sadly when I saw that his wife, Mildred, looked vaguely like Annie. She had dark hair, a sweet round face, and a slight smile that would not be denied even among the stern expressions her husband and children wore. "That's Will Junior, my great-grandfather," Bill said, pointing at a solemn-faced little boy who sat in his mother's lap, wearing a narrow-brimmed cap and a formal dark jacket with white shirtsleeves and lapels poking out at the cuffs and neckline. "He bought this farm with his share of the inheritance from Wright's Ocean House. Cost fifty dollars, which was real money, back in the day."

"Were there any family stories about him?" I asked Bill. "About Will Senior, I mean."

Bill frowned, thinking. "Well, he wasn't from around here. Not from the Shore, I mean. He was supposed to have come from Baltimore." He smiled. "My grandpa used to say he took the helm of the boat he served on during the Civil War, in a battle once when the captain was badly hurt, and that he led the men on to victory; but who knows about that sort of story, when it happened so long ago? He was supposed to have done lots of heroic things... catching a woman who had jumped off the top of a burning bank building... saving a man from drowning in the Pocomoke River... rescuing three children from a house fire in Salisbury..."

"But what was he like as a person?"

"As a person? How would I know? According to this obituary, he died in 1906," he said, holding up another yellowed newspaper clipping.

"You can see he was always fond of the sea," Jodie said, holding up a painfully detailed old-fashioned whaling schooner in a clear glass bottle. "Bill, we should clean this off and mount it in the living room. It'll make a great conversation piece."

I peered into the nearly empty trunk, wondering what it was I was looking for, after all. What were a lot of crumpled pieces of paper going to tell me? I couldn't even read what was on this one. It looked like it had been soaked and then dried out, leaving it all wrinkled and covered with streaks of blue ink. But the fact that it was handwritten drew my attention. It looked like a woman's handwriting. The only legible words were, "...love you always..." I glanced one more time into the trunk, wondering if there were other pages from the same letter that were in any better shape. I did find one—the second and final page, which ended in the middle of the sheet of paper. I picked it up and held it up to the light.

31

All night long the wind howled and howled. I lay wide awake on the Pearsons' sofa, wondering if it was ever going to stop. Bill and Jodie had finally said good night, after giving me sheets and a blanket so I'd be more comfortable on the downstairs sofa, and a flashlight so I could make my way through the blacked-out house. The trunk was closed again, but Bill said it was no problem to leave it there in the upstairs hallway and assured me no one would trip over it. We'd packed everything back where we'd found it except for the ship in a bottle and the brass uniform buttons. "We might as well have something nice around this place," Jodie had said, grimacing. "It's gonna look like even more of a shithole after Norma gets through with us."

"Hey, I thought we were trying not to use bad language around the kid," Bill said, nodding at me.

"Aww, fudge off, Bill," Jodie said, and we all chuckled. I went downstairs, made up the sofa and waited, staring at the ceiling and listening to the house creak ominously in the wind. My cell phone battery had already died so I didn't have any way of telling the time, but I waited till long after I was sure my hosts must have fallen asleep.

Then I reached for the flashlight and crept back upstairs. The trunk sat where we had left it, the broken lock beside it. I eased the lid open and started to move things around, trying not to rustle the papers or bump any of the picture frames and other hard objects against the sides.

The letter was where I had put it, towards the top of the heap. I grasped it gingerly, afraid of tearing the brittle old paper. My legs began to cramp up and I stood up a little too quickly, letting the trunk lid go so it slammed with a noise that sounded as loud as a gunshot to me. I froze, but there was no noise from Bill and Jodie's bedroom. So I tiptoed back downstairs, wincing at the ache in my leg and praying I wouldn't lose my balance and go tumbling down the steps.

Back on the sofa again I shined the flashlight on each page of the letter in turn, then folded it carefully and put it in my pocket. The wind screamed as it beat at the old house and the rain came in torrents that sounded as if dump trucks full of gravel were constantly unloading on the roof and outside walls. The words I had seen burned with lightless fire in the air above my head and I began to cry silently, hopelessly. I lay like that hour after dark hour. I don't think I ever shut my eyes, but I seemed to see Annie standing beside the couch, her glow rippling like the embers of a dying fire. "Why didn't you tell me?" I cried. "You promised to tell me everything!" She said nothing, just stared at me or rather through me with eyes like green suns. *Did you ever think you truly knew me?* she said without words. *Did you ever think you possessed my heart?* My thoughts chased each other through a maze with no exit. What kind of arrogance did it take to think I could help a ghost? That I could right wrongs committed when America was a land of ex-slaves who had just been freed and ex-masters who sought to re-enslave them, and slaughtering Indians was considered the height of civilized behavior? Could I even understand someone who had grown up in such a time, much less love her?

Gray light and quiet seeped gradually into my tormented awareness. I sat up dizzily and pulled at the dusty curtains to look outside. The wind was dying down and the rain had stopped, but the farmyard was a ruin. The chicken house had been smashed as if some unthinkably large creature had stepped on it, and despite Bill's efforts dead birds lay everywhere. The tool shed where Bill and I had found the storm shutters had vanished. Broken branches ranging from twigs to logs were scattered everywhere under a mulch of green and brown leaves.

"You awake?" a voice said, making me start. Bill had come downstairs so quietly I hadn't heard him. He drew in a breath when he saw the disaster area his property had become. No swearing, though. Some things are just too serious for words.

"Jodie's still in bed," he said. "She takes medicine to help her sleep. You want some fruit for breakfast? I want to run into town to pick up some stuff from the store." He chuckled ruefully. "Like maybe a bulldozer and backhoe."

"That's fine, thanks," I said, following him into the kitchen and taking a peach he handed me. "You can drop me off at my trailer and I'll be out of your hair." He pulled a skeptical face but didn't argue, just helped me load my bike into the 4X4.

The dirt road that led to the farm had vanished in a sea of mud, but though the tires spun once or twice, we got through. The cool, pleasant morning air belied the devastation Norma had left behind. It was a good thing the dirt road we had driven down last night did not lead through wooded country, or there would have been fallen trees everywhere.

When we reached Berlin, the town looked like it had been hit by a whole pack of tornadoes. Despite the evacuation order, plenty of people had stayed put, and they were wandering in a daze around their houses, which had suffered everything from broken windows to total collapse. Ambulances and police cars were parked every which way and rescue workers and volunteers were digging through collapsed buildings looking for survivors. When we arrived at my trailer we saw that the oak tree in the yard had fallen on it and crushed it as if it was a soda can. *Don't think about it,* I told myself. *About the way nature seems to be trying to kill you, and how it gets a little closer each time.*

The roof of the Pearsons' store had been torn off and lay in a mangled heap of corrugated metal in the parking lot, though the storm shutters Bill and I had put up remained neatly in place. Bill pulled into the gravel lot, swerving to avoid a fallen tree trunk, and got out of the 4X4. I followed him inside, and for a moment we both stood there gaping at the shattered glass display cases, tumbled shelving, and heaps of ruined food and sodden souvenirs.

"Do you want my help cleaning this up?" I asked.

"Well," he began, when a noise brought us up short. We looked up at the sky in time to see a wall of clouds shutting out the blue. Rain began to patter down. "It was the eye," Bill said, "it was only the god-damned eye of the storm. The second half'll be even worse. You'd better get back in the truck with me."

"There's something I have to check on first," I said, lifting my bike out of the bed of the truck.

Bill stared at me, then grabbed my arm hard and shook it. "Are you nuts? Ain't you heard what I just said? The storm's coming back!"

"I'll be all right," I said, shaking him off and climbing on the bike. "I got hit by lightning and got off with barely a scratch, remember?" He shouted at me but I was already pedaling furiously. The road to Assateague led through woods, and I had to maneuver around fallen trees. The sky was already dark and a stiff breeze from the south was blowing hard little drops of rain against me as I passed the National Seashore Visitor Center. I had to lift the bike over a chain that had been stretched across the foot of the Verrazano Bridge, with a sign dangling from it saying the

National Seashore and State Park were closed until further notice. I braked sharply as I reached the high point of the bridge and nearly went over the railing, the wind was blowing so hard.

An enormous chunk of concrete, a whole section of the bridge, had been torn half away from its moorings directly in front of me. There was no way I could ride my bike over that, and crossing on foot didn't look any too safe either. But I clambered over a section that was still intact and started down to the island, just as the storm struck with renewed fury. The wind gusts were so strong it felt like something solid, and enormous, was trying to shove me into the water, and I covered the last several yards on my hands and knees. *What if Annie isn't even there?*

But of course a ghost doesn't need to take shelter. Through the torrent of falling water I could see a bright glow next to a large dark object. Not until I was right next to Annie could I see what she was kneeling over—a dead pony. I called her name.

"He's dead, Darren!" Her eyes were twin globes of green fire.

"Who is?"

"Jamie! He drowned in the storm. He's dead! I don't know where Terry is… she might be dead too. But Darren, what are you doing here? You'll be killed! I've never seen a storm this strong!"

And that was saying something. I pointed east, toward the ocean. "Over there!" I screamed. "The State Park gift shop! I'm going to try to reach it!" And I started staggering toward the sea, not waiting for her response. I couldn't see where I was going, but I could still feel pavement beneath my feet, so I guessed I was heading the right way. Passing about where the State Park gatehouse should have been, I saw only a bare cement platform. I shuddered, trying to remember where the gift shop was exactly. *It's across the parking lot… a little to the right…*

Some of the boards that made up the wheelchair ramp

into the building were gone, and I had to take care not to twist my ankle, but at least the building was still there. Inside it was dark and deserted, and water was pouring through leaks in the ceiling, soaking the postcards and T-shirts that lay in a heap on the floor, blown there by the wind through a broken window in back. I didn't care. All that mattered was that Annie was still beside me, and the letter was still in my pocket.

"Darren, what is this? Why would you—?" Her eyes widened when I pulled the wet, stuck together pages out of my pocket. Her glow flared up, like a fire with gasoline thrown on it.

"Annie. This letter."

"That letter."

"The first page—the first page was warped and all the ink had run, as if someone had taken it outside in the rain. The only words I could read were 'love you always.' But the second page was perfectly legible."

She closed her eyes. I wished I could close mine; the light was starting to hurt my eyes. "...my dearest Jim," she quoted. "But I can write you no more. I must stand by my oath this time, and keep my vows to my darling Will. You deserve every blessing of happiness and love that this life can bring, not the affections of a silly girl who was never worthy of you. Nevertheless, I shall always remain—"

"Your loving Annie," I finished for her. "It's quite a letter. But what would Will have thought, if he only read the first page? He would have understood only that you still loved Jim, not him!"

"It is impossible that he saw it," she whispered. I looked just long enough to see her eyes were still closed, then looked away. Purple afterimages darted across the room as she spoke. "I wrote it the night before we left on that final trip to the mainland. There had been an early snowfall, you see... I was thinking about the times we used to go sledding down the dunes on that sled Will made me..."

"And so you wrote the letter that night, and hid it in the leather case behind the kitchen pantry with all the others. Yes. Maybe he felt a cold draft from back there—it was December, after all—and he went to plug it up—"

"No! It's impossible!"

I kept my voice gentle. "Annie, how did you find out there was a telegram for Will?"

"Why, Mr. Powers had sailed to Spence Landing early in the morning and told Will when he got back—"

"No, Annie. I didn't ask how Will said he had found out. I asked how you found out."

"Will told me."

Her voice sounded strange. I opened my eyes and found I could no longer distinguish the features of Annie's face and clothing. All were lost in a white glare. "He killed you, Annie…"

"No!" Her voice sounded like distant wind chimes.

"Yes, Annie. There never was a telegram. He told you that to get you out on the boat… he probably knew a storm was coming… and when it struck, so did he. The jibboom only swung because he pushed it."

"No, Darren…"

"But yes." The tears filling my eyes shattered the creature of light Annie was becoming into rainbow shards. There was an overpowering smell of ozone in the air, as there had been just after the lightning strike that nearly killed me. *It isn't fair. I gave her what she needed, the peace of knowing the truth. And my reward is to lose her forever!* I leaned into the light, groping for something solid. *Maybe I can pull her back.*

Someone was calling for me. Someone else. I didn't want to hear, but the voice was insistent. "Darren, man! What the hell are you doing? Bill called me all frantic…" I turned and saw Kevin's face almost lost in the light. But he wasn't even squinting. How could he not see it, when he was casting a sharp shadow? His uniform was soaked and torn, his face contorted as he reached for me. *No! I don't want to go with him!* I crouched and leaped toward the place where the light was brightest.

I was in a dark, featureless tunnel. Somewhere in the distance behind me was the gift shop and Kevin stumbling around inside it—but the view was distorted, as if I were seeing it through a fisheye lens. Somewhere ahead was a white light brighter than the sun. And in the space in between, standing next to me, was Annie. She looked shocked, then smiled sadly.

"Darren. You don't belong here."

I embraced her. She was solid and warm, and seemingly as alive as you or me.

"Darren, you can't come with me," she said, but she embraced me even tighter. Some force was tugging at us, pulling us apart.

I clung to her. "There is nothing back there for me without you," I said. A hot wind was rising, a wind that carried the stink of ozone. Annie's face began to lose definition, to blur into the light behind her. I could feel the floor, solid beneath my feet, and Kevin's grip on my shoulder. "Darren," he said, but something was wrong with his voice. The pitch? The timbre? He didn't sound quite like himself. He spoke my name again, his voice faltering. And then…

"Annie," he said. His hand dropped from my shoulder, and I stumbled and fell to the floor. The woman-shaped white light dimmed a bit and I could see Annie again, gazing at the man standing behind me. "Jim," she whispered.

"Annie," he said. His dark eyes were enormous and wet. His face was subtly different—older, perhaps. "I heard that you were drownded… I was living over by Princess Anne, but everybody was talking about it. It was even in the papers, how the 'Angel of Assateague' had been swallowed up by the very sea she had saved others from. I knew it weren't no accident, but what could I do? I was just a colored boy."

"Jim." She couldn't say anything but his name. Couldn't get the words out.

"I lived a good life, Annie. Married, had children and grandchildren, and died full of years, as the Bible says." He smiled a little. "Now I live again, my soul in the body of my great-grandnephew, but oh Annie, you are unchanged…"

"Unchanged," said a third voice. Kevin spun around. Bill Pearson was standing there, but he, too, looked different. Familiar, from the pictures I had looked at the night before.

"Darren is right, Annie," he said. "I only saw the first page of that letter. I was blinded by what I thought was your betrayal. I found the second page only afterward. I kept it all my life, so I would never forget what I had done. Millie was a good woman, but she wasn't you. I spent all my life atoning…"

"You killed her!" Kevin roared, and jumped. Both men went over with a crash and began grappling on the floor.

"Darren, stop them!" Annie screamed. But I stood frozen, until I saw Kevin start to fumble with one hand at his belt. I lurched toward him, tripped and fell. There was a flat bang, far softer than the rain drumming on the building. Something warm trickled down my side. Annie screamed again, wordlessly. But I didn't feel any pain. I groped around and put my hand on hot metal. With all my strength I yanked the gun out of Kevin's grasp and threw it the door, into the flood. "It's over!" I shouted. "Over, a hundred and fifty years ago! Don't you see?" I choked and started sobbing. "She's gone… and you're not the same men you were…" We all cried out as the room suddenly exploded soundlessly. Then everything faded into blackness.

EPILOGUE

All of that was more than twenty years ago. I never saw Annie again, but I stopped questioning that what I had experienced was real—the reality of my great and only love. Certainly my injuries were real enough, after that day when Hurricane Norma wreaked its havoc, and I spent weeks recovering, first in Peninsula Regional and then in Johns Hopkins up in Baltimore. I had plenty of company—Norma had hurt a lot of people, though I might have been the only one with a hurricane-related gunshot wound. Kevin and Bill were both concussed and confused, so it was left up to me to explain how, when they'd separately come to rescue me, we all ended up in a bruised and bloody heap on the floor of the Assateague State Park headquarters. Kevin's gun must have gone off somehow in all the confusion, I said innocently. In the chaos of the recovery from what everybody back then was calling "the storm of the century," nobody wanted to give a good and desperately needed cop any trouble. I even got a huge basket of flowers from Lakeisha, and later an invitation to their wedding. As for what I was doing out on an exposed barrier island in the middle of the worst hurricane anyone could remember, I claimed to have gotten a bit carried away doing my oceanographic research, and since everyone knew my head was in the clouds all the time, they took my word for it.

I started classes at UMES on time in January, with an almost-new car and a new wardrobe thanks to my parents, though the only possession I ever really cared about in my little apartment in Princess Anne, and the most precious one I've had in all the places I've lived in since then down here on the Shore, is a scrap of paper they found in my pockets that I had custom framed—a scrap on which is written, in blue ink in a slanting old-fashioned copperplate, the words "love you always."

I drove out to Assateague every weekend I was in college, and during the week as well when I could get away, and as I healed I made my hikes longer and longer until I could finally walk out to Green Run under my own power. Annie was gone, of course, and there was no hint she'd ever been there, though I found her grave easily enough. Following an old Jewish custom, I left a pebble atop it each time I visited—and I visited so often over the years that I ended up turning the grave into a virtual cairn. Sometimes I'd talk to her as if she was there and could hear, or I'd go through the whole ritual of reciting the entire Jewish morning prayer service, and then *El Malei Rachamim*, but more often I just sat by the stone and listened to the wind in the trees. There were times I was at peace with God and times when I raged at Him for the shortness of Annie's life and of our time together.

But I have much to be grateful for in my work as a marine biologist for the National Park Service. I'm the head of a scientific staff that has never numbered more than half a dozen people, measuring the impact of the rising sea level and ocean acidification on the Atlantic coast of Delmarva—I named our research vessel the *U.S.S Wilensky*, after my old professor in College Park passed away. Now the crew is down to just me, DeShonte Michaels and Haley DeCiprio, three crotchety middle-aged research Ph.D.s on an aging ship where we have to buy the fuel and do all the maintenance. And I can't even say I blame Uncle Sam much for his stinginess, not with all the problems the government has finally had to confront since climate change did what General Lee never could and forced the abandonment of the old capital at Washington.

So it's been left to just the three of us and the country's increasingly decrepit fleet of satellites to monitor the dramatic changes in the Atlantic barrier islands. Assateague itself isn't even a single island anymore, it's a chain of shrinking islets and submerged sandbars stretching from what used to be Ocean City Inlet in the north to the waterlogged stump of Assateague Lighthouse in the south, opposite the flooded ruins of Chincoteague. Green Run Inlet was actually one of the first of the old gaps that the hungry waves reopened, but it doesn't look much like the placid tree-lined waterway Annie told me about. In fact, it's usually too dangerous to sail the *Wilensky* through that choppy strait, so I had to give up making regular visits to Annie's grave. There came a calm summer day when I found an excuse to take the boat down that way and saw that the hill where Annie's tombstone had stood was gone, the sand saturated by the rising waters until it just crumbled away. Nothing abides.

Since then I've found a better excuse to go back to the Assateague Islands. In my free time I volunteer with the Assateague Pony Rescue League, which is trying to round up the last of the wild horses and evacuate them to the mainland as their old habitat vanishes around them. Piebald ponies are much more photogenic than drowning salt marshes, of course, and the League has managed to raise the kind of money DeShonte and Haley and I can only dream about as we putter around with our outdated instruments. I don't begrudge the League's boats their sleek computerized efficiency, of course, not in the service of Annie's poor companions, and I find comfort in this connection to her memory.

So it was that a couple of months ago I found myself on Green Run Island, chasing a colt whose band-mates had already been rounded up through a stand of shriveled red maple trees that had been killed off by the salt. If I could just get close enough, I could use my stunner, a gentler version of those Tasers the cops used to have, and the crew could trundle out the big robot lifter to load him onto the ship. But the stubborn animal kept trotting just out of range. *I'm getting too old for this*, I thought as I limped through the dead forest. It was the beginning of April, and already blazing hot.

"Need a little help?" a voice asked. An annoyingly peppy young voice. All I could do was nod and try to wipe the sweat from my eyes with the back of my arm. "I'm good with horses," the stranger said, and I saw a girl circle around to the far edge of the wood. A brown ponytail flopped around as she squatted and began to make soothing coaxing noises. Her face was shaded by the bill of a red ball cap, but I knew she wasn't one of my crew. However, she wasn't boasting about her equestrian skill; by the time I finished downing a liter bottle of water she had tempted the colt with some cookies and was leading it over to where I stood.

I started to thank her, but my voice died in my throat, because she was looking at me with brilliant green eyes. It was Annie, to the life.

"Annette," she said extending her hand. "Annette Pearson. And you are—?"

It took several false starts before I could say my own name, and I'm sure that was the limpest handshake she had ever received. "So, um," I croaked as the now-docile colt accompanied us over to my ship—there was a small, powerful-looking motorboat beached beside it, one of those new whizzy electric models—"wh-what brings you out here, Annie?"

"My name's Annette," she said, giving me a hard look. "Not Annie. Never Annie! That's a little kid's name, and I ain't no little orphan. I'll forgive you this once, 'cause we just met, but don't do it again!"

"Right, I'll try to remember that," I said faintly, as my crewmates herded the colt onto our ship. *Annette* explained that she loved these islands and the wild ponies, she'd been coming out here since she was little to swim and camp "and just hang out," and she was delighted that somebody was saving the poor animals. Of course she became a regular on the rescue trips, and of course I became the most enthusiastic volunteer. Annette and I started going out as if it was the most natural thing in the world—she just looked at me late one afternoon and said, "It looks like you could really use a trip to Dumser's Dairyland when we knock off," and so we went to that Eastern Shore institution on U.S. Route 50 that hardly gets any business anymore since Hurricane Gina wiped out Ocean City back in '32. She told me all about growing up in Berlin in this brave new world of Category 6 hurricanes (which they finally gave up naming five years ago, there are just too many of them) and "empathy implants" and invasive mangrove tree crabs from Central America. She knew Uncle Bill and Aunt Jodie, of course, or rather she knew of them because her father and her uncle weren't on speaking terms, which didn't stop Dad from losing it when his big brother and his sister-in-law drowned in the big flood of '32. "They were lovely people, it is a shame you never got to know them," I said, and then I told her about my work and DeShonte's horrible black bean stews and Haley's country music obsession, and we laughed and laughed and kissed and kissed some more, and Annette moved into my one-hundred-and-twenty-year-old farmhouse in Snow Hill this past Friday. I was all ready with a story about an old girlfriend when she saw the framed scrap with the copperplate writing on it, but she just looked at it, in its honored place on my living room wall, smiled and traced the letters delicately with her fingertip.

And of course, I had to know. I had to know, though

you can never know. You know? Because even if my memory of that long-ago day in the old State Park gift shop was reliable, what did it really prove? I'd stayed in touch with Kevin over the years, and with Bill before his death, and they'd never shown any sign of remembering the experience the way I did. So how could I be sure that Annie had finally "passed on" then, and had been reborn to return to me now? There were hints, like the way Annette always wore red bandannas or caps or even shoes, and I remembered how Annie's favorite color was red.

Well, maybe I could do a little experiment. I tried calling Annette "Annie" a couple of times this past weekend, as if absent-mindedly. The first time I got a sharp elbow in the ribs. The second time, we were out on Green Run Island and she pushed me into the bay. Tonight, I waited till she was sound asleep. I watched her lying on her side, wearing one of my old stretched-out UMES T-shirts (how did she get so comfortable with me, so quickly?), her chest rising and falling regularly, as magnificently corporeal as an Assateague pony, or the sea. And I spoke one word, softly but clearly. "Annie," I said. She mumbled something and turned over.

I can't be sure, but I believe it was, "Love you always, Darren."

ACKNOWLEDGEMENTS

Although this story is fiction, it is inspired by the real life and tragic drowning death at age sixteen of Emma Truitt, the daughter of Captain Jimmy Scott of Scott's Ocean House at Green Run, Assateague Island, Maryland. Like Annie Pearson, Emma was already married when she died in December 1874 and was buried on the island—and there is no reason to think the plot of my novel bears any real resemblance to Emma's biography. The real-life hotel and hamlet of Green Run are long gone, and Emma's lone gravestone is one of the few reminders of where they once stood. I have fictionalized the exact location at the request of the National Park Service.

No novel based on local lore can get off the ground without good background research, and I must thank the historian Edwin C. Bearss, Carl Zimmerman of the National Park Service, Bob and Kathy Fisher of the Worcester County, Maryland Historical Society, the helpful and friendly staff at Salisbury University Library and the Library of Congress, my sixth grade "Seminar" teacher Conrad Follmer for organizing the field trip on which I first visited Chincoteague and Assateague Islands back in 1981, Carla Coupe for invaluable editing work, and as always my wife Jackie for her boundless love, energy and helpful suggestions. Any remaining errors are my responsibility alone.

Front cover art: N. Heinz
Back cover photo of Emma Truitt's grave by the author.

ABOUT THE AUTHOR

Martin Berman-Gorvine is the author of the four-book "Days of Ascension" horror novel series: *All Souls Day* (2016), *Day of Vengeance* (2017), *Day of Atonement* (2018), and *Judgment Day* (2019), all published by Silver Leaf Books.

He is also the author of seven science fiction novels, many with an alternate history theme, including the Sidewise Award-winning *The Severed Wing* (as Martin Gidron) (Livingston Press, 2002); *36* (Livingston Press, 2012); *Seven Against Mars* (Wildside Press, 2013); *Save the Dragons!* (Wildside Press, 2013), which was a finalist for the Prometheus Award; *Ziona: A Novel of Alternate History* (as Marty Armon), an expansion of the short story "Palestina," published in Interzone magazine, May/June 2006 (Amazon/CreateSpace, 2014); *Heroes of Earth* (Wildside Press, 2015); and *Monsters of Venus* (Wildside Press, 2017).